SCENES FROM A COUNTRY BOOKSHOP

VICTORIA CONNELLY

Cover design by J D Smith

Published by Cuthland Press
in association with Notting Hill Press.

ISBN: 978-1-910522-15-8

To Rebecca, Patrick, Hudson and Figgy. Thank you for letting me spend the summer in your beautiful home where much of this novel was written.

CHAPTER ONE

Josh Nightingale stood in the centre of his bookshop, staring out of the window at the shop opposite and shaking his head at the noise.

'What do you think they're doing in there?'

Sam shrugged.

'No idea who's leased it?' Josh asked.

'No,' Sam said, 'although I heard a rumour it was going to sell lingerie.'

Josh frowned. 'Lingerie? In Castle Clare?'

'Apparently. Look at the letters.'

Josh looked out of the window again. As well as two workmen making a din with drills and hammers inside the shop, there was somebody outside painting the sign above the window.

'A Little Bit Bloo,' he read.

'Bloomers,' Sam said.

'No! *A Little Bit Bloomers* doesn't scan, does it?'

'What else could it be, then?'

Josh shrugged. 'Blooms? Could be a florist. But A Little Bit Blooms doesn't make any sense either, does it?'

'I suppose not.'

The two brothers looked on in wonder.

'I take it it's quiet at yours?' Josh asked.

'Grandpa Joe's holding the fort for a bit while Dad's taking Grandma to the doctors.'

'She okay?'

'I'm not sure. Dad says she's getting worse. Forgetting things and getting angry and confused.'

Josh frowned. He didn't like the sound of that. Their dear Grandma Nell was in the early stages of dementia and it was breaking the hearts of the Nightingale family to see those moments when she'd simply just slip away from them into another reality altogether.

'We have to be strong,' Josh's mother, Eleanor, had told him when he'd asked if there was anything he could do. 'We have to be there for your Grandpa. He needs us now more than ever.' And Josh had done his very best to do just that. Everybody had, whether it was cooking or cleaning or driving his grandparents to appointments, the Nightingale family had pulled together to make sure needs were met.

As the middle child of the five Nightingale children, Josh was, perhaps, the most serious. *Earnest* was the word his mother used to describe him and he accepted that because he knew he'd never be as carefree as Lara or have the natural warmth of Sam. Out of the five siblings, he was the most studious, the most solemn, the most *bookish*. He'd often been teased for resembling some of his literary heroes whether it be one of Chekhov's intense characters or a learned bachelor from an M R James story. But he took it in good humour and he was always the first to acknowledge his temperament.

~

It was around lunchtime that Josh noticed the sign was finished and he stared at it in wonder and smiled.

'Well,' he said to himself, 'that's a curious thing.'

After shelving three new copies of a Robert Macfarlane book that he was passionate about and frequently pushed with his customers, he scooted round to Sam's shop.

'Have you seen it?' Josh asked above the melodious tinkle of the shop bell.

'Seen what?' Sam asked from the top of a step ladder.

'The sign's finished,' Josh announced.

Sam quickly came back down to the shop floor and crossed to the window and they read the sign together.

A Little Bit Bloomsbury.

The two brothers looked at each other.

'Does that mean what I think it means?' Josh asked. 'Bloomsbury as in the Bloomsbury Group?'

'Could be Bloomsbury as in London.'

'Yes, but wouldn't that be odd?'

'There's a publisher called Bloomsbury,' Sam pointed out.

'You think they're opening a rival bookshop?'

'I've not seen any evidence of that. I saw someone taking some pieces of furniture in there before. I think that's what they're selling.'

It was as they were contemplating the meaning of the sign that the shop door opened and a young woman came out onto the pavement. She was wearing a long skirt in a sky-blue hue with a blouse in a bright floral print, over which she wore a necklace of chunky amber beads. But it was her long chestnut hair which really caught Josh's attention. It was the most astonishing colour he'd ever seen and was held back by a wide scarf tied at the nape of her neck.

'I'd say Bloomsbury as in the Bloomsbury Group for sure,' Josh said, trying not to stare at her in case she turned around. 'Just look at her clothes.'

'Only one way to find out,' Sam told him.

'What's that?'

'Go and ask her.'

Josh looked flustered by the suggestion. 'But I...' He swallowed hard. He was, by nature, introverted, and always felt a little uneasy introducing himself to new people.

'She's the new girl on the block and her shop is directly opposite yours,' Sam pointed out. 'I feel it's your civic duty to welcome her to Castle Clare, don't you?'

Somewhat reluctantly, Josh nodded. He could see the sense in Sam's argument and knew it would be the right thing to do especially when he saw her struggling to carry a large terracotta plant pot a moment later. Ever the gentleman, Josh was outside and across the road in an instant.

'Can I help?' he asked, his hands scooping around the pot.

'Oh!' the young woman exclaimed.

'I've got it,' he said. 'Where do you want it?'

'Just here, I think,' she said, pointing to the spot on the pavement to the left of the shop door.

Josh placed the pot gently on the ground.

'Thank you.'

'You're welcome,' he said. 'I'm Josh. Josh Nightingale. I run the bookshop across the road.'

'I'm April Channing.'

Josh nodded, noting the musicality of her name.

'My brother, Sam, runs the secondhand bookshop and our sister, Bryony, has the children's bookshop here.' He pointed to the other shops.

'A real family venture!'

'Absolutely. You might see Polly around too. She covers for us all from time to time.'

'Another sister?'

'Yes. There's Lara too, but she's away at university.'

'So there are five of you?'

'Yes. Like the Bennet family. Only... with boys as well as girls.'

'The Bennet family?'

'Jane Austen. *Pride and Prejudice.*'

'Oh, I see!'

'Sorry,' Josh said, loosening his shirt collar a little, 'I use a lot of literary references.'

'Well, thank you for the warning!' She smiled and it was only then that he noticed the glasses she was wearing had pink lenses. Rose-coloured glasses, he thought, wondering if that said something about the way she looked at the world or if it was a fashion thing. It seemed a bit early in their acquaintance to ask.

'So, you're selling furniture?' he asked instead.

'Upcycling,' April said. 'That's the popular word people are using now, isn't it? Taking something old and unwanted and breathing new life into it.'

Josh liked the sound of that idea. 'How did you get started?'

'Basically, my family's never had much money,' she began. 'All our furniture came from auctions or was handed down. One day, my mum bought me this really ugly piece of furniture for my bedroom and I thought, there's *got* to be a way to make this more beautiful! Of course, I didn't know what I was doing and used the wrong sorts of paint and glue, but it did ignite something inside me.'

'And did you make the piece more beautiful?'

'Well, it went from a rather dull brown to a very vivid pink, so it was definitely more beautiful to my twelve-year-old self.' She smiled again. She was very pretty when she smiled, Josh couldn't help thinking. Or even when she wasn't smiling. He pulled at his shirt collar again and cleared his throat.

'So, the name?' he began, looking up at the new sign above the door.

'It's as in the Bloomsbury Group?'

'I thought it must be,' he said. 'Your attire too.'

'They are a bit of an influence on me.'

'Then you're a Virginia Woolf fan?'

'Of course!'

'In that case, you might be interested in the book club we have here in Castle Clare. My brother, Sam, hosts it at his shop every other month. The next meeting's in July and they're reading *Mrs Dalloway*.'

'Wonderful! I think that's Woolf's best work,' April said.

'I'm sure they'd be delighted to welcome you at the book club.'

'Thank you. That's kind.'

'I take it you have a copy of the book already? Because I could order you one if you wanted. Or – well – any book.'

'I do have one. Two or three actually.'

Josh smiled at that. It sounded very familiar. 'I think you're going to fit in here very well.'

'I'm so pleased to hear that. It seems like a very special place.'

'Oh, it is. So, where are you from?'

'A little village just across the border in Norfolk.'

Josh sucked his teeth. 'Don't go telling people that around here!'

'Oh, really?' April suddenly looked anxious.

'Only joking!' Josh said quickly. 'You know the old Suffolk–Norfolk banter!'

'Yes. There's quite a rivalry between the counties, isn't there?'

'All nonsense of course,' Josh said.

'Exactly.'

'Suffolk is clearly *miles* better than Norfolk!' He grinned and she grinned back.

'You go on believing that!' she told him, and there was that smile again. And there was that tight feeling in his throat.

'Right, well I'd best get back,' he told her.

'Thank you for the welcome.'

'If you need anything...' he said, and then dried up.

'I know where to find you.'

'Yes!' He pointed to his shop opposite hers and then gave her a funny little salute which he instantly regretted. Honestly, what was wrong with him?

He crossed the road quickly and disappeared into the sanctuary of his bookshop. He could still see her from the window and couldn't help hoping that she'd go back into her own shop because she was proving an awful distraction and he had work to do.

Decidedly, deliberately, Josh turned his attention away from the window and back to his books, immediately going to the shelves and pulling out a single slim copy of Virginia Woolf's *Mrs Dalloway*. Sam had placed an order for several copies on behalf of book club members and they'd arrived last week and been paid for and collected by all but two members: Winston Kneller and Honey Digger. Josh shook his head in disapproval at the name Honey. He'd written *Hortense* on the order form because that was her proper name. Honey just wasn't dignified for a woman of her years or, indeed, for any woman as far as Josh was concerned.

He'd also ordered a couple more copies of the book for the shop in case there were any last minute requests and he opened one of them now, reading the famous opening line. Then he closed the book and put it back on the shelf and sighed in frustration.

As much as he hated to admit it, Josh couldn't help finding the whole adoration of the Bloomsbury Group somewhat perplexing. Some of the art was very beautiful – he'd been to a recent exhibition in London and had admired some of Vanessa Bell and Duncan Grant's paintings – but Virginia Woolf had never tickled his literary taste buds, he had to admit. Perhaps he shouldn't readily admit that to April Channing, though. He wouldn't want to put her off before they'd even become friends.

He turned and glanced out of the window again. She was still out on the pavement, primping some flowers in a little window box. The shop looked delightful with its newly-painted mauve-grey paintwork. It would be a pleasant change to look out at it rather than the vacant, unloved space which had greeted him over the last few months since the previous owner had vacated. It had been a bit of an eyesore for years if Josh was honest. More of a junk shop than an antiques shop. The owner had been quite an unpleasant man too. Basically, he didn't like customers, which wasn't a great trait in a shopkeeper. Well, the customers hadn't liked him either or his goods and he'd shut up shop and moved away. Castle Clare didn't miss him.

Josh was just wondering if he should make some sort of Bloomsbury window display, not only to please the new arrival but to coincide with the next book club pick, when Sam walked in.

'Hey! You spoke to her!' he said, a big smile on his face.

'I did.'

'And?'

'She's nice. Very friendly.'

'Well, that's good to hear. What's her name?'

'April.'

'Where's she from?'

'Norfolk.'

Sam sucked his teeth just as Josh had.

'I know. I teased her about that,' Josh admitted. 'She loves the Bloomsbury Group and is interested in the book club.'

'Excellent!' Sam said and then gave his brother a look.

'What?' Josh asked.

'Anything else?'

'How do you mean?'

'Did you – I don't know – ask her out for a drink or something?'

'No, of course not!'

'But you want to get to know her, right?'

'She knows where I am if she needs anything.'

'Oh, I see,' Sam said. 'Playing it cool.'

'I'm not playing it any way,' Josh said, moving across the shop to distract himself with a display that wasn't arranged quite to his satisfaction since a customer had randomly moved all the books earlier that morning before leaving the shop without buying anything.

'But she's pretty and you said she's nice,' Sam continued.

Josh sighed. 'Look, just because you're all happy and cosy with Callie, it doesn't mean I'm looking for a relationship too. I'm quite happy being single.'

'I wasn't talking about getting married or anything, Josh. Just going out for drinks. You know – chatting, laughing, getting to know someone!'

Josh straightened a neat pile of prize-winning titles. 'She's probably seeing someone. I mean, how could she not be?'

'You won't know if you don't ask.'

'It's too soon. We've only just met.'

'That's when to do it,' Sam said. 'And before anyone else steps in. I can tell you it won't be long before she samples Colin the baker's goods and he's single again after our Bryony broke up with him.'

Josh glanced out of the window. Sooner or later, everyone in Castle Clare discovered the goods sold at Well Bread, and Colin was a handsome man. Still, Josh wasn't convinced and shook his head.

'I knew the minute Callie walked into my shop,' Sam went on. 'The second I saw her sniffing one of my books.'

Josh couldn't help smiling at that. Sam and Callie had seemed destined to meet each other with their love of books, and he was so happy for his brother after the disastrous ending of his marriage. Sam deserved to be happy. He was a good guy. But Josh was happy on his own; he was one of life's natural bachelors. He had a set routine, a small home which was neat and orderly, he enjoyed cooking and eating on his own, and he took a pride in his work. He led a fulfilled life. He didn't feel he lacked anything or needed anyone, and yet the arrival of April Channing had definitely rattled something inside him, and Sam had obviously noticed too.

Josh would simply have to deny it, he decided.

'Look,' he began, 'I'm single. She *might* be single. But that's no reason to fling us together within five minutes of us meeting each other. It's presumptuous and – well – embarrassing.'

'I wasn't *flinging* anybody together,' Sam said. 'I just noticed the sparkle in your eyes when you saw her.'

Josh flinched at the very idea of anything about him *sparkling*.

'I'm not wrong, am I?' Sam persisted. He wasn't going to let this go, was he?

Josh picked up a copy of a literary novel which had been described by a respected critic as the best debut in a decade, but which Josh privately thought was a piece of pomposity.

'Have you read this?' he asked Sam, turning its cover round.

'No,' Sam said, grinning in a way which told Josh that he knew he was avoiding the subject. 'Look, I'm not going to go on about this.'

'Good.'

'I'd just like to see you happy.'

Josh frowned. 'But I *am* happy!'

'I know. But you *could* be even happier.' Sam came forward and play punched him on the arm and Josh watched as he left the shop. A blissful silence followed. It was just Josh and the books. He closed his eyes and inhaled the all-pervading smell of new books. Different, but just as engrossing as the scent of old books, it calmed Josh down, bringing him back to what was important in his life.

And, as he moved around the familiar domain of his shop, straightening a book here and swapping a book there, he knew that a pretty woman was all very well, but she could never hope to usurp the place which books held in his heart.

CHAPTER TWO

Callie Logan was signing copies of her latest novel in Bryony's bookshop. It was so kind of Bryony to always make sure she had a stock of Callie's books on display with a little note letting her customers know that Callie was that most special of celebrities: a local writer!

'There we are,' Callie announced at last. 'All done.' She put the lid on her fountain pen and placed it safely in her satchel.

'Lovely!' Bryony said, taking the books from her and arranging them on a table near the till. 'Have you heard the latest gossip?'

'About the new shop?'

'The new shop *owner*,' Bryony said. 'April Channing.'

'Sam told me about her. Apparently, she sells lovely pieces of furniture and she's very pretty and wears unusual clothes.'

'*Beautiful* clothes,' Bryony enthused. 'All flowing and romantic. Very Bloomsbury.'

'I'll have to pay her a visit. I've been looking for a bedside table for a while. I wonder if she'll have something suitable.'

'I'm sure she will,' Bryony said. 'Cup of tea? You deserve one after all that signing.'

'Love one.'

Callie followed Bryony into the private area of the shop that was stacked with boxes and where there was just about enough room for a kettle and a biscuit tin. Bryony opened the tin now and peered inside.

'It's at times like this that I regret choosing Ben over Colin the baker.'

Callie laughed.

'Don't tell Ben I said that!' Bryony quickly added, her dark eyes wide.

'I won't! But I'm sure he'd understand,' Callie told her, looking at the remains of a rather dejected garibaldi. 'Would you like me to pop next door and get us a little something?'

'Oh, there's no need for that.'

'Judging by that garibaldi, I'd say there was,' Callie said, grabbing the purse out of her satchel. 'I'll be back in a mo.'

She left the bookshop and entered the baker's and there, standing by the counter, was a beautiful woman with long chestnut hair and a sage-green skirt that kissed her ankles. Callie tried not to stare, guessing this was the very person she and Bryony had just been talking about. She watched her interaction with Colin for a moment.

'See it as a welcoming gift,' Colin said, handing the woman a paper bag.

'That's very kind of you. Thank you.'

The woman turned around. She was wearing rose-tinted glasses and smiled sweetly at Callie as she left the shop.

'Wow!' Colin said after the door had closed behind her.

'I take it that was Ms Bloomsbury?' Callie asked.

'Is that her surname?' Colin said.

'No!' Callie laughed. 'The shop's called A Little Bit Bloomsbury – after the Bloomsbury Group of artists. She's April Channing.'

'Ah,' Colin said. 'I don't know much about art.'

'I disagree,' Callie said. 'You are an artist in pastry and dough.'

He beamed at that. 'What can I get you?'

'Two of whatever Bryony adores most.'

'Raspberry tarts,' Colin informed her. It was sweet that he remembered, although it was probably a courtesy he had for all his customers, Callie thought, watching as he placed two perfect tarts in a paper bag.

'Bryony okay?' Colin asked as Callie paid.

'Yes. Very well.'

'She looks happy. When I see her.' He gave a smile that was half-joy, half-pain, and Callie realised that he still wasn't completely over Bryony and her heart ached for him.

'You'll find someone,' she told him.

'Yeah?'

Callie nodded. 'Love was the very last thing I was looking for when I came to Castle Clare, and see what happened?'

'I don't think I'm a naturally lucky person in that department,' Colin confessed.

'Oh, I don't believe that. Just give it time.'

The door to the shop opened and a young mother came in with a babe in arms.

'I'll see you, Callie,' he said.

'Bet on it!' she said, motioning to her bag of goodies, as she left. She entered Bryony's shop a moment later. 'I'm back with sustenance!'

Bryony, who'd been hidden behind a low bookcase, bobbed up. 'Lovely! What have you got?'

'Colin said these were your favourites,' Callie said, handing her the bag.

'He did?'

'He remembers.'

Bryony sighed. 'He's a sweetheart.'

'Yes, he is.'

'Just not *my* sweetheart.'

'He might have found himself one.'

'Really?'

'Ms Bloomsbury,' Callie announced.

'What do you mean?'

'She was in Well Bread when I went in and Colin was giving her a freebie.'

'Oh, no!' Bryony said, looking instantly crestfallen. 'Colin *can't* fall for her. Our Josh has his eye on her.'

'Does he?'

Bryony pursed her lips. 'Well, he probably does. We're teasing him about it anyway because he's the only one of us who's still single.'

'So is Lara seeing somebody? Callie asked, thinking of the youngest of the Nightingale brood.

'Oh, Lara's *always* seeing somebody. That's what students do, isn't it? But Josh never went through that stage at least not seriously. Nothing was ever long-term. He's always been married to his books. That's not normal, is it? Not to fall in love!'

'You mean he never has?' Callie asked, trying to imagine that.

'Not really. Not *truly*.'

'And you're all match-making him with Ms Bloomsbury?'

'Match-making is such a loaded term, isn't it?'

Callie grinned at that.

'We're just making encouraging noises,' Bryony added as she took a tart out of the bag and then passed the bag to Callie.

'So what about Colin?' Callie asked before taking a bite of her tart.

'What about him?'

'Is he ever allowed to fall in love?' she asked with a wry grin.

'What do you mean?'

'Well, you said he can't have April and he's certainly not allowed you.'

'Oh, Callie! You make me sound just terrible!'

'Sorry, I didn't mean to.'

'I'm very fond of Colin. It's just – well – he wasn't the right one for me. You know how that is, don't you?'

Callie nodded. After her first, brief marriage had ended, she knew only too well when a relationship wasn't working. For a moment, she looked at the much-loved satchel that went everywhere with her, thinking of how her estranged husband had hated it so much that he'd threatened to throw it into the River Thames on more than one occasion. And then she'd met Sam. She'd known pretty quickly that he was the right man for her when he'd admired the very same satchel. She smiled now as she remembered. Sometimes, it was the little things that made all the difference.

'Don't feel guilty. You're meant to be with Ben. Anyone can see that,' Callie told Bryony. 'But don't you think it's a little dangerous to match-make people? I mean, it never works out in books, does it? Just think of Jane Austen's *Emma*. And I have a feeling it never works out in real life either.'

'But I've got a good feeling about this.'

'Have you talked to her?' Callie asked.

'Not yet, but she *looks* right. Does that make sense?'

Callie considered this for a moment. 'I think it's probably what Josh thinks looks right that counts here.'

Bryony popped the last piece of raspberry tart into her mouth and nodded. 'I suppose you're right. But I can't help worrying that he's never going to find someone. His nose is always in a book and, if he ever does look up for long enough, it's usually to find yet another one!'

Callie smiled sympathetically. 'Still, I'd be tempted to leave things to nature.'

'Nature!' Bryony scoffed. 'He's going to let life pass him by with nothing to show for it but the world's biggest to-be-read pile.'

Callie finished her own raspberry tart, making a mental note to treat herself to them more often – perhaps when she finished each chapter of her new novel which was proving more difficult to write than normal.

'The romantic in me would adore seeing Josh fall in love,' she told Bryony as she grabbed her satchel, 'but the realist thinks it's probably best not to meddle.' Callie leaned forward and hugged Bryony. 'Thanks so much for today.'

With that, she left the shop, noting the look of deep disappointment on her friend's face.

It was no good, though. Bryony just couldn't help herself and, as soon as Callie had left, she closed her shop and nipped across the road to Josh's.

'He's giving her free sweets!' she blurted as soon as she'd entered.

Josh looked up from where he was stacking a shelf.

'What?'

'Colin! He's giving April free pastries. You've got to do something!'

Josh glanced out of the window in consternation, as if he might catch Colin in the act.

'I think you should give her a book or something,' Bryony went on, whispering as a customer came into the shop. 'To welcome her.'

Josh grimaced. 'But that's so cheesy and contrived.'

'So? It's still a nice gesture.'

Josh shook his head and then approached the customer – a young man with a very long beard.

'Can I help you with anything or are you happy to browse?'

'I'm looking for the first *Game of Thrones* novel. Do you have it?' the bearded man asked.

'I don't,' Josh said. 'But I'd be happy to order it for you. The whole George R R Martin canon has to be ordered. Takes up too much shelf space, you see,' Josh explained, thinking of the great fantastical tomes written by the master of the genre.

'Oh, okay. I'll do that then.'

'No problem.'

Bryony watched in frustration as the minutes ticked by while Josh took the man's order. Minutes in which Colin could be planning to make a move on April. Finally, the man left the shop.

'Give her a book!'

'Pardon?'

'April – you need to keep up with Colin – make an impression.'

'I've already said hello.'

'Well, say hello again – with a gift for her.'

Josh shook his head. 'I'm really not going to get any peace from you and Sam until I'm married, am I?'

Bryony ruffled his hair. 'Nope!'

He sighed. 'I was actually thinking of taking her the new edition of *Mrs Dalloway*.' He moved towards the shelf and pulled out a copy. 'But she already has several copies.'

'What about something *you* love?'

'Oh, well, I didn't think of that.' Josh scanned the shop, his eyes alighting on a little pile of books on a table in the centre of the room. Not the pompous debut novel. No way. But a little hardback next to it published by a small press. He walked across the room and picked it up, showing his choice to Bryony. She nodded.

'Don't forget a bookmark.'

~

Once he'd made his mind up, Josh didn't waste any time. He popped the book inside a paper bag together with a bookmark and then nipped across the road to A Little Bit Bloomsbury. April was at the rear of the shop as he came in, her back to him, a paintbrush in her right hand.

'Hello,' he said.

She turned around. 'Josh! How funny.'

'Funny?'

'I was just thinking about you.'

'You were?'

'Yes. I was thinking that I could do with some books to pop in this little bookcase.'

Josh walked forward and took in the piece of furniture she was painting with dusky rose paint. It was very pretty. Very feminine.

'Funny you should mention books because I've brought you one.'

'Really?' April stood up, putting her paintbrush down and turning to face him, wiping her hands on the cream apron she was wearing over her skirt.

'It's one of my favourite books,' Josh said, handing her the paper bag.

April took it with a smile.

'*River Diary*,' Josh announced. 'By Ronald Blythe. One of his beautiful collections of essays.'

She held it in both hands, Josh noticed, almost cradling it so that it was safe. He liked that. He liked her hands too. She had long, slim fingers with silver rings and big coloured stones.

He watched, mesmerised, as she looked at the book, bringing it close to her face and, for one heart-stopping moment, he thought she was going to sniff it just as Callie had in Sam's shop, but she didn't.

'I love the grey-green of these trees,' she said. 'Who's the artist?'

'John Nash,' Josh told her. 'He lived in the Stour Valley and painted the area extensively. The house he lived in on the Essex–Suffolk border was left to Ronald Blythe.'

'Ronald Blythe,' she read, turning the book over to take in its sky-blue back and spine. 'I've not heard of him.'

'Not enough people have, I'm afraid, but I'm trying to remedy that by always stocking his books and putting them in front of customers who I think will enjoy his writing. Each of his books is a little diary of a passing year. He's in his late-nineties now and has only recently retired from writing. Beautiful prose. His observations of nature and the changing seasons are second to none and it's written with such a gentle, loving touch and with plenty of humour too.'

'Sounds wonderful.'

'He's a very special writer. I hope you enjoy it,' Josh said, feeling supremely happy that he'd plucked up the courage to give her this gift, which had to beat anything from Well Bread. Pastries were all very well, he thought, but they couldn't hope to compete with fine prose.

'It's a very thoughtful gift,' she told him.

'Perhaps we can discuss it sometime,' Josh said and then saw her face cloud with hesitation. 'Sorry, I don't mean to force my reading tastes upon you. I'd never want to do that.'

'No, no!' she interrupted. 'I do want to read it. But I'm not the world's fastest reader.'

'No worries, really. The last thing I'd want to do is to put pressure on you. Especially with a book like this which needs savouring slowly.'

'Then that's exactly how I'll read it.' She smiled, her eyes bright through the pink lenses of her glasses.

Josh hesitated. He wanted to say more, but didn't know what. He felt a little lost outside of his bookshop and inside somebody else's realm.

'Well, I'll let you get back to work,' he said as he shuffled awkwardly towards the door.

'Josh?'

'Yes?' He'd opened the door and was half in, half out.

'Can you recommend any pubs around here?' April asked him.

'I can. There's a couple in Castle Clare. The George just off Market Square and The Happy Hare at the end of our road.'

She nodded. 'I was thinking of going for a drink after I close the shop today.'

'Right. Well, both are great.' His hand hovered on the door handle.

'I think our shops close at the same time. Five, right?' she said.

'That's right.'

There was a pause. She was smiling at him as he hovered.

'Would you like to come with me?' she asked.

'Oh!' he cried. She was asking him out for a drink. What a dimwit he was not to have picked up on that instantly. Honestly, he really had no idea when it came to this sort of thing, did he? 'Yes. I'd love to.'

'Good.'

'I'll meet you here? At five?' he said.

'Right.'

They stared at each other for what seemed like an extraordinary length of time to Josh who had to almost shake himself back into normality.

'Right!' He gave a funny little salute again. Honestly, what was it about this woman that kept making him want to salute?

He was mightily relieved to return to the sanctuary of his own shop. He checked his watch. It was after three. In less than two hours, he'd see her again. He swallowed hard. He'd never been more nervous in his life.

CHAPTER THREE

Five o'clock came all too swiftly for Josh. This thing – this going to the pub – seemed much too soon. He knew it couldn't be thought of as a date, and yet his stomach churned with nerves because he knew word would get back to his family. Somehow, in the not-too-distant future, Bryony and Sam and maybe even Polly would hear about him sitting in a pub with April Channing, and he didn't feel ready for that kind of scrutiny yet. He wanted to do things his way – slowly getting to know April with no pressure from the outside world. Like C S Lewis and Joy Gresham, or Helene Hanff and Frank Doel who'd written letters to one another. How beautiful that seemed to Josh – for a relationship to develop through the written word – the *proper* written word: ink, paper and envelopes. Not the insanely fast communication of the email or the text or those appalling boxes that popped up on various apps and social media sites. They were quite intolerable to Josh. The modern world was far too fast for him.

He went through to the back room of the shop and the tiny cloakroom where he combed his dark hair, straightened his shirt and waistcoat and then just stared at his pale reflection. Josh was always pale. He generally didn't like the sunshine. Even as a young boy, he'd forgone the pleasure of running around the garden or kicking a football around in favour of sitting in a shady spot with a book in his lap.

Looking at himself so critically wasn't something he spent much time doing and he never really thought about how others saw him, but he wondered about that now. April must have thought there was something likeable about him in order to suggest a drink. You wouldn't do that if you had taken a dislike to someone, would you? Unless she was just being kind. Or maybe she was genuinely lonely in Castle Clare and was using him to get to know others. Or maybe she'd not only suggested a drink to Josh, but to others too. Like Colin. What if Colin was coming to the pub too?

Josh took a deep breath in an attempt to calm down. What was he getting so worked up about? It was none of his business if April had asked the whole of Castle Clare to have a drink with her and, if she had, he'd have to do his best to make sure he stood out from the crowd.

He groaned. Josh had never been good at that. He was a stand-at-the-back kind of person – the sort to slope away at parties or at large gatherings in order to find a quiet space of his own.

He looked at his watch. He was one of the few people he knew to still wear one and not to rely on their mobile phones for the time.

'Five,' he said, moving quickly to the front of the shop. He'd done his usual end of the day tidy up and only had to lock up now.

April was just coming out of her shop as Josh turned from locking his own door.

'Hello,' he called over.

'Hi!'

'Had a good day?' he asked as he crossed the road to join her even though the pub was on his side of the road.

'Very good. Two sales today.'

'Excellent!'

'You?'

'A slow but steady stream,' Josh recounted. 'Oh, and a man with a bad cold who sneezed on *Madame Bovary*. I wiped the cover after he left.'

April laughed. 'So, where are we going again?'

'I thought The Happy Hare on the corner here.' He gestured as they approached the pub, noting that, if she hadn't known where they were going, then she couldn't have invited anyone else. Like Colin. Unless she was going to call them once they were in the pub, Josh thought. Maybe she was one of those people who sat with a real life person in front of them, but spent all their time looking at their phone. Josh sincerely hoped not. He hated mobile phones. He actually had a sign up in his shop asking people not to use their phones. He knew what a lot of them were doing, of course – checking prices of books online and then not buying his. That was bad enough, but there were also those who actually spoke on their phones and, to Josh, that was as bad as talking in a library. Bookshops were meant to be quiet, contemplative places, where thoughts could be free to roam. He didn't want that process sullied by modern technology. Surely people could switch off for the time it took to browse a few books.

There was also that time Josh had objected to a young woman who'd been taking endless photos on her phone which he'd felt was some kind of violation. She'd given him a heated glare and had left in a huff. When Josh had told Sam about it, Sam's mouth had dropped to the floor.

'But that was Bookshop Becky'

'Who?'

'She's one of those Instagrammers – she takes photos of bookshops and posts them online. She's got hundreds of thousands of followers.'

Josh had looked her up afterwards and, sure enough, saw that her account had over two hundred and eighty thousand very engaged followers. He'd sworn quietly and put it down to experience. How was he expected to keep up-to-date with all this modern technology? He still wasn't used to the new till he'd bought. Anyway, Josh was yet to be convinced about the effectiveness of all those social media sites. Bryony had recently made sure that the Nightingale bookshops weren't left behind and there was a very attractive website, a page on Facebook and an Instagram account. Bryony was good at that sort of thing. She was generally a much more sociable sort of person and found great enjoyment in photographing her shop and engaging in online book discussions with her customers as well as complete strangers who would probably never visit the shop.

'The point is to *talk* about books,' she kept telling Josh, 'and that doesn't just happen in bookshops anymore, but in all these virtual spaces.'

Virtual spaces indeed. Josh preferred *real* ones where you could see and touch and – yes – smell a book.

They entered The Happy Hare and walked to the bar.

'What can I get you?' he asked April.

'Let me,' she said. 'After all, you've already given me a gift.'

'No – no – it's my treat.'

'But *I* asked *you* for a drink.'

'Doesn't matter,' Josh insisted with a shake of his head. As far as he was concerned, this was his duty. 'Now, what can I get you?'

'A white wine would be lovely.'

'Two white wines.'

A moment later, they were sat at a table by the window.

'So, are you one of these rare old-fashioned guys who always picks up the bill and holds doors open for ladies?'

'Not just ladies,' he said.

April smiled. 'You seem...' she paused, 'unusual.'

'I've been called worse.'

'You have?'

'Fusty, stuffy, outdated, antediluvian.'

'*Antediluvian* – really?'

'That's one of my favourite ones actually,' he told her with a certain sense of pride, as if he'd been given a badge of honour. 'What can I say? I'm out of my time.'

'Yes,' April said. 'I feel like that too sometimes.' She toyed with her string of amber beads. 'Do you ever wish you'd been born in another century?'

'Frequently,' Josh said, taking a sip of his wine, 'but then I remember the hygiene standards and quickly change my mind.'

'Yes, we've a lot to be grateful for in the twenty-first century,' April agreed, and it was then that she reached into her handbag and took out her mobile phone. 'Like these gadgets. Where would we be without them?'

Josh tried not to openly grimace. So, she was one of those people who couldn't hold a real-life, in-the-moment conversation without getting fidgety fingers and reaching for one of those god-awful contraptions. He sighed. What a shame. He'd so hoped she'd be different.

'There,' she said a moment later, putting the phone back in her bag. 'Sorry about that – I meant to turn it off before. I do hate being followed around by a phone, don't you?'

'Well, yes!' Josh said, almost spluttering on his wine.

'It's so rude when people have their noses glued to a screen when you're right in front of them, don't you think?'

'Absolutely!' he said, barely able to hide his relief. He watched as she took a sip of her wine and he began to relax.

'So it's going well so far at the shop?'

'I think so,' April said. 'I've had some early sales and some requests for make-overs already.'

'Is that people bringing furniture to do up'

'That's right. It's great fun transforming something from an unloved piece to one that has new life. I adore seeing the owners' faces when they come to collect them.'

'It sounds so rewarding.'

'But your job must be equally rewarding, isn't it?'

Josh smiled. 'Oh, it is.'

'Do you get any feedback? I mean if a customer has read something you've recommended?'

'With the locals, yes. They'll come in and either rave or rant. I've got into trouble before for recommending books which weren't wholly enjoyed.'

'Oh, dear!'

'Yes, you can't guess people's taste all the time, I'm afraid. You can only point and suggest and hope for the best.'

'And what would you recommend for me?' April asked, her eyes seeming to sparkle with mischief behind her pink glasses.

Josh hesitated and then leaned forward and whispered, 'I'd have to get to know you a little better.'

She laughed coquettishly. 'But you know I'm interested in the Bloomsbury Group.'

'And that you've probably already read around that subject extensively.'

'True.'

'So perhaps I'd recommend some local reads.'

'Like the Ronald Blythe book you gave me?'

'Exactly. Try Roger Deakin too and Richard Mabey. Beautiful writers with a real sense of place.'

'Are they favourite writers of yours?'

'Indeed they are. I love nature writing and autobiographies so these are perfect reads for me.'

'So what happens if a real fantasy geek comes into your shop looking for suggestions? Are you able to help them?'

'Well, it's a bookseller's job to know a bit about all the genres. I could certainly help, I think, but you'll often find people come in knowing what they want.'

There was a pause and Josh panicked, floundering for something else to say. He never struggled when a conversation was about books, but they seemed to have covered that topic already.

'Tell me about your family,' April said and Josh breathed a sigh of relief as a new subject opened for him.

'You know there are five of us?'

'Yes.'

'My brother Sam's the oldest. Then there's Polly. She's got a gorgeous son called Archie. Then there's me and then Bryony who runs the children's bookshop, and Lara who's at university.'

'So what's Lara studying?'

'Literature.'

'Well, of course.' April gave a wry smile.

'You can't escape it in our family,' Josh said. 'Books are part of our DNA.'

'And is there a bookshop for Lara to run when she graduates?'

'Actually, no. But I think she's going to be a writer. You'd like her. She's a real live wire. She's passionate about everything. She helps organise Castle Clare's Literary Festival each August.'

'There's a festival?'

Josh nodded with pride. 'You'll see the posters and bunting going up pretty soon. It was slow to get going. There are a lot of festivals to compete with these days, but it's been steadily growing over the years and it's getting quite popular now. It's great fun. It brings all sorts of interesting people to the town – writers, publishers, journalists and, of course, lots of book lovers. It's always a busy time for our bookshops.'

'I can't wait.'

'Yes. Make sure you have plenty of stock in for the tourists.'

'I will.'

'So, what about your family?' Josh asked. 'What are they like?'

'Not as interesting as yours, I'm afraid. Mine's very small.'

'Any brothers or sisters?'

She hesitated for a moment. 'Just me.'

'And parents?'

'They live in Norfolk.'

'Are you close?'

'Yes.'

Josh paused in his questioning, feeling her obvious resistance and waiting for her to elaborate only she didn't, and he scanned his mind quickly for something else to talk about.

'So your art – your love of painting and restoring things – where do you think that comes from?'

'My mother and...' she paused, 'my father.'

He watched her as she spoke. Again, she seemed hesitant, almost reluctant, to talk about her family which seemed like an odd thing to Josh, although he knew his own situation was becoming more rare and that not everyone had the sort of family he did with a father and mother who had been happily married for nearly forty years, and siblings that not only got along, but were able to run the family business together too.

'Both artistic, then?' Josh prompted.

'Very.'

He nodded. The conversation had stalled again. So, she was close to her parents, but she didn't want to talk about them. Why was that, he wondered?

'Have you bought a place here?' he asked.

'I'm renting,' she told him. 'It's just a small place on the edge of town.'

'I hope you're happy here. Castle Clare's a pretty special place.'

'Yes, I can see that.' She smiled and there was another awkward pause. 'I'm sorry if I'm being a bit vague.'

'No,' Josh said, even though he thought that she was. 'I'm sorry if I'm asking the wrong questions.'

'You're not.' She looked down into her wine glass. 'Let's talk about something else, shall we?'

'Whatever you want,' Josh encouraged.

'How about you tell me more about you?'

'What do you want to know?'

'Everything!'

'Well, that shouldn't take long. My name's Joshua William Nightingale and I'm the middle child of Frank and Eleanor. I've already told you about my siblings and what they do.'

'And did you always want to run a bookshop?'

'Oh, yes! I remember the first time Dad took me to his shop. It's the one Sam runs now. Back then, it was the only shop we had and we sold everything under that one roof – new, secondhand, children's – every kind of book. It was a magical place. Still is. But there was something special about it then. It was a secret world and I could lose myself for hours there. The shelves reached the ceiling and it seemed to me, as a youngster, that the whole world was made of books, and there was always some new volume to discover. That was the real joy – finding something for yourself. It's always great to be given a book, and heaven knows that each of us Nightingale children were given book after book over the years, but it always seemed doubly sweet to find one for yourself. Like a secret discovered.'

Josh smiled as he remembered those early, formative years surrounded by books.

'I was five when I sold my first book to a customer,' he went on. 'I still remember that intense joy. I'd been in the back room and had sped through a picture book about snails. It was filled with lots of glorious images of slime – just perfect for little boys – and there was a woman in the shop with her little boy and I remember reaching out to grab her arm and telling her that she had to buy her son the book.'

'And she did?'

'Oh, yes!'

'Did you get any commission for that?'

'Probably a mint humbug!'

April laughed. 'You're a born salesman.'

'Only when it comes to books. I don't think I'd be very good at selling anything else.'

'So what happened after the age of five?'

'School and books. And books and school. Then sixth form – English and History, and then university and even more books.'

'And dare I ask what you studied?'

'Literature – of course.'

'Of course!' April echoed.

'Shakespeare, nineteenth-century literature, and a little bit of modern.'

'And you never wanted to teach or do anything other than sell books?'

Josh took another sip of wine. He couldn't remember the last time someone had shown this much interest in him. It was a new experience for him and one that wasn't at all unpleasant.

'I thought about teaching, but that isn't so much about the books as the pupils, is it? And I don't know if that would be a good fit for me.'

'You don't like children?'

'It's not that. I like children well enough. I adore my nephew. But the thought of trying to get thirty great hulking fifteen-year-olds interested in Shakespeare is a bit daunting, isn't it?'

April grinned. 'I suppose it is.'

'It takes a special sort of person to be a teacher.'

'And an equally special one to match people to books.'

'Well, thank you.'

'Tell me more about your job. What's it like?'

Once again, he was surprised by her interest and her question. He just wasn't used to being such a focus of attention.

'Other than the fact I'm surrounded by books all day, there are some definite highlights to the job,' he began. 'I'd say one of my favourite things is helping someone to find that perfect book. Say a random person comes in and they're looking for a gift for a spouse or their child. If you can pick *just* the right book for them, well, that's a magical moment. It's like the best little link in the universe.'

'I love that. Making those types of connections must be so special.'

'It is. I also love trying to guess what it is customers might be looking for. It's a little game I often play with Sam when we're together, and you really never can tell what it is a person enjoys reading,' Josh confessed. 'Just last week, an elderly man came in and he'd been browsing for some time before I asked him if there was anything I could help him with, and he asked what I could recommend in YA. Young Adult. He was absolutely addicted to all those dystopian novels. Well, that's something Bryony has more knowledge of than me, so I sent him over to her shop.'

'So what did you think he'd be interested in?' April asked.

'Thrillers, histories, autobiographies,' Josh said. 'You see? I was typecasting him based on his gender and age, and you never really know and you should certainly never try and guess. That's one of the lessons bookselling has taught me.'

'So what are the negatives? Are there any?'

'Oh, yes!' Josh said with a laugh. 'When you're dealing with customers, there are *always* going to be negatives.'

'Do tell!'

'Well, most of them come from their expectations of what I know. Now, I've been around books all my life so I like to think I've got a pretty good knowledge of what's been written in the past, and I pride myself on keeping up-to-date with what's being written and published now, but there are customers who expect you to know everything – and I mean *everything*. Like the woman who came in a couple of weeks ago asking for a book she'd read as a teenager. She said she thought it had a red cover and that the heroine was called Holly and it was set in Scotland.'

April laughed. 'Not very specific?'

'No author name, no idea what the title was. Even having the publisher's name might have helped to track it down. Believe it or not, and it pains me to say it, but booksellers don't know every single book that's ever been published. Then there are the people who have the ability to take a book down from a shelf, but don't seem to have the skills to put it back. That drives me crazy!'

April smiled and nodded in sympathy.

'But the positives far outweigh the negatives. Like making a new display when fresh stock comes in. Deciding how to arrange all those beautiful books and what should go in the window – which books you want the passing world to see.'

He paused. Was he talking too much? His heart was racing, he could feel it, which told him he was probably a little bit too hyper. But that's how talking about books made him feel. He should really stop talking and try and turn the conversation back round to her again.

'So, did you grow up around books?' he asked.

'Oh, yes. Art books mostly. But plenty of fiction from the library. My mum never liked us spending money on fiction. She used to say what was the point of something that was made up?'

'Really?'

'I'm afraid so. But she didn't mind books from the library so I got my fill and, when I started earning my own money, I could buy my own books.'

'And you studied art?'

'Yes. It was always going to be a part of my life in some way and I think I've finally found what I love to do the most – turning something unloved into something beautiful and making it a part of a home. I don't think I had it in me to be a real artist and stand and paint portraits or landscapes all day, and still lifes bore me, but having a great hulking piece of furniture to restore is special. It's something I can wrap my imagination around as well as my whole body too. I adore that. It seems more real to me than a painting. You can move it around it. It's useful, it has a purpose.'

'And that's important, is it? That it should have a purpose?'

'I think so. I've thought about this a lot,' April said, 'and I've noticed that you stop looking at art after a while. I've lived with beautiful things all my life – paintings and ceramics, textiles – lovely handmade things, and it's a privilege to be surrounded by them, but you do stop looking at them after a while. But a piece of furniture – you can't not look at that if it's functioning properly.'

'So, every time you take a pair of socks out of a drawer you've decorated, or eat your dinner off a table that you've restored–'

'You'll notice it!' April said. 'That's what I believe, anyway. I still think art is important. I couldn't live without beautiful things in my life, but I don't feel the need to contribute more of it to the world. Does that make sense?'

'Absolutely.'

April looked down and pulled her sleeve back to reveal a slim gold band.

'I still like to wear a watch,' she said.

'Me too,' Josh said, pulling his own sleeve back to reveal the ancient watch which had been a gift from his Grandpa Joe.

'And I'm afraid I really should be going.'

'Oh,' Josh said, fearful of showing his disappointment. He'd been nervous about them getting together but, now that it was over, he wished he could do it all over again.

'Can I drop you anywhere?' he asked as she stood up and grabbed her bag.

'Oh, it's okay. I've got a lift.'

'Right.' He waited, expecting her to say more about this lift as they left the pub together, but she didn't. 'I can wait with you if you like.'

'There's really no need.'

Josh looked around. It was still light and Castle Clare was pretty safe, but it still didn't feel right leaving a young woman on her own.

'I don't mind waiting.'

'I'd really rather you didn't,' she told him and there was a sharp edge to her voice, but she quickly smiled. 'Really – you don't need to.'

He shuffled his feet, feeling awkward now. 'Well, if you're sure.'

'Thank you for the drink. I've had a lovely time,' she said.

'Me too.'

She smiled. 'I'll see you tomorrow, no doubt.'

'Yes,' Josh said. 'No doubt.'

He turned to go, pausing to look back just once at April Channing. He was still delightfully surprised by her arrival in Castle Clare. He wasn't sure what it meant yet – if, indeed, it meant anything at all – but he was grateful and happy that she was there.

CHAPTER FOUR

It was the next day when Winston Kneller came into Josh's bookshop as soon as it had opened. He was wearing his old felt hat, despite the warmth of the May morning, and a red and white polka-dotted neckerchief added a dash of vibrancy to his appearance.

'No Delilah today, Winston?' Josh asked.

'No, she's at home sleeping her breakfast off as was I until about twenty minutes ago.'

Josh smiled. Winston was in his late-seventies and was a great character in Castle Clare.

'How can I help you?'

'I believe you have a book for me,' he said Josh.

'Ah, yes! That's right. *Mrs Dalloway.*'

'Decided to treat myself to a new copy of this one,' Winston said. 'Besides, Sam didn't have one secondhand. He usually looks out for them for me, but this one was proving elusive.'

'There was a very nice Penguin Modern Classic a few years back. Had a painting of Virginia Woolf on the cover painted by her sister Vanessa Bell,' Josh told him. 'Actually, it's a bit of a spooky image. Bell seems to have forgotten to paint in Woolf's face.'

Winston's mouth gaped open. 'Did she have bad eyesight?'

'No,' Josh laughed. 'I think it was just the style of the painting.'

'A portrait with no face? Just sounds like bad art to me!'

Josh nodded in agreement, dreading to think what April might make of their disparaging comments on the art of the Bloomsbury Group.

'Let me get your book,' Josh said, going behind the desk and retrieving the brand new copy of *Mrs Dalloway* with its colourful cover depicting... Josh paused. What exactly was it depicting? Leaves and fruit possibly. It was hard to tell. What was it about Virginia Woolf's work that demanded odd covers? He rang it through the till and Winston paid for it and Josh handed it to him in the customary brown paper bag with the shop's logo stamped upon it and a bookmark inside.

'It better be good,' Winston said.

'Not your usual fare, I'm imagining.'

'You can say that again,' Winston said with a chortle. 'This book club business is stretching the old grey matter, which is no bad thing, I hear. Keep all that dementia stuff at bay.'

Josh flinched, thinking of Grandma Nell and her lifetime of reading. Had that helped her, he wondered? Would she have succumbed even earlier if she hadn't been a bookworm?

'Reading is the best medicine around,' Josh agreed. 'You'll have to let me know how you get on with it.'

'Sure thing. You not coming to the book club, then?'

'I might look in, yes. But it's not really my kind of thing.'

'But you love books, don't you?'

'Of course,' Josh said, wondering how he'd explain that it was the social aspect of the club that he'd find tricky. He was much more of a one-to-one sort of person. He didn't bloom in a room full of people. 'I'm just not a fan of book clubs.'

'Fair enough although you're missing out on some pretty fine baking treats.'

'So I've heard.'

Winston nodded. 'Although there was a chicken feather in the last offering from Flo.'

'Something else I've heard,' Josh said and they exchanged smiles.

'I see the new shop is open for business,' Winston said, looking out of the window. 'What's it selling?'

'Furniture and household items. Upcycled.'

'Up-what?'

'Cycled.'

'Oh, you mean that fancy secondhand stuff? All flaky paint in pastel colours, eh?'

'They're beautiful pieces.'

'And who's running it?'

'She's called April Channing.'

'Is that her now?'

Josh looked across the road just as April stepped out onto the pavement. Her long chestnut hair caught in the breeze and his breath caught in his throat.

'Yes.'

Winston looked at Josh and then back at April.

'She's lovely,' Winston said. 'Kind of reminds me of someone.'

Josh tore his eyes away from April and looked at Winston. 'Who?'

He shook his head and waved a hand in dismissal. 'Oh, nobody.'

Josh observed him, noticing the slight flush of his cheeks and the brightness of his eyes.

'Nobody – *really?*'

Winston glanced up at him and then looked out of the window as April watered her plants with a small blue watering can.

'Somebody,' Winston conceded. 'Somebody... special.'

'Who?' Josh asked gently.

Winston took a moment before answering. 'Marguerite,' he said at last.

Josh smiled. 'Lovely name.'

'For a lovely woman.'

'How did you meet her?'

'At a dance.'

'Here in Castle Clare?'

He nodded. 'At the town hall. Believe it or not, before it became a home for the occasional bric-a-brac sale and all those boring council meetings, people used to dance there. They'd come from miles around. Every week. And the music!' Winston's eyes glazed over as he travelled back in time and his old body started to sway right there in the shop. 'Food too,' he added with a chuckle.

'And that's where you met her?' Josh prompted.

Winston sighed and stared out of the window again. 'Chestnut hair – just like hers.'

Josh looked across the road at April again and it was then that the shop phone rang.

'Hold it there, Winston. I'll be right back,' Josh said, running to the desk to take the call, making a note of the order the customer wanted.

When he finally got off the phone and looked across the shop, Winston had gone. Josh sighed. He'd so wanted to hear more about Winston's girl with the chestnut hair.

He looked around the shop. Nobody had come in whilst he'd been on the phone so he took the opportunity to sneak across the road to see April. He'd spent most of the night before thinking about her, playing their conversation over and over in his mind and remembering the attentive way she'd looked at him and her genuine interest in all he did.

Opening the door to A Little Bit Bloomsbury, he called her

name.

'April?'

She emerged from the back room, a pot of paint in her arms. Her chestnut hair was half swept up, half tumbling across her shoulders and she was wearing a long dress in a pretty fabric of tiny pink and blue flowers.

'Hello,' she said. She wasn't wearing the pink glasses today and it was the first time he'd seen her eyes properly. Like her hair, they were a warm chestnut-colour and he could see that her pale skin was scattered with tiny freckles.

He swallowed hard, trying not to stare. 'How are you? Did you get home okay?'

She looked confused for a moment. 'Oh, yes.'

'Good. I really enjoyed last night.'

'Me too,' she said, perhaps a little hesitantly, Josh couldn't help thinking.

'Perhaps we could do it again sometime?'

'Erm, sure,' she said.

Josh nodded. This wasn't going as well as he'd thought it might. She felt a little cooler to him, as if a barrier had gone up. He hadn't felt that the night before. That had gone well, hadn't it? He thought it had.

'Okay,' he said, nodding awkwardly. 'I'll leave you to it.' He turned to leave, feeling somewhat deflated and puzzled by the change he felt in April.

'Josh?' she called as he reached the door.

'Yes?' he turned around.

'Come back tomorrow. I've got to work on a commission now.' She gave him a smile and there was the April he recognised once more.

'Okay,' he said, relieved. 'I'll see you tomorrow.'

~

Winston Kneller was feeling somewhat shaken after his conversation with Josh Nightingale. He'd gone into the shop to buy a book and then the great secret of his past had reared up in front of him. Marguerite. He hadn't thought about her for years. No, that wasn't true. Months maybe. He'd been doing a lot of thinking about his past since his wife, Sally, had died three years ago.

Three years. Was it really so long? It seemed just like yesterday when he'd lost his dear partner of fifty years. Theirs had been a long and happy marriage. They'd been the very best of friends, sharing in the highs and lows of life – the arrival of their son and daughter, the loss of jobs and the finding of new ones, the buying of their first home and the subsequent selling of it when Winston's pension turned out to be worth a fraction of what they'd banked on. Oh, yes, they'd experienced all that life had to offer and then she'd died. It had been so sudden and swift – a blessing really after her diagnosis of pancreatic cancer – but such a shock. Winston had been lost. His children, Andrew and Katie, had been wonderful, helping with all the arrangements and then sorting through the house and making sure Winston knew how to take care of himself. But they had their own lives to lead and, the truth was, he didn't see them as much as he'd like to.

Thank goodness for Delilah his chocolate Labrador, he thought. She was his constant companion now. And thank goodness they'd made the move into Castle Clare. The terrace on the edge of the town was easy to manage and handy for everything, and Winston had been so grateful for having his friends nearby, and things like the book club had been a real lifeline, occupying some of the space which Sally had filled. He'd never read so much in his whole life as he had since Sam had started the book club. He'd even joined the library and had a new pile of books on his coffee table every three weeks. Okay, so he didn't read them all cover to cover. But he dipped in and out of a fair few, making up for all the years that he'd spent without reading anything more than the local newspaper.

Reading, however, could only fill so many hours. He'd soon come to realise that retired widowers had a lot of time on their hands – a lot of thinking time – and Winston started to think about things he hadn't had a chance to think about for years, and one of those things had been Marguerite Taylor. He closed his eyes now as he remembered her. Only he couldn't tell if it was Marguerite he was remembering or if it was April. This morning had confused his memory and now he couldn't be sure whose face he was seeing in his mind's eye.

How well could you truly remember somebody you hadn't seen for over fifty years? Surely you couldn't really hope to recollect them clearly. And why was he even trying?

Winston went upstairs, suddenly spurred on by the need to know. There was a tin somewhere – a large tin full of old bits and bobs – the sort of thing other people know not to look in because it's full of the personal clutter of somebody else's life. Winston hadn't thought about the tin for years, but he desperately wanted to find it now. But where was it? He stood in the middle of his bedroom and looked around. Top of the wardrobe? No, that was the resting place of all of Sally's hat boxes which he still hadn't been able to part with. Under the bed? No, that was full of suitcases whose travelling days were long over. He scratched his chin. Spare bedroom, then?

He walked through, looking at the single bed that hadn't seen a guest for a good few months now. He pulled up the valance sheet and peered underneath. There was something under there all right, but he couldn't make out what. Getting down onto his knees, which wasn't as easy as it once had been, Winston peered underneath the bed and then sighed. It was a shoe box. Not the old tin.

It was as he was hoisting himself up that he saw the chest of drawers in the corner of the room and something clicked. He walked towards it, opening the bottom drawer, and there it was: his old tin. His hands were almost shaking as he pulled it out, feeling the weight of it for the first time in years and the roughness of the metal which had rusted after years of being kept in a leaky shed at the bottom of the garden.

Gently, as if it was made of gossamer rather than rusty tin, Winston carried it to the bed where he sat down, placing it on his knees. He prised the lid off and smiled at the contents, neglected for so long, but never forgotten. There were postcards and cinema tickets, ticket stubs from bus journeys he couldn't quite remember, but which had obviously had some significance, a receipt for his wedding suit for an eye-watering sum even in today's money, a couple of old buttons, a lollypop stick with a joke which had made Sally laugh so much that her nose had run, a piece of ribbon that Katie had worn in her hair on her first day of school, and photos. Lots of photos. He picked these up now – they were funny little photos with rounded edges, the colours faded. Not like the digital images you got these days, he thought. But he loved these old, tactile memories. Moments you could hold in your hand or put in a frame. They would never crash or be deleted by accident or lost inside one of those awful computer contraptions. They would live safely forever in the sanctuary of his tin.

His fingers moved quickly through the rest of the contents now, trying to find that one particular photo – the one he'd buried years ago, the one he'd hidden from Sally. Well, she'd known about it. He was pretty sure about that. They were always honest with each other and he knew that she'd had boyfriends before he'd come onto the scene. He'd seen the love letters she'd kept from one of them. There'd been no harm in that, he'd thought. After all, she'd married *him*, hadn't she? And Winston had kept that one photo. But where was it?

He shifted another little heap of faded photos aside and that's when he saw it, amongst the black and white photos from what seemed like another age. Which it was, of course, he thought to himself, smiling as his mind travelled back to the days when he'd had a full head of hair and when backache and arthritic joints were simply unimaginable. He pulled the photo out from the others, letting them fall back into the tin. He didn't care much what they were of. This was the one he wanted.

Marguerite.

It was a crying shame that the photo was black and white but, all the same, he could see the bright chestnut of her hair in his mind's eye, and the pink glow of her cheeks after dancing the night away with him. And the dress? Had it been blue or green? He couldn't remember now. But that didn't matter. All that mattered was the smile that greeted the man taking the photo. Him. Winston. *Young* Winston. He could still feel the flush of heat on his own cheeks from an evening of whisking her around the floor to the music played by the band. Gosh, he'd loved to dance. He couldn't remember the last time he'd taken a woman by the hand and danced. Had it been his wedding to Sally? Had they really not danced after that? Maybe they had and he'd just forgotten. It was so easy to forget things these days.

And yet he hadn't forgotten Marguerite. He felt almost guilty for the strength of that particular memory. Did it mean he'd loved his wife any less? Certainly not. But there had been something undeniably special in that first love. And, after it had ended, it had taken Winston a whole five years before he'd let himself fall in love again.

He sat on the bed for a little while longer and then he put the lid back on the tin and returned it to the drawer. But he kept hold of the photograph because there was somebody he needed to show it to.

~

Josh was reorganising the central display table in the bookshop when the bell chimed. He looked up and there she was. Wearing a lime green linen dress and with a yellow ribbon tying her chestnut hair back, she was a vision of spring loveliness.

'April!' he said, putting down the book he was holding which, only a moment ago, had been the centre of his world.

Her face seemed creased in anxiety.

'Are you okay?' Josh asked.

She walked into the shop until she was standing quite close to him.

'I'm sorry about yesterday,' she said.

'What about it?'

'If I was a bit... off,' she stated, and then her forehead creased again. 'Was I? *Was* I a bit off?'

Josh frowned, not quite sure how to respond. It seemed like some kind of female trap and that he couldn't win whatever he said and so he simply shrugged.

'I was, wasn't I? I'm sorry.'

'You were busy,' he said as tactfully as he could.

She shook her head. 'That's no excuse. I'm sorry.'

'No need to apologise.'

'I'm afraid that sometimes, not always, but sometimes, I can seem a little bit...' she paused.

'Brusque?' Josh volunteered and then he wished he hadn't in case it sounded rude.

Luckily, she laughed. 'Yes! That's it exactly. And it's not because I am brusque,' she added. 'It's just that I have things on my mind. I'm not always in the here and now. I'm thinking of things – colours mostly, or patterns or combinations of things like which piece of furniture would best suit the new chalk paint I've just discovered. Or can I get away with using these enamel knobs on this set of drawers? I'm afraid my head is full of such things and I don't always function well as a civilised human being.'

Josh smiled. 'Then we have something in common.'

'We do?'

'Yes. I'm often told I'm in a world of my own, only mine is the printed world of books.'

'So you understand? I mean, you don't mind?'

'Of course I don't mind. I totally understand. I think it's all part of the creativity of being an introvert, isn't it?'

'You're an introvert?' she asked.

'Aren't you?'

'*Yes!*'

Josh grinned. 'It's still not very popular to admit to such a thing, is it? Our world is all about leaders who shout the loudest and people willing to put every little detail about their lives onto every single social media platform.'

April nodded with enthusiasm.

'But at least it's beginning to be understood,' Josh went on. 'Us bookworms, and those who prefer a quiet night in to a noisy one out, we're not being dismissed as – well – geeks anymore.'

'I never really minded the geek label.'

'You didn't?'

'No. I guess I've been brought up to be proud of being different – of not following the herd.'

'There's definitely something in that,' Josh agreed.

'So, are your brothers and sisters all introverts too?'

'Well, Sam definitely is, but Bryony and Lara are more gregarious and love an evening out. And Polly? She's somewhere in between.'

'And your parents?'

'Mum likes to throw a party every so often, but Dad prefers to potter around the garden. I actually think he prefers plants to people. What about your parents?'

April, who'd been smiling, now turned away from Josh to look at the shelves in front of her, idly pulling out a book.

'Erm, I guess they like their own company,' she said without looking at him and, once again, Josh felt her pulling away slightly at the mention of her family. 'Can I take a look around?'

'Of course,' he said, gesturing to her with an open hand, glad that the momentary awkwardness had been replaced by enthusiasm once more.

'Or, even better, could you *show* me around?'

Josh smiled. 'It would be my pleasure.'

As with all of the Nightingale's bookshops, Josh's was a modest size but, like his brother and sister, he had made the very most of the space, cramming it with as many interesting tomes as possible and, while it wasn't quite as crammed to the rafters as Sam's was, it was certainly very full indeed. Josh loved order and didn't like to double-stack or have books lying horizontally on top of other books. That wouldn't do at all. Nor did he like piles of books on the floor. That worked for Sam's secondhand offerings next door, but not for his new books. Everything had to be just right in Josh's shop and if he was accused of being too particular and too precise then that was fine. That's what he was.

'Well, you can see practically everything with one glance,' he began. 'Fiction at the front, biographies there, history and art here, cooking, gardening, DIY there. Crafts over here.'

'And in the back?'

'Come on through,' he said, leading her into the small back room. 'All sorts in here. Drama and poetry, dictionaries and science, travel and self-help. Actually, there's a shelf I've recently created that I'm rather fond of.' Josh walked across to a little shelf which he thought of as very special indeed.

April peered closely through her pink glasses and then gasped. 'A whole shelf of books about introverts!'

Josh nodded proudly. 'I like to empower my own people.'

'Wonderful!'

Josh leaned forward and pulled one of the titles out. 'I can highly recommend this one.'

April took the book from him and flipped through it, her face close to the pages.

'I could give you a little discount if you wanted it,' he whispered.

She placed the book back on the shelf. 'Actually, I kind of prefer audio books,' she told him.

'Oh,' he said. 'Right. Well, they're marvellous too.'

'I mean, I'll read the book you gave me as a welcome present.'

He held his hand up. 'I'm sorry – the last thing I should do is pressure anyone into reading anything. It's a sure-fire way of turning someone off.'

'No, no – you're not pressurising me. You're just being enthusiastic.'

'Can't help that, I'm afraid.'

'It's a wonderful shop. A whole world, really.'

'Yes. Books are kind of like citizens, aren't they? Each one standing their ground and making their own unique statement.'

'I like that.'

'They're friends too. Is it crazy to say?'

'Not at all,' April said. 'I think of colours as being like friends. My paint pots and boxes, my pastels and my pencils. They're definitely companions.'

'It's good to find somebody who understands these things,' he said.

She smiled and Josh felt an unexpected lightness, as if he'd suddenly lost all the weight of his body. It was the strangest feeling and not altogether unpleasant.

And that's when the shop bell rang.

'I'd better leave you to it,' April told him and Josh watched helplessly as she quickly left the shop. There was a part of him that very nearly made him reach out to take her arm and ask her to stay there with him. He wanted to go on talking to her and Josh never normally wanted to go on talking to people. He usually wanted to get away from them. But April was different and, as he watched her go, he couldn't help begrudging the customer who'd interrupted them.

'Can I help you?' Josh asked the gentleman, polite despite his internal frustration.

The gentleman, who was in his sixties, was looking shifty. 'I'm after that book.'

'Which book?'

'You know – that book that's been all over the place and made into a film.' He leaned forward and shielded his mouth with his hand. 'That *racy* one.'

Josh sighed, unable to believe that people were still requesting it. 'We don't have it.'

'You don't?'

'I don't stock erotica.'

'Why not?'

'Because that's my choice as a bookseller.'

'But that's prejudiced.'

'Maybe. But you can order it easily online.'

'Surely that's not good for business.'

'It's a choice I've decided to make.'

'Can I order it?'

'Not from me, I'm afraid, but there are hundreds of other books that I'm sure I could interest you in.'

The man shook his head and tutted in frustration as he left the shop.

Josh watched him go, knowing that he really shouldn't pass judgement on what people read, but quite helpless to stop himself from doing so.

CHAPTER FIVE

Sunday lunch at Campion House was something of a Nightingale tradition and woe betide anyone who made an excuse to miss it. It was when four generations came together, from Grandpa Joe and Grandma Nell, and Frank and Eleanor to Sam, Polly, Josh, Bryony and Lara – when she nipped home from university – and Polly's son, Archie. Sam's girlfriend, Callie, Polly's partner, Jago, and Bryony's boyfriend, Ben, were also very much a part of the gathering. Grandpa Joe would often joke that they'd have to extend the dining room out into the garden once everybody was partnered up and had children. Eleanor would always smile at that. She wouldn't mind at all. She loved nothing more than having a big, happy brood around her.

That Sunday was a particularly cool one after a spell of warm weather and Eleanor, Polly, Bryony and Sam were busy in the kitchen preparing a roast when Josh arrived. He'd popped his head round the door to the living room where his father and grandparents were sitting, while Jago, Archie and Callie were on the floor playing some board game Josh didn't recognise.

'Think they need my help in the kitchen?' Josh asked.

'Always something to do,' his father told him.

'Is that why you're sat in your armchair with the paper?' Josh teased.

'Hey, I grew the greens we're going to be eating!'

Josh laughed. His father was very proud of the produce he grew for family meals.

Taking his shoes and coat off, Josh made his way to the kitchen.

'Josh!' His mother flew across the kitchen and hugged him. It was as if she hadn't seen him for a year rather than just a week.

'Anything I can do to help?'

'You could peel and chop some of those carrots and then start on the broccoli.'

'What are we having?'

'Our favourite roast,' Polly told him. 'I'm making Yorkshire puddings to help combat the unseasonable cold.'

'And I've got a Bakewell tart for pudding, to be served warm,' his mother told him. 'We all need warming up today.'

'Wonderful!' Josh said as he got to work on the carrots. He liked working in the kitchen. He appreciated the precision of the utensils, and nobody peeled and chopped carrots quite like him. He might not have been the quickest, nimblest of workers in the kitchen, but he was the neatest.

'Is Lara home?' he asked.

'She certainly is,' Polly said. 'She turned up on Friday night with three bags of washing and a jumper with a hole in it which she begged Mum to mend for her because, in her words, her stitches were, "Beyond the horror of Frankenstein".'

'Is that right?'

'It certainly is,' Eleanor said. 'Well, the jumper's as good as new now.'

'She's got you wrapped round her little finger,' Sam chipped in from the sink where he was washing glasses.

'Talking of fingers,' Eleanor said, 'look what she did as a thank you.' She flexed her fingers and Polly gasped at her nails.

'They're purple!'

'Iridescent – look!'

Polly wasn't impressed. 'You look like you've slammed your fingertips in the door!'

'Oh, nonsense! They're delightful.'

Josh smiled. Polly rarely wore anything as decadent as nail polish and, if she ever did, it would be clear or a subtle shade of pink.

'I can't wait to see what the ladies make of it at our coffee morning next week,' Eleanor said with a naughty laugh.

A couple of minutes later, Lara tumbled in through the back door having just given the dogs, Brontë, Hardy and Dickens a quick run around the garden.

'Hey, Josh!' she called, pushing her long hair out of her face. 'Blimey, it's windy out there.'

'Hey, Lara!'

'Paws wiped?' Eleanor prompted.

'Oooops!'

'I'll help,' Polly said. 'After all, a third of those paws belong to me. It's only fair.'

It didn't take long before Polly and Lara were back in the kitchen, the dogs' paws duly wiped.

'Hardy was the only one who was really mucky,' Lara announced. 'He ran across Dad's new veg bed.'

Eleanor gasped. 'Don't say a word to your father!'

'I wouldn't dare,' Lara said as she sniffed the air. 'Smells yummy! Any mashed potato?'

'We're roasting them,' Polly told her.

'Can we have mash too?'

'If you're happy to prepare it,' Eleanor told her youngest.

'I can peel the potatoes if you like,' Josh said.

'What an angel you are,' Lara said, only now taking her coat off. 'How can it be so warm and springlike one day and then freezing cold the next?'

'British Summertime,' Polly said.

Sam laughed. 'Wonderful reading weather. At least it's good for business.'

'And how are the shops?' Eleanor asked.

'I've got a new display of Callie's books,' Bryony said.

'It looks great,' Sam told her. 'She's delighted.'

'So are my customers. They love her signed books.'

'Sam?' Eleanor asked.

'Yeah, good. A school librarian pulled up the other day with a stack of boxes. Just wanted rid of the lot. Said he'd binned the really grubby copies, but a few had sneaked through. There are some nice titles in there. I'm just sorting through them all now.'

'And what about you, Josh?' Eleanor asked.

He shrugged as he made a start on Lara's potatoes. 'Things are good.'

Eleanor shook her head at his brevity. 'Would you like to add anything to that?'

'Not really. It's pretty normal.'

Bryony turned around from where she was chopping herbs at the table. 'What a great fat liar you are!'

'What do you mean?'

'It's not a *normal* week at all!'

'What's this about?' Eleanor demanded, putting down the tea towel she'd been holding and giving Josh her full attention.

'Josh is in love!' Bryony chimed.

Josh felt his face flare with colour. The fact that Bryony could still do that to him, even though he was an adult, annoyed him intensely. She was *such* a child.

'You're talking rubbish – as usual!' he said, hating how childish he sounded.

'Oh, come on! You must admit that you like her at least,' Bryony insisted.

'Who are we talking about?' Eleanor asked.

'April...,' Bryony paused. 'What's her last name?'

'Channing,' Josh said.

'See! You know everything about her!'

'Stop teasing him, Bryony.' Her mother warned her with a stern look.

Bryony grinned. The admonishment had been worth it.

Josh turned his back on them, hoping against hope that the conversation would move on.

'Josh?' His mother wasn't giving up.

'Yes?'

'Tell me about April.'

Josh sighed as he put his potato peeler down. 'She's opened the shop across the road.'

'The one that's been empty all this time?'

'Yes.'

'I'm so glad somebody's in there at long last. What is it she does?'

'She upcycles furniture,' Josh explained.

'She's a really gifted painter,' Bryony chipped in.

'And what's she like?'

'She's...' Josh's words dissolved on his tongue as his mother waited to hear them. How was he going to explain how he felt about April without looking like a fool? She'd only been in Castle Clare for such a short time and yet his feelings were totally out of proportion. It was ridiculous and he couldn't hope to explain them in front of a room full of eager family members.

'She's nice,' he said.

Eleanor sighed. 'For a bookworm, your vocabulary is sometimes horribly limited.'

'I told you he was in love,' Bryony dared to say again, receiving another warning look from her mother.

Josh took the distraction as an opportunity to return to his potato peeling.

'I'd love to meet her,' Lara said.

'Me too,' Sam said. 'I've only seen her in passing.'

'Yes, and me,' Polly added.

'Well, I don't want to be left out,' Eleanor said. 'Why not ask her to lunch next week, Josh?'

Josh shook his head. 'No way. It's *much* too early to spring you lot on her.'

'Oh, rubbish!' Bryony said. 'The sooner the better, I say. She should be well informed about things.'

'But we've only just met.'

'You took her for a drink, didn't you?' Sam asked.

'Yes, but–'

'*Did* you?' Bryony cried. 'Why didn't you tell me, Josh? Or you, Sam?'

'Invite her to lunch. Next week,' Eleanor repeated.

'Best to get it over and done with if you ask me,' Sam told Josh with a grin. Josh sighed. Sam was probably right.

Monday in the bookshop was usually a slow day as the people of Castle Clare got back into the swing of the workday week. But there was one customer who came in that Josh hadn't expected. Winston.

'Hello there,' Josh said, delighted to see him.

'Okay if Delilah comes in?' Winston asked, hovering half inside with the chocolate Labrador on the pavement outside.

Josh hesitated, well aware that Delilah's age brought with it a host of issues which might not be customer-friendly.

'Sure – come on in,' he said, crossing his fingers and hoping for the best.

'I've brought you something,' Winston said as he crossed the shop towards Josh. 'After our little conversation.'

'Oh?'

'You remember what we talked about?'

'I do. Marguerite.'

Winston smiled at hearing the name from another's lips. 'That's right. Here.' He handed Delilah's lead to Josh and then popped his hand inside his waistcoat pocket and brought out a little black and white photo. 'I wanted to show you this.' He handed it to Josh as he took Delilah's lead back.

Josh looked down at the photograph of a young woman.

'She's lovely,' he said and he truly meant it. The woman in the photo was a real beauty and her smile was utterly captivating.

'Same chestnut hair as that young lady across the road,' Winston said.

'Do you have a colour photo of her?' Josh asked as he returned the photo.

'No. This is the only one I have. But I remember it!' he said, tapping his head. 'There's no forgetting a thing like that – mark my words.'

They exchanged knowing smiles.

'You were telling me about the dances at the town hall and how you met her there.'

'That's right,' Winston said.

'I'd love to know more.'

Winston smiled, his cheeks high and bright with pleasure. 'Would you now?'

'If you've a mind to tell. I could make us some tea.'

'Now, there's an invitation,' Winston said.

A few minutes later, tea made, Josh gestured to behind the till where there was a stool and Winston happily sat upon it, Delilah settling by his feet. Slowly sipping his tea, Winston's mind rolled back to the past as he began.

'It was the highlight of every week, the dance. It was what got me through sometimes. I was working as a farm labourer and it was pretty hard work, but there was a good gang of us and we'd look forward to the weekends when we could get dressed up a bit.' He chuckled. 'Believe it or not, I used to cut quite a dash when I was nineteen.'

'I *do* believe it!' Josh told him, trying to imagine a nineteen-year-old Winston. 'You still do.'

Winston smiled as his hand self-consciously felt for his lime-green neckerchief.

'It's different when you're young, though. You primp and preen like a peacock.'

Josh frowned. He wasn't sure about that. He liked to be clean and presentable, but he wasn't aware that he ever primped.

'Anyway,' Winston continued, 'there I was that Saturday evening in June. It had been a warm day and the evening was still light as the dance got underway. I'd taken my jacket off. It was an old thing anyway and it was pretty hot in the dance hall that night.'

Josh watched as Winston looked across the shop at nothing in particular, his focus still in the past.

'I saw her as soon as she came in,' he began again after taking a sip of his tea. 'She was wearing a light dress that seemed to float. She didn't seem real. But she was because she laughed. She was with friends and one of them said something to her and she laughed. It was the loveliest sound I'd ever heard and it made me smile and that's when she looked at me and our eyes just sort of locked and she stopped laughing. I didn't know what to do. I felt trapped by indecision, knowing this was one of those moments in life when you had to make your mind up – and fast. And so I walked towards her – even though I didn't have the confidence of having my jacket on. I walked towards her and offered her my hand. I'm Winston,' I told her, 'and I'd love to dance with you.'

Winston paused and Josh found himself leaning forward. 'And what did she say?'

'Nothing at first. I was left hanging in one of those awful silences. I heard one of her friends giggling and I felt myself beginning to deflate, but my hand was still out towards her and, after what seemed an age, she took it. I couldn't believe it. I'm sure one of her friends was protesting, but her hand was in mine and I was going to dance with her.'

Josh smiled. It was one of the most romantic moments he'd ever heard about and he knew he'd always think of it every time he walked past the town hall from now on, and he couldn't wait to hear what happened next, but...

'Oh, lord!' Josh exclaimed, grabbing the nearest book and covering his nose in a protective barrier.

'What is it?' Winston asked, putting his mug of tea down.

'I think Delilah might need to go outside,' Josh said as tactfully as he could.

'Really? Oh, dear! You know, my sense of smell isn't as strong as it was.'

'Trust me on this,' Josh said. 'It's bad!'

'Perhaps we should be off, Delilah,' Winston said as he hopped down from the stool and clicked for Delilah to follow him. 'I'll catch you later, Josh!'

'Yes!' Josh said from behind the book. 'Oh, leave the door open, Winston.'

Winston waved his goodbye just as Sam walked in.

'I wouldn't come in here if I was you,' Josh warned.

But it was too late; Sam was inside. 'Why not? Oh, *Christopher Robin!* That's bad!'

'I'm going to have to fumigate the whole shop,' Josh said, still wearing the book as a shield.

Sam was backing out fast.

'What was it you wanted?' Josh called after him but, whatever it was, it wasn't half as important as fresh air.

It took a while for the smell to clear, but something else lingered in Josh's shop after Winston had left – the image of Winston as a young man, walking purposefully towards the beautiful young woman with the chestnut hair and reaching out towards her and asking her to dance. Josh held that image in front of him as he looked out of his shop window towards A Little Bit Bloomsbury. He could see April in there, reaching up to place something at the top of a little shelf. She half-turned, but didn't seem to see him. But that was the moment when he made his decision. Just like Winston at the dance hall, Josh knew what he had to do.

Monday lunchtime came and went without Josh leaving his shop. He'd spent a fair bit of time staring across the street at April's shop, but a constant stream of deliveries and customers had put paid to his idea of going over there. Josh was shy at the best of times and he knew he'd never be able to ask her to Sunday lunch in front of any sort of an audience. So he waited. And waited.

Two o'clock, three o'clock, four o'clock came and went and still he hadn't ventured over. If he lost his nerve and didn't do it today, he knew he never would and so, when he felt sure both her shop and his were empty of customers, which was at about ten to five, he crossed the road towards A Little Bit Bloomsbury, opening the door and finding her crouching on the floor painting a chair leg sky-blue.

'Josh! What a surprise,' she said as she stood up.

'Hello,' he said. She was wearing the pink glasses again today and looked like spring personified in a blossom-pink dress and a turquoise bead necklace. He found himself just staring at her, wishing he could pass the whole day like that. But that would be creepy, wouldn't it?

'Are you all right?' April prompted.

'Come to lunch!' he blurted.

She frowned. 'But it's nearly five o'clock.'

'Sunday. Sunday lunch.'

'Oh, well, that's kind of you. Where? At the pub?'

'Actually, at my parents' house.'

'I see.'

Josh shifted awkwardly. 'I know what this seems like and I don't want you to have any preconceptions or fears, or for you to think I have any sort of expectations or anything like that. It's just that – well – everybody's heard about you and they want to meet you. My mother invited you especially. She's delighted that you've opened a business here and she wants to get to know you. And I'd like you to meet them. They're good people and lunch – Sunday lunch – is always something special.' He stopped, fearing that he was pushing way too hard. 'Am I overselling this?'

She shook her head. 'Not at all. I'm enjoying hearing about it all and I'd love to come with you.'

'You would?'

'Yes.'

'Well, that's great,' Josh said, feeling somewhat surprised. He'd genuinely thought that she'd say no. 'Listen, I'll understand if you change your mind. We're quite a rabble.'

'But I've said yes and I rarely change my mind once I say yes.'

Josh smiled. 'Well, you might change your mind once you get there and hear the noise. Even I find them too much sometimes and I'm related to them!'

April laughed. He loved her laugh. It was like the sound of springtime and he couldn't help thinking how perfectly she fitted her name. April Channing. It chimed of spring.

He cleared his throat, suddenly feeling self-conscious at the thoughts that were dancing through his mind.

'Listen, I know that I – that we – find social interaction more difficult than some, and I don't want to put you off, but you should know that my family is large and loud and likes to joke around, but they're...'

'What?'

'They're the best.'

She smiled. 'I'd be honoured to meet them all. And I promise I won't get stage fright or be overwhelmed. After all, it's only lunch, isn't it? It's not like it's a full-blown party with blaring music or anything.'

'Just lunch,' Josh confirmed.

She smiled again. 'It's funny, isn't it? I can be invited to a party and I'll look forward to it for days in advance and I'll enjoy getting dressed up and deciding what pieces of jewellery to wear and how to have my hair. And I'll get there and, for a few minutes, it'll be nice to see people, but it isn't long before the noise starts to overwhelm me and I'll start feeling claustrophobic and have this urge to get away – even if that means wandering into a room I'm not supposed to be in or sneaking out into the garden. I've lost count of the number of friends' gardens I've hidden in at parties.'

Josh grinned. 'Well, we've got quite a substantial garden should you need to escape.'

'That's good to know although I'm sure I won't need to.'

'I promise to look out for you, okay?'

'Okay.'

Josh hesitated for a moment, clapping his hands together in a nervous manner. The deed was done and he didn't quite know what to say now.

'I guess I'll see you before then, won't I?' she said. 'To arrange a time and a pick up?'

'Yes, although twelve would be good if that suits you.'

'And could you pick me up here?'

'You'll be at the shop?' he asked in surprise. Was she really working on a Sunday?

'There's something I want to do so it'll be easier to meet here.'

'Okay, then. Twelve here on Sunday.'

'I'm looking forward to it.'

Josh smiled. So was he.

CHAPTER SIX

Winston was just coming round from his post-lunch nap when he heard the doorbell ring. He was sitting in his favourite chair, with his favourite plump cushion and his favourite mug beside his new copy of *Mrs Dalloway* which had sent him nicely off into a doze. Waking abruptly now, he looked down at Delilah, who didn't bother much about doorbells these days.

'Who's that then?' he asked the Labrador who looked nonplussed by the question. 'Better go and see.' Winston hoisted himself up, using his arms as levers. His knees were weak these days, despite all his dog walking.

Who would be calling on a mid-week afternoon? It couldn't be Andrew or Katie because they always rang ahead and gave plenty of polite notice. Oh, god, Winston suddenly thought. Was it election time? Might there be some dreadful MP on his doorstep? Well, they wouldn't get Winston's vote, that was for sure. Anyone who disturbed a person in the privacy of their own home during a post-lunch nap didn't deserve his cross in a box.

But it wasn't any local MP. It was his brother, Montague Kneller.

'Monty?'

Winston kind of wished it was an MP after all.

'Hello Winston. Can I come in?'

Winston looked down and saw the large suitcase by his brother's feet. This didn't look good.

'What are you doing here?'

His brother gave a wan sort of a smile. 'Cup of tea first?'

Winston nodded and held the door open wider.

He watched as Monty entered, leaving his suitcase on the doorstep for Winston to pick up. And this is just the beginning, Winston couldn't help thinking, as he obliged his brother, taking the suitcase through to the hallway.

'You still got that smelly dog?' Monty asked as he walked through to the kitchen.

'Her name's Delilah.'

'Not dead yet, then? She must be some age.'

Winston couldn't reply because he was silently seething. Nobody came into his home and criticised his beloved dog.

He looked on, half fascinated and half horrified, as Monty got on with the business of making himself a cup of tea. Winston wondered if his brother was going to offer to make him one but knew he'd prefer something slightly stronger at that moment – like a double whisky – to help him cope with this sudden invasion.

'Any jammy dodgers?' Monty asked, opening a cupboard.

'No.'

'Ginger snap?'

'No.'

'Custard cream? *Any*thing?'

'There might be a rich tea in that tin over there.'

Monty shook his head in despair. 'Of all the biscuits in the world, you choose to fill your tin with the world's most boring one!'

Winston bit his tongue. It was always the same with Monty –

he always wanted what he couldn't have. If there *were* custard creams, he'd ask if there wasn't a Viennese whirl.

'Ah, that's better,' Monty said a moment later, sipping his tea. 'A nice sit down now, I think.'

Winston led the way to the front room and watched as Monty sat down in the chair he'd been occupying only minutes before. Winston didn't say anything. Instead, he sat on the sagging sofa whose springs had died a long time ago.

'What brings you to Castle Clare, then?' he asked.

Monty sipped his tea and then put the mug down on top of Winston's newspaper.

'I'm not coping,' Monty said in a low voice.

'Ah,' Winston said simply, acknowledging the fact that his older brother did, indeed, look as if he needed help. 'Well, it's early days, isn't it? I'm not sure you're actually *meant* to be coping yet.'

'I miss her,' Monty said, his voice thick with emotion.

'I know.'

Winston remembered only too well the desolate days after Sally had died. He'd felt cast adrift in a sea of grief and there were still some days when it felt so raw. He'd reached out to Monty back then, but his brother had told him that these things happened and that he'd get into a new routine soon enough. There was a part of Winston that wanted to remind Monty about that conversation now, but he thought better of it. Now was not the time to score points especially as Rebecca had only passed seven months ago.

'I didn't think I'd miss her so much,' Monty admitted with a sigh. 'I know it was expected and I thought I was prepared.'

'Nothing can prepare you for such a thing,' Winston told him, thinking of how fast and cruel the cancer had come just as his Sally's had. 'You have to give yourself time, that's all. Be kind to yourself.' Winston hated rattling out the same old platitudes he'd been told after Sally had died. They seemed so hollow and inadequate. But what else could one say? And one had to say something; he sincerely believed that. Saying something – even if it was clichéd and awful – was better than saying nothing, wasn't it?

'I just had to get away,' Monty said. 'Get out of those walls for a while.'

Winston nodded, although he hadn't wanted to go anywhere after his Sally had died. He'd wanted to burrow even deeper into his home and never leave it. It had taken months – years, really – before he'd felt normal and had connected with society again and done crazy things like joining a book club. He smiled as he remembered. The book club had been like a lifeline.

'Have you tried reading?' Winston asked his brother now.

'What?'

'Books. Do you read?'

Monty looked at him as if he were quite mad.

Winston reached across and retrieved his copy of *Mrs Dalloway* and passed it to Monty who screwed his eyes up behind his thick glasses.

'Virginia Woolf? At your age?' He made a dismissive noise.

'Why at *my* age?'

'I thought she was an author you got out of your system in your teens. Rather pretentious, no?'

'Perhaps. But I'm broadening my outlook. Giving the old grey matter something to think about.'

'Think I'll stick to the crossword,' Monty said, throwing the book onto the sofa. Winston winced, hoping Monty hadn't bent its brand new cover.

'So, how long are you staying?' Winston dared to ask.

Monty shrugged. 'Long as I need. I'll just take it day by day.'

Winston silently seethed at his brother's vagueness and then caught himself. He must be charitable even if it grieved him.

'I'll get the guest room ready,' he said, heaving himself up from the sofa.

'Could you take my suitcase up for me, Win? I seem to have hurt my back again.'

Winston nodded. Monty had one of those backs that seemed to flare up at the most convenient moments like when a stack of logs needed chopping or a pile of heavy boxes needed moving. But Winston didn't say anything; he never did. Instead, he moved to the foot of the stairs and picked up Monty's suitcase, marvelling at the weight of it and wondering, once again, just how long his brother was planning on staying.

When he got to the top of the stairs, he heard Monty behind him.

'The bed's already made up,' Winston told him as he led him into the spare room which was a rather poky affair. 'Always keep it ready for the kids, but I don't see them as often as I'd like.'

Monty stepped into the room and sniffed disdainfully, no doubt noticing the sun-faded curtains and the tatty, threadbare rug on the floor.

'Where's your room?'

'At the back.'

'Can I see it?'

'Why do you want to see it?'

Monty was already out of the room and had crossed the landing. 'Here?' He motioned to a door.

'Yes.' Winston watched as Monty opened it and stepped inside.

'Nice,' he said. 'This is more like it. Quiet.'

'But this is my room, Monty. You're in the spare.'

'No, no, no.' He shook his head. 'You know I sleep lightly.'

'Do you?'

'I'd be better in your room at the back away from the street outside.' He gave a little smile. 'Bring my suitcase in, will you?'

~

Those first few days living under the same roof as Monty were very trying for Winston. Monty seemed to want to do nothing but hang around the house, eating toast in his pyjamas while watching daytime television.

'Look at that idiot!' he'd shout at the TV. 'I can't believe he's really going to buy that house. It's a dump. An absolute dump!'

Like this house, Winston thought, looking around him in horror at the empty mugs and plates that were collecting on every surface. Winston sometimes didn't have the energy to clean up after himself some days, let alone anybody else.

By day four, Winston knew he'd have to say something.

'You need to get out,' he told Monty.

'Pardon?' Monty looked shocked by this.

'I think you need to get out and about – go into town. Talk to people, do some shopping. It isn't healthy hanging around the house all day in your nightwear.'

Monty looked thoughtful for a moment. 'I suppose they could do with a wash.'

Winston nodded. He hadn't liked to say anything, but there was a large strawberry jam stain just above the right knee which had been bothering him for a couple of days.

'Why don't you get washed and dressed and we'll go into town together?' Winston suggested.

Monty sighed and levered himself up from the armchair he'd been living in.

'If you think that's a good idea,' he said in a tone that suggested he thought otherwise.

'I do,' Winston said, noticing, as Monty got up, that there were toast crumbs all over his favourite cushion.

Bryony Nightingale still couldn't believe that Ben Stratton was back in her life. Having met at primary school and become instantly inseparable, the whole world had believed that nothing could part them and, for many years, nothing had. They'd studied together right the way through school and had then taken places at Cambridge for their degrees so that they could be together. But then, a year after graduation, Ben had upped and left Castle Clare for six whole years. Bryony, who hadn't been able to bear the thought of leaving her family or her home town, had been devastated. And then Ben had come back just last month. Had it really only been a few short weeks since he'd re-entered her life? They had been the most turbulent in her life, and she'd said and done a few things that she regretted, but they were together now and she was pretty sure that nothing could ever part them again.

She watched in adoration as he stood at the top of a small step ladder, a tube of polyfiller in his hand.

'You really don't need to do that, Ben,' she told him.

'You can't have gaping holes in your walls.'

'It isn't gaping. It gives the place character! Besides, this is your day off. You shouldn't be working.'

He finished what he was doing and came back down to earth, his dark eyes and his smile bewitching her as they always did.

'I like helping out in the shop.'

'And I love having you here.' She walked towards him and gasped as he put his arms around her. 'Ben! A customer might–'

He stopped her with a kiss.

'Or they might not,' he said.

'Don't forget that I'm working,' she said, gently pushing him away and returning to the stack of books on the counter by the till.

'I know I'll always come a very poor second to your beloved books,' he said.

'Ben Stratton – that is *not* true!'

'Oh, come on – it is just a little bit!' he said with a teasing grin.

Bryony smiled back at him. 'Well, I do love my books. I can't deny that,' she said, her hand stroking the cover of one on the top, 'but I love you more.'

He crossed the shop towards her and was just about to lean over the counter and kiss her again when the door opened, ringing the merry bell above it, and a customer walked in. It was a regular. One of the young mothers of Castle Clare who enjoyed browsing the stock after dropping her daughter off at school and she wasted no time today, picking the latest in a much-loved series and taking it to the till.

'Good choice,' Bryony told her.

'Amber loves these books,' the mother said. 'Can't get enough of them.'

'I hear this one's the best yet,' Bryony said, popping it into a paper bag together with one of the Nightingale bookmarks.

'I hope this series runs and runs.'

'Oh, so do I!' Bryony said, thinking of how she could never replenish the shelves fast enough when a new book in the series was released.

'There's a happy customer,' Ben said after she'd left the shop.

'Nothing quite like it,' Bryony agreed. 'It's a good day's work when you can give someone so much pleasure simply by selling them a book.'

'Remember that time you sold your old books at school and got into trouble with Mr Cobley?'

Bryony laughed. 'I was just stretching my wings. If I remember rightly, I'd spent the last couple of weekends working alongside Dad in the main bookshop and I guess I caught the bug.'

She went into the stock room to get another copy of the book she'd just sold, knowing that she'd have to order some more before the week was out.

'You know what we should do after we close?' she called through to Ben.

'What?'

'Go and see Flo. It feels an age since I last saw her and I feel awful for not helping her out more in the garden. I did promise I would, but then you turned up, didn't you?'

'Have I been a distraction, then?' Ben asked as she came back into the shop.

'You know you have! But a rather wonderful one.'

'I like Flo.'

'She's wonderful, isn't she? It'll be fun to catch up with her and see how Sonny's doing,' Bryony said.

'And the animals.'

'And the garden. We'd better wear something sensible if we're going to offer any help.'

'Yes. The last time I was there I picked up one of those hens and – well – let's just say that hens aren't toilet trained,' Ben mused.

Bryony laughed at the memory and grew even more excited about seeing Flo and her menagerie again.

Winston and his brother had walked into town. It was only a five minute walk, but it was obvious that Monty wasn't used to any sort of walking at all.

'You'll have to get yourself a dog,' Winston told him, nodding to Delilah who was with them.

'I haven't got time to look after a dog!' Monty complained.

Winston frowned. 'You've got nothing *but* time.'

Monty sighed. 'I can barely look after myself let alone a fellow creature.'

Winston left it at that. 'Come on. I'll introduce you to Josh in the bookshop.'

The entered the shop, the bell ringing merrily.

'Winston!' Josh cried in greeting.

'Hello, Josh. I've brought somebody to meet you.'

Josh came forward as Monty entered the shop and that's when something strange happened.

'Well, hello, young Josh!' Monty said, a huge smile upon his face. 'What a marvellous place you have here. Simply marvellous! I was telling Winston that I needed to find myself some good books to read and did he know of anywhere? And I have to say this looks like a splendid place. Really splendid!'

Winston almost did a double take at the change in his brother's manner. Just a few moments ago, he'd been morose Monty. Now he was positively sprightly.

'Well, thank you very much,' Josh said, looking somewhat startled but pleased by the praise.

Winston cleared his throat. 'This is my brother–'

'Monty. Montague Kneller,' his brother interrupted.

'Yes,' Winston said. 'That's him.'

Josh and Monty shook hands.

'So, tell me how long you've been running this place,' Monty said, clapping a hand on Josh's shoulder. Winston was instantly invisible. He'd stupidly forgotten what Monty could be like. As soon as he had an audience – any audience – he turned into this manic performer, charming everyone around him. Winston scratched his head and looked down at Delilah in despair. The Labrador didn't look a bit surprised.

Winston made the most of being in the bookshop, perusing the shelves and pulling down a few interesting looking volumes as Monty ploughed on with his charm offensive. Josh, who was young and probably didn't know any better, was lapping up the attention. Winston couldn't blame him. Monty was very good at what he did.

Finally, Monty stopped talking and moved through to the back of the shop.

'Well, your brother's something else,' Josh told Winston.

'Yes, he's that all right.'

'You know, you're nothing alike!'

'Thank you.'

Josh grinned and then whispered. 'I'm detecting a little tension between you.'

'You don't say!'

'Ah, sibling rivalry. There's nothing quite like it, is there? You should have seen me and Bryony growing up. We'd bicker constantly. There always seemed to be something to fight about. We're fine now. Well, she loves to tease me, but it's all good. One tends to grow out of these things.'

'Some people do!' Winston said. 'Others endure it for a whole lifetime.'

'Oh, dear.'

Winston shook his head. 'What can I say? We're related, but that's the beginning and the end of it.'

'But he's staying with you, isn't he? That's what he told me. He came to you when he needed to.'

'Oh, yes. There is that.' Winston sighed. 'I'm being too hard on him. He recently lost his wife.'

'I'm so sorry.'

'He's taken it badly. It's...' Winston paused, 'it's unlike him to be so unsure of himself.'

'He seemed pretty sure of himself just now,' Josh pointed out.

'Yes, he's always loved an audience.'

Josh smiled. 'Hey – while we've got a moment, I wanted to ask you what happened next.'

'With what? I've not finished *Mrs Dalloway* yet,' Winston said, panicking.

'No, not *Mrs Dalloway* – with you and Marguerite.'

Winston swallowed hard.

'Remember,' Josh continued. 'You met at the dance. You

plucked up the courage to ask her to dance with you. I can't stop thinking about what happened next.'

Winston shifted uneasily. 'I can't really talk about it now.' He nodded towards the back room where Monty had disappeared to.

Josh frowned. 'Why not? Is he... involved?'

It was then that Monty came back into the room.

'What are you two gossiping about, then?'

'Oh, just books,' Winston lied.

'Well, it's the right place to have that conversation,' Monty said, giving Josh a friendly slap on the back.

'See anything you liked?' Josh asked.

'Actually, I was hoping you could recommend something,' Monty said. 'Something with a bit of a mystery to solve, but not too gory. I don't like all these dead bodies on every other page. Puts you off your toast.'

Josh laughed. 'I think I may have just the thing.' He walked across to a shelf. 'New author who has a lovely style of writing. Plenty of mystery and plenty of atmosphere. Good reviews too.'

Monty took the book from him and peered at the blurb. 'Yes, seems like it might do.'

Winston watched as his brother paid for the book.

'Thank you,' Monty said as he took the paper bag from Josh.

'And thank you. It's good to meet you,' Josh said.

'You too, young man,' Monty chimed as he turned to leave the shop. Winston waved a hand to Josh.

'Well, what do you think?' Winston asked once they were outside.

'Very nice,' Monty said and Winston could see that he was quickly sliding back into his old morose self now that his audience had gone.

'Fancy a tea and cake while we're in town?' Winston asked.

'No,' Monty said with a sigh. 'I think we should head back. Maybe have some toast at home, eh?'

Cuckoo Cottage was looking splendid in the May sunshine. It was a perfect English country cottage with its thatched roof and Suffolk pink walls and it was a favourite with photographers, despite its slightly rundown appearance. But maybe that added to the charm. Bryony certainly thought so as she and Ben arrived that May evening, and she inhaled the sweet scent from the honeysuckle and admired the deep red roses that hung over the front door.

'I don't think there's any point knocking,' she said, noticing one of the windowsills was stuffed with trays of seedlings. 'On an evening like this, she'll be in the garden.'

Ben nodded and the two of them made their way round to the back of the cottage, passing cities of terracotta pots and trays of young annuals waiting to be liberated now that the threat of frost was over. There were also the ever-present weeds and nettles that no amount of work seemed to put an end to.

And there was Flo Lohman, waist deep in a bay of compost.

'Bryony, my dear! And Ben!' She climbed out of the bay and walked towards them, embracing them both, and enveloping them in a cloud of white curls. 'What a lovely surprise.'

'We've come to help in the garden,' Ben said. 'Is there anything we can do?'

'How long have you got?' Flo laughed. 'Come and see the chicks first.'

'You've got chicks?' Bryony asked.

'I've never had a broody hen before,' Flo told them as she led them towards a long, low coop positioned on the lawn. 'And, of course, I don't have a cockerel so the eggs she'd been collecting would never hatch.'

'Which hen is it?' Bryony asked.

'Portia – the buff.'

'Oh, she's lovely!'

'She's a pretty good mother too. I felt a bit sorry for her sitting on eggs that were never going to hatch and then a farmer friend said I could take some of their eggs and – well – you can see what happened!'

Bryony and Ben crouched down and watched as the eight perfect yellow chicks cheeped and fluttered around their mother, their dark eyes so round and bright.

'Can I hold one?' Bryony asked, unable to resist.

'If you can get hold of one,' Flo said. 'They're getting confident now and can move pretty fast.'

Bryony opened the door in the roof of the run and popped a hand inside, scooping up a sweet yellow chick.

'It's adorable!' Bryony cried.

'Don't drop it!' Ben told her.

'I'm not going to drop it!'

'They're proving quite a distraction,' Flo told them. 'I have to drag Sonny away from them to do his homework.'

'How is Sonny?' Bryony asked, carefully returning the chick to its mother and standing up.

Flo nodded towards the donkey field where Sonny was grooming Belle.

'He's doing remarkably well,' she said, a proud smile on her face. 'I think he's feeling proper settled here now. We're doing his room up just how he wants it and he's talking – *really* talking to me.'

'That's so great to hear,' Bryony said, remembering the shy boy who used to come into her bookshop and be too afraid to say anything.

Flo shook her head. 'When I think of the years he's suffered with that no good nephew of mine! Oh, I could *shake* myself for not intervening sooner.'

'You weren't to know what was going on, Flo,' Ben told her.

'But I should have made it my business to know,' Flo said, clearly still blaming herself for the whole sorry mess. 'I guess we just assume everything is good and normal with people, don't we? Especially our own kin.'

Bryony nodded and, not for the first time, felt incredibly grateful to have the family that she did because she knew that not everybody was like the Nightingales.

'Now, what would you like us to do?' Ben asked, clapping his hands together.

Flo's face broke into a smile. 'Grab those sheers and that fork over there, you two, and follow me!'

CHAPTER SEVEN

Sunday came round a lot faster than Josh had imagined it would. It had been a brisk week of business in the shop. Several customers had been buying books as gifts and Josh had sold a number of glorious hardbacks which were always a pleasure to handle.

He'd seen April a couple of times since her acceptance to Sunday lunch at Campion House and they'd talked casually about the upcoming date. Josh smiled as he took one last look in the mirror. It was a date, wasn't it? Yes, he thought it must be. Sunday lunch was definitely a date even if it wasn't a posh restaurant, but rather his family home. He straightened the collar of his shirt. He'd gone for the navy one over the white. Bryony had told him that he suited darker colours better and he trusted her opinion.

Leaving his home, he drove the short distance into Castle Clare and pulled up outside A Little Bit Bloomsbury. He could see April at work in the shop and recognised a fellow workaholic when he saw one. Or at least, somebody who was passionate about the work they did.

He got out of the car and opened the shop door.

'Hello,' he said. 'Ready for lunch?'

She looked up. She wasn't wearing her little pink glasses today and he got a good look at the warm hazel-colour of her eyes. The freckles on her nose seemed more noticeable too, he thought.

'Yes, I'm ready.' She gave a somewhat faint smile and he put that down to nerves.

'Everyone's really looking forward to meeting you,' he said and then regretted it. Maybe that would make her even more nervous.

'I'll just tidy up here,' she told him.

Josh nodded. Was it his imagination or was she a little cool with him today?

He looked around the shop as she went into the back room with the brushes she'd been using and he heard the sound of running water. She'd been working on a little chair and it was a charming piece which was painted a chalky blue. Josh peered closely at it and noticed there were a few paint drips on it. Being the fastidious person he was, he couldn't help but say something.

'April? You've got a few drips here.'

She turned the tap off. 'Yes, I know. They've dried, I'm afraid. I'm going to have to sand it down another day.'

She came back through to the shop and he took in the pretty jade-green dress she was wearing which made her chestnut hair look so wonderfully bright.

'You look lovely,' he said.

She smiled, but didn't say anything.

'Ready?'

'Yes.'

They left the shop together and Josh opened the passenger door of his car for her. She slid into the seat and placed her small handbag on the floor.

'It's a lovely day,' he said as he got in beside her. He suddenly felt very awkward, as if he didn't know this woman at all, and he began to worry that he'd tried to move things forward too fast, but it was too late to do anything about it now. His family was expecting them and they'd never forgive him if he let them down. 'Have you explored much of the countryside here since you arrived?'

'No,' she said. 'I'm afraid not.'

'You should. I mean, if you get the chance. This part of Suffolk is very pretty. Lots of little valleys and rivers. And churches too. I've got a marvellous old copy of M R James's book *Suffolk and Norfolk* where he tours all his favourite churches. It's great for ideas for days out and you never know what you're going to see in a country church. There are some marvellous surprises.' He stopped. He was babbling and he wasn't sure April was at all interested, which was funny because they usually connected whenever they talked, but he wasn't feeling it today.

'Tell me more about your family,' she suddenly said and he was glad that she wanted to open the conversation up a bit.

'Who do you want to know about?'

'Everybody!'

'Didn't I tell you about them in the pub?'

'I don't think so. Maybe just the bare bones.'

'Yes, you're probably right.'

'And I feel as if I should be prepared.'

Josh smiled at that. 'Okay then. Let me see. Well, there's Sam who runs the secondhand bookshop. He's quiet and decent and kind. He's seeing Callie who's a children's writer. She's lovely. Really sweet. Then there's Polly. She's a real organiser. You can always turn to Polly if you're in trouble which is pretty amazing really because she's had more than her fair share of trouble. Her husband left her.'

'What happened?'

Josh winced. 'It's a long story. Suffice to say he was no good. Left his own son too. Archie. He's a sweetheart. You'll love him. Everyone does. Anyway, Polly's seeing Jago now. He nearly ran Archie over on his motorbike.'

April gasped.

'Don't worry – he didn't actually hit him. Archie was running out into the road to pick up some litter.' Josh laughed. 'Little eco warrior that he is.'

'Who else is there? Another sister, right?'

'Two more actually. Bryony runs the children's bookshop. She's zany and spirited and loves colour. Clothes too. Like you only her colour choices can be a little...'

'What?'

'A little too daring for my taste. I know – I'm too conservative. But there you go. But you've met Bryony, haven't you? She told me she'd come into your shop the other day.'

There was a pause. 'Oh, yes. Of course.'

'Well, Bryony's seeing Ben. They were childhood sweethearts until he left suddenly six years ago. Bryony was devastated. But he's back now.'

'Why did he leave?'

Josh hesitated. 'I'm not really sure it's my story to tell.'

'Now I'm intrigued.'

'I'll tell you about Lara instead. She's the youngest. She's studying English Lit at the UEA and she's a real live wire. I'm never sure what colour her hair's going to be and she's pierced parts of her body which really shouldn't be pierced.' He saw April smile at that.

'What are your parents like?'

'Well, Mum's the best mum in the world. She's strict, mind, but she's always there for you if you need advice or just a slice of cake. Dad's great too. Quiet. A thinker. And a gardener. He's either got his nose in a book or a spade in his hand. Oh, and there's Grandpa Joe and Grandma Nell. They live at Campion House too. Grandma's in the early stages of dementia and it's really sad to see her slipping away from us, but we're all determined to keep her at home. It's killing Grandpa, though, seeing her like this.'

'I'm so sorry.'

'Thanks. It's pretty sad. You'll love them, though.'

'It's a big family.'

'And that's before I tell you about all the cousins!'

'There are more Nightingales?'

'Absolutely. Uncle Ralph – Dad's brother – lives nearby with Aunt Bonnie. They've got three children: Tristan, Luke and Megan. Megan's the librarian in Castle Clare.'

'You're all really crazy about books, aren't you?'

'Pretty much. Dad and Uncle Ralph used to run the bookshops together before handing over to me, Sam and Bryony.'

April nodded. 'A real family affair.'

'Yes. I often wonder what we'd all have done if it wasn't for the bookshops.'

Josh slowed down as he turned into the quiet country lane which led to Campion House. The roadside verges were a sea of swaying cow parsley and creamy elderflower bloomed along the hedges. The bluebells were past their best now, but you could still smell the wild garlic in the woods, and bright pink campion was flowering by the ditches. It was a magical time to be in the countryside.

'Well, here we are,' he said as they approached the Georgian house and he pulled into the gravel driveway.

April sat there in silence, staring up at the facade of Josh's family home and, for a moment, he tried to see it as a stranger might. It was certainly an impressive house with its large sash windows and enormous front door. Polly had always said it looked like a doll's house. That couldn't be scary, could it, Josh thought?

'Ready?' he asked April, wondering if he should reach across the space between them and give her hand a comforting squeeze, but deciding against it.

She nodded and they got out of the car. Josh watched her closely. It was as if an internal switch had been flicked and she'd sunk somewhere deep inside herself, but maybe that would change once she realised that his family was a friendly bunch even if his youngest sister, Lara, was waving at them from the living room window like a maniac. He could just imagine the scene inside. Lara had probably been waiting for them to arrive and would have sounded the alarm off, shouting through to the kitchen where, no doubt, everybody was. There'd then be a scrum for everyone to be as close to the door as possible while trying to look like they naturally belonged there.

'Okay,' Josh said as he reached the front door and opened it. He looked down the hall. Mercifully, there was nobody there. 'Hello!' he called.

'We're in the kitchen, Josh, come on through!' his mother called and he was relieved that she hadn't forced a welcoming committee onto them.

Lara, however, now sprang through from the living room.

'I'm Lara!' she announced, extending a hand towards April while totally ignoring Josh. 'Lovely to meet you!'

'And you,' April said.

'Hi Josh!' Lara gave her brother a perfunctory hug, her eyes never leaving April. 'Come on into the living room. Grandma and Grandpa want to meet you.'

Josh gave April a reassuring smile as they followed Lara who, he noticed, had blonde hair this week as opposed to the red of the week before.

Grandpa Joe had been sitting in his favourite armchair, but he got up as soon as they entered the room, a huge smile on his face.

'Well, well. Let me take a look at you!' he said, clasping April's extended hand in both of his. Despite his years, Grandpa Joe could still appreciate an attractive young woman.

'This is April, Grandpa. April – this is Grandpa Joe.'

'Pleased to meet you,' she said politely.

'Welcome to our home. Thank you for coming, my dear. Now, come and meet my Nell.'

Josh looked at his Grandma Nell who was sitting in a chair by the window. She liked to look out into the garden and watch the birds in the trees. She looked well today, he thought. Her eyes were bright and clear.

'She's having a good day,' Grandpa Joe whispered to him and Josh smiled.

'Grandma? I'd like to introduce you to April. She's just moved to Castle Clare and has opened a shop opposite mine.'

Grandma Nell's face lit up as April approached her, her pale skin luminous with joy at the sight of Josh's new friend.

'How lovely you are, my dear,' Grandma Nell said.

'It's a pleasure to meet you,' April said politely, shaking Nell's delicate hand.

'You're joining us for lunch, aren't you?'

'She is,' Josh said.

'And staying?'

April looked flustered and Grandma suddenly looked confused.

'Not staying?' Grandma asked.

'Just here for the afternoon, Grandma,' Josh said.

'Well, that's nice.'

'Josh?' Bryony's voice called through from the kitchen. 'Mum wants to meet your date, but can't take her eyes off the cooker just now!'

'We've been summoned,' he said, glancing at April who looked even more panic-stricken now. 'Come on – there's bound to be wine to soften things a little.'

They walked down the hallway and entered the kitchen which was a large room at the back of the house, overlooking a grand sweep of garden. It was full of light, Sunday roast smells and Nightingales.

'Josh!' Bryony called. 'And April – you came!'

Suddenly, April was surrounded as introductions were made, hands were shaken and kisses exchanged. Josh couldn't help feeling a little sorry for April who was completely engulfed for a good couple of minutes. There was Bryony and Ben, Sam and Callie, Polly, Jago and Archie and Lara who'd come in from the living room so as not to miss all the fun.

'Will somebody please let me see her?' Eleanor Nightingale called from the cooker where she was keeping an eye on things.

'Mum, this is April,' Josh said, guiding her through the crowds towards his mother.

'Mrs Nightingale – it's so good to meet you.'

'Please, call me Eleanor.'

Josh smiled as he saw the look of genuine pleasure in his mother's eyes. She liked April, didn't she?

'Where's Dad?' Josh asked, suddenly realising that he hadn't seen his father yet.

'Gone to get some of his precious chard,' Bryony teased.

'Don't make fun,' Polly said. 'It's fabulous stuff.'

'I know it is,' Bryony said. 'Actually, I keep meaning to ask for some seeds from him. I'm going to grow some in my garden.'

Sam looked surprised by this assertion. 'Since when have you been into gardening?'

'Since I started helping Flo in hers. I told you about it, didn't I?'

'We go over some evenings and weekends to help out,' Ben said.

'How is Flo?' Eleanor asked.

'She's well,' Bryony said. 'Sonny too. He's really thriving at Flo's.'

'That's good to hear,' Eleanor said. 'His father should have been locked away for treating that young boy the way he did.'

It was then that Josh's dad opened the back door, his arms full of rainbow chard.

'Here we are. Fresh enough for you?' He placed it on the draining board and Polly and Jago got to work washing and chopping it.

'Dad? Come and meet April,' Josh said after his father had washed his gardener's hands.

Frank approached them. 'Good to meet you and welcome to Suffolk. I hear you're a Norfolk girl.'

'Please don't hold that against me,' April said with a little smile.

Everyone laughed.

'Let's get that bottle of wine open, shall we?' Frank said.

'Oh, at last!' Lara said.

'It's the only reason you come home, isn't it, Sis?' Josh teased. 'Free alcohol.'

'And free washing facilities, don't forget,' Polly added. 'I think there were three bags of washing, weren't there?'

'Like you guys weren't the same in your time!' Lara said.

'Didn't Josh once bring his roommate's bedding home to wash?' Sam asked.

'Only because he never washed it himself,' Josh told them.

'Ewww, that's gross!' Lara cried.

'It really was,' Josh said, 'but let's not talk about it before lunch.'

Everyone laughed again and Josh glanced at April. She was looking totally overwhelmed by it all.

'Mum?' he said. 'Is there time for a quick walk around the garden?'

'As long as it *is* quick,' she said. 'I'll be serving shortly.'

He nodded.

'Take the dogs for a little breather,' Eleanor added.

'Sure thing,' Josh said. 'April – come and meet the other three members of the family.' He led the way into the utility room where two Springer spaniels and a pointer were sitting in their baskets. 'Hardy the pointer and Brontë and Dickens the spaniels.'

April reached out to greet them as Josh opened the door into the garden and, after a fuss, they all went outside. The three dogs tore across the lawn and were instantly lost in the greenery.

'This place is wonderful,' she said.

'Dad's paradise,' Josh told her. 'He's very proud of his garden.'

'It's beautiful. It reminds me of the one at Charleston especially that lovely old wall over there and the planting in front of it.'

'Really? Dad will be thrilled to hear that.'

'You've been?'

'Yes. We all went down for the festival a few years ago. We loved the garden. Dad took masses of photos and kept on about how our garden just wasn't floriferous enough.'

'It's one of my favourite places in the whole world.'

'You're fascinated by the Bloomsbury Group, aren't you?'

'They're my life,' April told him earnestly.

Josh was surprised to hear such an assertion. 'Really?'

'Their work, the way they chose to live – the boldness of it all in such a conservative time. They were wonderful. I wish I could be more like them.'

Josh nodded as if understanding. He'd always secretly thought the Bloomsbury Group a bit strange, but he thought better than to say that.

'They were certainly a fascinating bunch,' he said, feeling safe with that statement.

They walked down the slope of lawn towards the vegetable beds. Wigwams of canes had been erected for peas, and clumps of chives threw their purple flowers towards the sun.

'Is it all a bit much?' Josh asked at last. 'My family, I mean?'

April knelt down beside a large terracotta pot and pinched a mint leaf between her fingers.

'Well, I was expecting a large family, but I didn't quite realise...' Her voice petered out as she sniffed her scented fingers.

'We don't have to stay long. If you don't want to. We can leave after lunch.'

'Oh, no – that would be rude,' she said, standing back up again.

'But the option's there if you need it.'

She gave him a faint smile. 'We should head back.'

'Yes, before Mum sounds the gong.'

'She has a gong?'

'She does. She uses it when Dad's lost himself at the bottom of the garden.' Josh laughed and April smiled. He was pleased to see her smiling again. She hadn't been smiling nearly as much as usual, he thought. She seemed like she wasn't completely there somehow – like there was a screen between herself and the rest of the world. But he couldn't really blame her. He'd be feeling pretty daunted if he had to meet a family as large and as loud as the Nightingales.

He turned to whistle for the dogs who appeared from out of a border, Brontë the spaniel with a tangle of goosegrass tying her ears together. Josh bent down to sort it out and then they returned inside.

'Ah, just in time, Josh,' Polly said. 'Grab that bowl of carrots and bring it through, will you?'

Josh did as he was told, following Polly into the dining room where lunch was being served. As ever, the dining table looked resplendent. His family had really made every effort to make it look as appealing as possible from the matching white plates and crystal glasses to the vases of freshly cut flowers from the garden that ran down the centre of the table.

Josh guided April to the chair next to his and pulled it out. Bryony was on the other side of her and she placed a hand on April's arm.

'Take a deep breath and try to relax,' she told April.

'She's not kidding,' Josh said.

'Bryony – don't be mean,' Polly said. 'You'll make her more anxious than she already is.'

'We don't bite, my dear,' Grandpa Joe chuckled from the end of the table. 'Not when there's a delicious lunch in front of us.'

'It's good to have you join us,' Frank said. 'Have some chard.'

Bryony laughed. 'You know you'll be instantly evicted if you don't eat a mountain of Dad's home-grown chard!'

'Sam, how's the book club going?' Eleanor asked as she passed the bowl of peas down the table.

'Good,' he said. 'We've just read *The Darling Buds of May*.'

'Ah, what a perfect novella!' Frank enthused.

'Or *perfick*!' Jago joked, nudging Archie who giggled.

'He was saying everything was perfick when he was reading that book,' Archie informed them.

'And what's next?' Eleanor asked.

'Well, the next meeting's in July and we're reading *Mrs Dalloway*,' Sam said.

'An acquired taste, that one,' Grandpa Joe said.

'April's a big fan of the Bloomsbury Group,' Josh told them.

'Of course – your shop is named after them, isn't it?' Eleanor said.

April nodded.

'I must pop in some time. I'd love to see your pieces. I bet they're beautiful.'

'So you like Virginia Woolf, April?' Frank asked.

'Of course,' April said.

'Don't find her dull or static?' Grandpa Joe added.

'Never. She's a genius.'

Silence fell upon the table for a moment at April's abrupt declaration.

'She has been called one, yes,' Frank agreed.

'You don't agree?' April's forehead creased in alarm.

Josh cleared his throat and shifted in his chair.

'Well, I can only speak for myself, but I find her prose a little stilted, although the ideas she explores are always fascinating and innovative.'

'And we've always greatly admired what she and Leonard Woolf achieved with the Hogarth Press,' Sam added.

'I loved all the beautiful covers by Vanessa Bell,' Polly said.

'The Hogarth Press was about more than pretty covers,' April stated.

'Well, of course it was,' Frank said.

Josh glanced at April, feeling her hostility. 'More wine, anyone?' he asked, reaching for the bottle and offering it to April.

'No, thank you,' she said.

Bryony reached around and took the bottle from him. 'I think we could use some down this end.'

'I came across an interesting little paperback in the shop,' Sam said, diplomatically filling the awkward silence.

'Oh, yes?' Frank said. 'What was that?'

'*The Common Stream* by Rowland Parker. Published in 1975.'

'Bit of a classic in certain circles,' Grandpa Joe said.

'Yes, I believe so,' Sam said.

'What's it about?' Polly asked.

'It follows the history of a village in Cambridgeshire from its first human settlement through Roman and medieval times to modern times.'

'Sounds riveting!' Lara teased.

'Well, I know it won't tickle every bookworm, but there are some fascinating insights like the reference to butts.'

Archie giggled.

'Not *those* sort of butts, Archie,' Sam told him. 'Butts were archery targets and every village had them at one time so that people could practise their bow and arrow skills. Well, it's reported that Foxton's were in a deplorable state and that the whole village was going to be fined because they weren't being looked after. It sounds like being ready for possible invaders was a serious business,' he finished, looking across the table towards April. 'April – if I come across any books about the Bloomsbury Group, would you like me to keep them for you?'

'I have them all,' she told him.

Josh flinched at her abrupt delivery.

'Oh, right,' Sam said, taking a sip of water.

The rest of the meal consisted of polite but stilted conversation in which they tried to engage April, but her monotonous replies made it very difficult. Josh was feeling decidedly awkward. He'd never have put her through this ordeal if he'd known the effect it would have on her. But how could he have known? She'd always been a little shy around him, but she'd also been very sweet too. He wondered where that sweetness had gone now.

After the meal was finished, Eleanor, Polly and Jago went through to the kitchen with the plates.

'What do you make of her, Mum?' Polly asked when they were quite sure they were out of earshot.

'I'm not sure what to make of her,' Eleanor confessed. 'Although it must be incredibly intimidating for her being surrounded by all of us. Maybe that explains her – well – prickly behaviour.'

'Nonsense!' Polly said. 'Jago didn't behave like that when he first came to lunch, and everyone was ribbing him mercilessly too.'

'I still wear the scars,' he teased.

Polly smiled at him.

'She wasn't opening up to any of our questions,' Polly said.

'We weren't too intrusive, were we?' Eleanor asked, her face etched with concern.

'Not from where I was sitting,' Jago assured her. 'She just wasn't very happy talking, I guess.'

'I wonder what Josh sees in her,' Polly said as she began to stack the dishwasher. 'I mean, she *is* very pretty.'

'Yes,' Jago agreed. 'Pretty and prickly.'

'Like a flowering cactus,' Polly said.

'Oh, Polly!' Eleanor cried. 'Maybe she'll improve after a cup of tea.'

'You think it's a caffeine withdrawal thing? You're too kind for words, Mum!'

It was then that Josh popped his head round the kitchen door.

'I thought you should know, we're off,' he announced.

'Leaving – now?' Eleanor said. 'You're not having a cup of tea?'

'No, thank you.'

'I thought you'd be joining us for the walk.'

'Not today. But thanks for a lovely lunch. I'll give you a call, okay?'

'Josh?' his mother called as he was leaving.

He came back into the kitchen just as Bryony was joining them with the empty wine bottles.

'Is April all right?' Eleanor asked.

'Yes, of course.'

'It's just... well, she seemed...'

'Yes, what's wrong with her, Josh?' Bryony asked, obviously not as keen to walk on eggshells as her mother.

'Nothing. I think she's just shy.'

'But I thought you said she was lovely,' Bryony said. 'She was just plain rude during lunch.'

'She *is* lovely. Well, she was the other day. Believe me, I'm as baffled as you are.'

'Well, let's put it down to nerves,' Eleanor said.

'Yes, she's certainly got a nerve behaving like that,' Polly said.

'Shush!' Josh said, flapping his hand.

'Ah, April,' Polly said as she appeared in the hallway behind them. 'We were just going to make some tea. Would you like one?'

'No, thank you. I've got to go, but thank you for a lovely lunch. You have a beautiful home, Mrs Nightingale.'

Eleanor blushed with pride and it seemed that some of her belief in the potential of the young woman before her was restored.

Five minutes later, Josh and April were in the car. She hadn't said anything to him since leaving Campion House and Josh was feeling pretty wretched. He'd known it wasn't going to go swimmingly, but he hadn't expected it to go quite so badly. The look of disappointment and confusion he'd seen on his mother's face as he'd entered the kitchen was proving hard to shake. He knew with all his heart that his family had wanted to like April, and they simply hadn't. And, the truth was, he wasn't sure he liked her anymore – not after the way she'd behaved, and yet there had been glimpses and glimmers of the April he'd been attracted to. Every now and then, she'd peeped through the abrupt exterior to make him smile.

She wasn't peeping now, though, he thought as he turned to glance at her. She was sitting stony and silent and Josh felt crushingly defeated. This thing between them – whatever it was – was too strange. It wasn't like the simple, easy love that had blossomed between Sam and Callie, nor was it like the fun and light-hearted relationship that Polly and Jago had. This was... what was it? Josh couldn't seem to find any words to describe it and, being a bookworm and something of a wordsmith, that made him feel even more anxious.

'Where would you like me to drop you?' he asked once they'd

nearly reached Castle Clare.

'At the shop, please.'

'Not at home?'

'No. At the shop.'

Josh frowned. 'Don't you have a home to go to on a Sunday?' He tried to make his question sound casual, but he honestly wanted to know.

'I want to do some work.'

He sighed as they pulled up outside the shop.

'I wish you'd talk to me, April,' he said once he'd parked.

'What do you want to talk about?' She turned to face him and he saw that her eyes were a little warmer now, but she still had that guarded look about her.

'I don't know – anything!'

'What do you mean?'

'What I mean is, I can't help thinking you're hiding something from me.'

'Like what?'

'Well, for starters, you won't tell me where you live, you don't share anything about your family with me...' he paused as something occurred to him for the first time. 'Are you married? Is that it?'

'No, of course I'm not married.'

'Then what are you hiding?'

She didn't answer.

'April? Please – this is all too weird for me.'

He saw her swallow. 'I'm sorry,' April told him. 'Things aren't quite what they seem.'

'What does that mean?'

She looked down at her hands in her lap which were clasped together, as if she was holding onto herself for support. And then she looked up at him, her eyes clear and bright.

'I think it's probably time you knew the truth,' she told him.

CHAPTER EIGHT

April didn't get out of the car at the shop as she'd said she would. Instead, she directed Josh to a little road on the edge of Castle Clare. It was easy to find and they pulled up outside a Victorian villa a few moments later.

'It's the ground floor flat,' April explained as they got out of the car.

Josh couldn't help feeling anxious. What was April about to reveal? She'd told him she wasn't married so Josh knew he wasn't about to be introduced to a husband. Maybe she had a house full of children. But that really wouldn't explain the change in personality he'd witnessed, would it?

He waited as she fished her key out of her bag and opened the front door straight into a living room with high ceilings and a fireplace with a pretty tile surround. He recognised it as April's immediately with the pieces of painted furniture and the shelves of books about the Bloomsbury Group. A print of a Vanessa Bell painting was propped on the mantelpiece, and a poster for an old Virginia Woolf exhibition hung on the wall.

'So, what's all this about?' he asked.

April, who'd been fiddling with her handbag, turned to look at him now.

'I think you should sit down.'

'I don't need to sit down.'

April took a deep breath and then walked to the door on the far side of the living room.

'April?' she called. 'Josh is here.'

Josh frowned. Why was April calling for April? And then someone who looked just like April walked into the room.

'I think I need to sit down,' he said.

'Hello Josh,' April said. Or *was* it April? There were now *two* Aprils in the room.

'What's going on?' he said, feeling helpless as he looked from one to the other.

'*I'm* April,' said the one he hadn't just brought home from Sunday lunch.

'And I'm May,' the other one said.

'We're identical twins born either side of midnight at the change of the month,' April explained. 'I was born at five to midnight on the thirtieth of April, and May was born at eighteen minutes past midnight on the first of May.'

Baffled, Josh listened to this explanation.

'So *you're* April?'

April nodded.

'And I took May to Sunday lunch?'

'Yes,' May said.

'I hope you behaved,' April told May. 'I hope you weren't rude.'

'I was very civil.'

'Was she, Josh?'

Josh's mouth fell open.

'Oh, May! What did you do?'

'What?' May cried. 'I didn't do anything. But you know I don't like big gatherings.'

'I know. Thank you for going for me.'

'How are you feeling now?' May asked.

'A little better.'

'Still in pain?'

'No, the pain's gone now.'

'Good. Let me make you some ginger tea to chase it all away.'

Josh watched as May left the room.

'You've not been well?' he asked April, noticing that she did look a great deal paler than usual.

'No. I get a lot of headaches and migraines,' she said. 'May's great at stepping in for me when I'm not well.'

'So it *was* you I asked to Sunday lunch?'

'Yes it was.'

'And it was you at the pub and you I've been chatting to in the shop?'

'Apart from one time, I think.'

Josh's mind reeled back. 'Ah, yes. I remember a slight difference in you one time.'

'May mentioned it. She hoped she hadn't ruined things between us.'

'So that was May? Why didn't you tell me you were a twin? I thought I was going crazy today!'

'I'm sorry, Josh.'

'So – let me get this right – it's been *you* working in the shop?'

'Most of the time, yes. May prefers to work at home. She's not so easy around people as I am.'

'But you told me *you* were an introvert.'

'Well, I am. But I'm a little less of an introvert than May is.'

Josh shook his head, still trying to comprehend everything.

'So that evening in the pub when I asked if you had any brothers or sisters – you lied to me.'

'I'm sorry,' April said and she looked genuinely mortified.

'Why did you do that?'

She sighed and sat down next to him on the sofa. 'I don't know. I didn't want to, but we've always had this role, you see. May's shy and doesn't always want to go out much, but she sometimes does so it's just easier if she's me. We kind of share a persona.'

Josh's eyes widened. 'I've read about that in books, but I didn't think it really happened.'

'You'd be surprised. It's great fun actually.'

'And very confusing for those around you.'

'I'm so sorry. I shouldn't have put you through all that. I didn't think it would do any harm. It was clear when we wanted to open the shop that I'd be the one running it on a day to day basis, while May would be in charge of the paperwork and do odd bits of restoration here at home. It seemed ideal. I had no idea that – well – that I might meet somebody.'

Josh shifted a little. 'But that was bound to happen sooner or later, surely. You *have* been in a relationship before, haven't you?'

April shrugged. 'Not really. Not seriously.' She paused. 'You see, I have this problem.'

'What problem?'

'With my eyes. I have a condition.'

'What sort of condition?' Josh asked gently.

April shook her head. 'I don't want to bore you with all the medical terms. It's just something I was born with.'

'Gosh, I'm so sorry, April. How does it affect you?'

'Well, May can be quite protective of me for one thing, but I'm absolutely fine most of the time. I'm just...' she paused again. 'I'm super-sensitive to light. That's why I wear those glasses.'

'The pink glasses?'

'Yes.'

'So I'll always know it's you if you're wearing the pink glasses?'

'Pretty much.'

'And they help you?'

'A bit, I suppose. But I suffer from headaches and migraines and my peripheral vision is pretty poor so I tend not to go out much. At least not like a normal person might. And that's fine. It suits me really. I don't feel that I'm missing out on anything,' she confided. 'I often think that, even if my eyesight had been perfect, I'd still be a bit of a recluse.'

'So May doesn't have it?'

'No. The doctors aren't quite sure how one of us has it and the other doesn't. We were put through endless tests as children. I think we're a bit of a medical mystery.'

'And does it affect your work?'

She nodded. 'I'm afraid it does. I tend to do the first coats of paint and May does all the finishing touches. She says I sometimes leave drips.'

Josh remembered his surprise at seeing some on the blue-painted chair earlier that day.

'You've chosen a tricky profession,' he pointed out.

'But I didn't choose it – it chose me. I'm not sure I could do anything outside the art world.'

'But how did your sight affect your studies?' Josh asked. 'I don't mean to be rude, but I'd have thought art would be particularly tricky to study if your vision isn't – well – good.'

April smiled. 'Don't forget I've never known anything other than bad vision. I just got on with things. I've never let it stop me doing what I love. It might restrict me in a few areas, but I've never let it rule my life.'

It was then that May came back into the room.

'Everything sorted?' she asked, handing a mug of ginger tea to April.

'Sorry, Josh – can we get you a tea or coffee or something?' April asked.

'No, thank you. I'm fine.'

'I'll leave you both to it, then,' May said. 'If you're sure you're all right, April?'

'I'm fine. Just a bit woozy after last night,' she admitted, taking a sip of her tea.

'Don't tire her out, please, Josh,' May told him sternly. 'She was up all night.'

'It's okay. I'm fine just sitting and talking.'

They waited as May left the room.

'I see what you mean,' Josh said.

'Yes, she may be the younger twin, but she definitely acts like an older sister.'

Josh smiled at that.

'Listen, Josh, I know this is all a bit much to take in and I feel really awful for not telling you the truth because I really like you, but I won't blame you if you just want to walk away.'

He frowned. 'Are you kidding? Things are just getting interesting around here.'

April laughed and he remembered how much he loved her laugh and how he'd missed it earlier that day, wondering where the old April had vanished to. He hadn't been with April at all. But he was now and that made him intensely happy.

CHAPTER NINE

Josh felt a little adrift after he left April and May's and so he simply got in his car and drove back to Campion House, knowing that everyone would still be there. For a few moments, he sat parked in the driveway as he took in everything he'd learned that day.

Twins! How could he not have known or at least suspected? The clues had all been there – the changes in April's behaviour towards him and the reluctance to talk about her family. He should have known that the woman he'd taken to Sunday lunch was not the woman he'd been so wholeheartedly attracted to.

He got out of the car and walked across the driveway, opening the front door and taking his shoes off in the hallway.

'Josh is back!' Lara cried as she was the first to spot him.

'Josh?' his mother called down the hallway. 'Everything okay?'

He entered the kitchen.

'Josh, darling, you look quite pale,' his mother said. 'Sit at the table here and have some tea.'

Josh let himself be looked after for a moment. The truth was, he needed his family around him because he was finding it hard to take in what had unfolded that afternoon.

A couple of minutes later, they all moved through to the living room with their tea and biscuits. Even on a bright spring afternoon, a lamp had been turned on next to Grandma Nell's favourite chair. Josh saw that she was reading a book although he wondered whether she was truly reading it. Grandpa Joe said that her mind tended to wander and she'd often stare at the same page for hours.

'Tell us what's happening, Josh,' Bryony asked, bringing his attention back to what had made him return home. He watched as everyone seemed to lean forward in their seats. Even young Archie was looking anxious.

'I took April home,' he began. 'Only, she wasn't April.'

'What do you mean?' Sam asked.

'Her name's May.'

'April's May?' Lara said with a frown.

'Why did she change her name?' Polly asked. 'Does she prefer one month to another?'

'No,' Josh said. 'It's because there's an April *and* a May.'

A stunned silence greeted him.

'April has a sister?' Frank was the first to ask his son.

'Not just a sister,' Josh announced. 'A twin.'

'Twins!' his mother exclaimed.

'Identical twins,' Josh confirmed.

Bryony gasped. 'So which one did we meet?'

'May,' Josh said.

'But we thought you were seeing April,' Polly said.

'Yes. So did I!'

Lara giggled. 'So you thought May was April?'

'I did. Only I kind of didn't,' Josh said. 'I mean, I felt she was different, but I couldn't quite work it out.'

'She was a different person – that's why she was different,' Grandpa Joe said with a guffaw.

'I know that *now*!' Josh told him.

'Well, I was fooled,' Bryony said, 'and I'd had a good look at them both.'

'So, let me get this straight,' Ben said. 'They're called April and May?'

'That's right,' Josh confirmed. 'They were born either side of midnight when the months changed.'

'Oh, I love it!' Callie said.

'How delightful!' Eleanor cried.

'And are they absolutely identical?' Polly asked.

'May has a few more freckles,' Josh said. 'April tends to stay out of the sun.' He paused. 'She has an eye condition which means she's sensitive to light.'

'Is that why she wears the pink glasses?' Bryony asked.

'Yes.'

'I thought that was more than just a fashion statement.'

Josh shook his head. 'I'm feeling a bit stunned by all this, I don't mind saying.'

'I think we all are,' Grandpa Joe said.

'Does this mean you're dating both of them?' Jago asked.

'Jago!' Polly cried, obviously shocked. 'Of course it doesn't!'

Jago shrugged. 'I just mean – well – twins can be close, can't they? And he has been seeing both of them.'

'By *accident!*' Polly said. 'But that's all been sorted out now that he knows the truth and can tell them apart.'

'And you're *sure* it's April you're interested in?' Lara asked.

'Absolutely,' Josh said.

'Thank god!' Lara said. 'Because May was just awful!'

'She wasn't *that* bad,' Frank said.

'Oh, come on, Dad, she was dreadful!' Lara told him.

'I think that's a little harsh, love,' Eleanor told her.

'But you said she was uppity too, Mum!' Lara said.

Josh looked at his mother who was turning red. 'Mum?'

Eleanor's face screwed up in consternation. 'I might have said *tricky*, Lara.'

Lara shook her head. 'You definitely said *uppity*. But she was, wasn't she, Josh?'

He sighed. 'She was certainly different from April.'

'Let me get this right,' Sam said. 'It was May we met today, but it's April that you're seeing.'

'Yes.'

'So we've still not met the girl you're seeing,' Sam pointed out.

'That's *right!*' Grandpa Joe said. 'I mean, I've seen her across the road, but that isn't the same thing at all, is it?'

'We've *got* to meet her,' Polly said.

'Yes!' Callie agreed and everyone chorused the same sentiment.

'So, will you be bringing April – the *real* April – to Sunday lunch next week?' his mother asked him now.

'Oh, yes – you must!' Lara exclaimed. 'I'll come home specially even though there's a pretty good rock group coming to perform.'

Josh grinned. 'I'd be happy to ask her.'

Everyone chatted for a bit longer over the tea and biscuits and then Josh stood up.

'Listen, I'm exhausted.'

'But you haven't had any biscuits,' Archie informed him.

'You eat them for me, Arch.'

Archie eagerly reached for two fingers of sugary shortbread.

'One at a time, greedy!' Polly warned him.

Everybody was on their feet hugging and kissing Josh goodbye, but only his mother followed him into the hallway.

'Josh?'

He paused by the door as she approached him. 'Yes?'

'April's very special to you, isn't she?'

He smiled. 'She is,' he confided. 'I didn't think I could become so fond of somebody so quickly, but...'

'It happens to us all sooner or later.'

'It just happened to be later with me.'

'Oh, you're still a young man!'

'I feel ancient sometimes.'

'You were born with a mature mind, that's all.'

'Perhaps.'

Eleanor wrapped him up in a warm hug. 'Dear child! Call me if you need me, won't you?'

'I will.'

'And tell April...' she paused. 'Tell her to come and see us soon.'

'I will.'

Monday morning at the shop felt so very different from last week, Josh couldn't help thinking. Now, when he looked out of his shop window at A Little Bit Bloomsbury, it was with the knowledge that there was not only an April but a May too, although it was April in the shop today, he noted. They'd waved at each other a couple of times and he was going to pop over as soon as he could. In fact, after he'd placed an order and helped a customer to choose a book for his wife, he scooted right across.

'April?' he called as he entered the shop.

She appeared from the back room, her chestnut hair piled on top of her head in a gorgeously messy bun and a floral apron tied over a pale denim pinafore which skimmed her ankles.

'It *is* April, isn't it?' Josh teased.

She smiled. 'Very funny!'

'Just checking! I did know, you know. And not just because of the glasses.'

'You did?'

'I think I always kind of did.' He walked towards her and cocked his head to one side. 'Maybe not physically – that had me stumped – but I instinctively felt that you weren't – you know – you. *May* wasn't *you*.'

'But we're so alike.'

Josh shook his head. 'You're more different than you think.'

'Really? How?'

Josh paused before answering. This was tricky. How was he going to explain it to April without insulting May?

'Well, you're – erm...'

'What?'

'You're such a warm person.'

'And May isn't?'

'Well, what I mean is, you're warmer than her. Maybe. I don't know.'

She grinned. She looked like she was enjoying his discomfort in all this.

'Perhaps you're like a book I want to read,' he went on. 'You know that moment in a bookshop when there are two books next to each other and you know, instinctively, the one that's right for you – the one you want to pick up?'

'You want to pick me up?'

'Oh, goodness! I'm not explaining this very well.' Josh paused again. 'What I'm trying to say is that you're April. I know the difference. I *feel* it. And I like you.'

'So you don't like May?' She was teasing him again. At least, he hoped she was.

'I *like* her well enough. But,' he smiled and then whispered, 'not as much as I like you.'

She smiled back at him and it was a bright warm smile that

seemed to spread through her entire being and right into Josh as well, telling him he'd finally said the right thing.

She moved an inch closer to him.

'I'd know too.'

'Know what?' Josh asked, confused.

'If you had a twin brother. I'd know that it was you I liked best.'

He smiled. 'You would?'

'Definitely. I feel there's this connection between us. Does that sound pretentious?'

'No!'

'And it's not too weird to say this so soon after meeting you?'

Josh shook his head. 'No! I feel the same way.' They smiled at one another. 'Listen, seeing as it was you I wanted to introduce to my family, and seeing as it wasn't *actually* you, I think you should come to the next Sunday lunch.'

'Are you sure?'

'Of *course* I'm sure! I want everyone to meet you, and for you to meet everyone.'

'But will your family really want to after what May and I did?'

'As long as it's *you* who comes with me, I'm sure they will.'

'Then I'd love to. Only, I was going to invite you to meet my family too.'

'Really?'

'In the spirit of being honest going forward.' She looked down at her apron and started to pick at a blob of bright blue paint on it. 'I think you should meet them.'

'Okay,' Josh said. 'When?'

'I've got to go over on Wednesday to pick some things up and I thought you might like to come. Can you get away from the shop?'

'I can ask Polly if she's free.'

'Great,' April said, but her face seemed clouded with anxiety.

'What is it? What aren't you telling me? You aren't going to reveal you're actually a triplet, are you, and that there's a June as well?'

'No, of course not!' She laughed, but then her expression became serious again. 'But – well – you'll see.'

'You are one mysterious girl, April Channing,' Josh told her, wondering what surprise he was in for next.

CHAPTER TEN

Leaving his shop in the capable hands of Polly on Wednesday morning, Josh crossed the road to A Little Bit Bloomsbury, a bunch of flowers in his hand.

'Ah!' April said when she saw them. 'Are they for...?'

'Your mum.'

'May I?' She held her hand towards him and he handed her the bouquet.

'Anything wrong with them?' he asked as she disappeared into the back room.

She appeared a moment later, the flowers now wrapped in paper.

'Mum can't abide unnecessary plastic.'

'Oh, I'm sorry. I didn't think of that.'

'It's okay. It's just that it's a plastic-free home as much as a home can be.'

'Really?'

'Oh, yes. Wooden toothbrushes, hessian bags – that kind of thing.'

'So I wouldn't have made a great first impression?'

April grinned. 'No, and she would have told you too – given you her "saving the planet" speech. At least you've saved yourself that!' She grabbed her handbag from a nearby stool and they left the shop with April carrying the flowers which she placed on the back seat of a little car parked just by the church.

Josh was surprised that it was April who was going to drive them out to Norfolk. Thus far, he had seen no evidence that she drove and, with her eye condition, he hadn't even been sure she did drive.

'You look shocked,' she said when he got in the car beside her.

'I thought May might be driving.'

'She doesn't go everywhere with me, you know.'

'Oh, I didn't mean... I just thought – your eyes...' he stopped.

'Don't worry. I'm allowed to drive. Only not at night.'

Josh smiled as they pulled out into the main street of Castle Clare.

'So are you going to tell me what to expect before we get there? I don't know a thing about your family apart from the fact that your mother is an eco warrior.'

April laughed. 'But you've met May.'

'Of course.' He glanced at April's face which had a pensive look. Was she concentrating on driving or was she thinking about how to answer his question?

'You might...'

'Might what?' he encouraged.

'I should warn you...'

'About what?'

'You might find things *unusual*.'

'How so?' Josh asked.

'My family. It's not like a regular family.'

Josh frowned. 'Okay.'

'It's not like your family for example with a mother and father all married and everything.'

'Does that mean your parents are divorced?' he asked.

'Oh, no. Not divorced. Never married actually. Well, not a legal sort of marriage.' He saw her frown again. 'I'm not explaining it very well, am I?'

'Erm, not so as I can understand.'

She smiled. 'Then I'll be straightforward. I have two fathers and they both live with my mother. Daddy Jeff and Daddy George.'

Josh took a moment to comprehend this. 'Two fathers?'

'Yes.'

'Is it a big house?'

'Not at all. It's an apartment, really – part of a big house. You'll see.'

'And they all live... *together*.'

'That's right,' April said matter-of-factly. 'A bit like Charleston. You know Vanessa Bell's house in Sussex?'

'Yes, I know it,' Josh said. 'I was telling May that we had a family trip there a few years ago.'

'Well, Vanessa lived there with her husband and her lover and his lover too. It was all wonderfully mixed up.'

'And that's what your family home is like, is it?'

'A little bit. It's not quite as wild. It's just Mum and Daddy Jeff and Daddy George. Most of the time. Daddy Jeff was seeing somebody else for a little while, but he got bored of her. Said she couldn't even hope to compare to Mummy.'

'Okay.'

April laughed. 'You're shocked, aren't you? I *knew* you would be!'

'No, no,' Josh said quickly. 'I'm just trying to process it all.'

She glanced at him. 'You've turned quite pink.'

'No I haven't!'

'You have! You're blushing from head to toe!'

'Well, it's warm in here, isn't it?' he said, opening the window.

She laughed again. 'Honestly, Josh, don't worry about it. You'll see how wonderfully normal and natural it is.'

'They're all going to be there, then? Both fathers?'

'Of course! Daddy Jeff has taken some time off work to meet you. They're all really excited about it. And you'll love them. Daddy George is just gorgeous! He's very funny too. Loves to throw a party. He's an artist and can get a bit moody if his painting isn't going well, though. Daddy Jeff is more serious. He loves a good conversation. He's the business head of the family. He works in London and nobody's quite sure what he does. It's something deadly dull like moving money from one place to another. But it earns him heaps of money which helps run the apartment and keep Daddy George in paint because he doesn't sell many paintings, to be honest. They're a bit – how shall I say it? Vague.'

'Vague?'

'Yes, they're hard to make out.'

'You mean abstract?'

'Some of the time. Others are just a bit washed out like there's a layer of paint missing or something.'

'And Daddy Jeff doesn't mind that he keeps everyone?'

'Gracious, no! He hasn't an artistic bone in his body, you see, and this is his way of living an artistic life.'

Josh took all this in, trying to picture just how these two very different men lived together.

'And your mother? What's she like?'

'Her name's Arbella. She's an artist too. She's dabbled in all sorts of things over the years. She started as a life model and then decided that she'd prefer to keep her clothes on and do the actual painting. But she's been a potter too and worked with ceramics and all sorts of textiles. I don't think there's an art she hasn't tried. She says that life is too short to stick to one thing and that we must experience lots of different things. Choosing one art, she once said, would be like wearing only one colour all one's life.'

Josh smiled. 'I like that.'

'Do you believe it?'

He frowned. 'I guess.'

'So you won't be running that bookshop your whole life? You'll try other jobs?'

'Ah, well, no. Probably not. I mean, I like the idea in principle, and I did spend a couple of years living in London, but it wasn't a natural fit for me. I guess I'm the sort to suit one job in one place.' He paused. 'How about you? Are you planning on running A Little Bit Bloomsbury forever?'

A look of hesitation hovered over her face. 'Forever's a long time, isn't it?'

They drove on through the country lanes, slowly making their way towards the Norfolk border where the population seemed to peter out altogether and the fields stretched widely to the horizon, peppered only with church towers and pine trees. The sky was high and blue and Josh had to admit that it felt good to be out amongst it all. He couldn't help feeling that he was being wickedly naughty like he had skipped school or something. It was so rare for him to take time off during the week. The bookshop pretty much dictated his life and, while he didn't regret that for a moment, he acknowledged the fact that being here with April, driving through the country lanes on a beautiful summer's day felt very good indeed.

They drove on, passing through a pretty village with a windmill overlooking a village green and then they turned into a narrow country lane where the thick hedges scratched at the car and the grass growing in the middle of the road tickled the undercarriage.

'Here we are,' April said a moment later as she turned into a tree-lined track. Josh briefly saw a sign which read Fairley Hall and noticed the pleasant, open farmland with myriad footpaths on either side of the track. There was a pretty little wood too which would cool one's limbs and restore one's soul on a hot day such as this. But they weren't there to walk.

April slowed the car down further. The track, it had to be said, could have done with a bit of attention for it was littered with enormous cracks and giant potholes.

'Don't look so alarmed,' April said. 'I can navigate my way round these blindfolded.'

Josh tried to relax, but it didn't come naturally to him. He looked out of the window and saw that the field soon gave way to a well-tended garden with fenced off areas and raised beds full of produce. There were a number of people milling about, some holding tools and others baskets and boxes.

'Is this… is this a *commune*?' Josh asked.

'Not really. It's more of a… fellowship.'

'Isn't that the same thing?'

'Not judging by the way you view the word *commune*!' April told him. 'Don't look so shocked!'

'I'm not shocked. I don't know why you keep thinking that I'm shocked.'

'Not everybody lives like you do.'

'What do you mean by that?'

April pursed her lips together. 'Not everyone is so very traditional.'

'You think I'm traditional?'

'Your whole family is, isn't it? That's what May told me.'

'Is it?'

'Don't you think it's traditional? That whole Sunday lunch thing where everyone gathers together?'

'I don't know. It's just normal.'

'Exactly! Like this is normal to me.'

'Now you're saying the word 'normal' as you're saying I'm saying the word 'commune'.

April laughed. 'As long as we both understand that we were brought up differently.'

'I totally understand that,' Josh assured her.

'Good.'

A moment later, April pulled the car up alongside a beaten up old Land Rover and they got out.

'The flowers!' Josh said, watching as April reached inside for them. 'Although I see there are plenty here.' He nodded towards the raised beds which were full of colour. Josh recognised alliums and peonies, but there was a lot he didn't recognise too.

'It was Mum who insisted on growing flowers alongside the fruit and veg,' April told him. 'She and Daddy George paint them and the others sell them to local shops and at the market.'

She led the way across a path strewn with starry daisies and thyme until they came to a green-painted door. 'This is it.' She lifted her hand to a large metal wind chime and set it ringing before opening the door. A wide square hallway greeted Josh with several rooms leading off it.

'Hello!' April called. 'They're probably upstairs.'

Josh wasn't sure what he had been expecting when April had told him about her parents' lifestyle. Perhaps he'd imagined a place filled with crystals and the obligatory Buddha head, but it wasn't like that at all. He looked around. There were plants, lots of plants in pots, in baskets, and in galvanised containers. Josh even saw one in an old cracked teapot. There were books too which instantly had a calming effect on him, and masses of paintings on the walls.

'Wow!' he said. It was all he could manage really.

'You like it?'

'It's... it's...' He looked around, taking it all in. 'I do.'

April turned to beam him a smile. 'Good.'

'You grew up here?'

'Yes. And, for a long time, May and I didn't want to leave. The outside world seemed so big and scary and, well, ugly compared to this place.'

'I can see why.'

'We've always had everything we needed here so why look for something you don't need somewhere else?'

'Good point.'

A woman's voice from upstairs interrupted them. 'April? Is that you?'

'It is!'

'Well, come on up, then!'

April grinned. 'I think somebody's impatient to meet you!'

Josh took a deep breath and followed her up the stairs into a large open plan space which, like what he'd seen of the house so far, was full of plants, books and paintings. With its enormous windows, it looked like a cross between a greenhouse and an art gallery. He'd never seen a room quite like it before with its paint-splattered wooden floorboards and easels standing at regular intervals. There were a couple of small sofas covered in silky shawls and cushions but, other than that, he couldn't really see much in the way of furniture. This room, he thought, was all about art, and perhaps its occupants were too busy making more art to spend time sitting down.

A woman appeared from behind a giant banana tree which stood near one of the windows.

'Mummy!' April cried and the two women embraced. Josh looked on, taking in the wondrous splendour that was April's mother. She had long silver hair right down her back and was wearing a large pair of hooped earrings threaded through with turquoise beads. She was like an exotic bird, Josh thought, and he could see where April and May had inherited their beauty from.

'So, you're Josh, are you?' she said, making no attempt to disguise her curiosity as she looked him up and down a couple of times.

'Very pleased to meet you, Mrs Channing.' They shook hands.

She made a funny sort of scoffing noise. 'Mrs indeed! Call me Arbella. Everybody does.'

'Arbella,' Josh said. 'That's a very unusual name.'

'Who'd want a *usual* one?' she countered.

'I bought these for you.' He handed her the flowers.

'Thank you. Nice paper,' she said, examining it. 'I can use that for something I'm working on.' Josh glanced April who winked at him. He had passed the first test.

'What an amazing view,' Josh said as he walked towards one of the floor to ceiling windows and looked down into the garden and out across the parkland.

'It's not too shabby, is it?' Arbella said with a sniff, and then she gasped and ran towards a pair of doors which opened onto a small balcony overlooking the vegetable and flower garden. 'Stefan! Don't you *dare* cut those peonies!' she shouted. Josh was taken aback by the volume, sure that half of Norfolk had heard her cry.

Arbella came back in from the balcony, shaking her head. 'You've got to watch him. He'll have the heads off before they're committed to canvas. I've been keeping my eyes on those, waiting for the moment when they're just right.'

'But you eat his potatoes, Mummy.'

'That's different. Any fool can grow potatoes.'

Josh grinned and then he spotted something glowing amber, scarlet and violet all at once.

'Wow!' he said for the second time that day when finding himself at a loss for words. 'I love that stained glass.' He pointed to a large rectangular frame.

'Really?' Arbella said, sounding shocked. 'I was going to recycle it.'

'Oh, don't do that, Mummy! It's lovely.'

'*Not* one of my best.'

'If that's not one of your best, I'd love to see the ones you think *are* your best,' Josh told her.

'Don't worry, she'll show you!' April teased.

'Only if he wants to see them,' Arbella said.

'Oh, I'd love to see them.'

Arbella's hazel eyes widened just a fraction. 'I think I like this young man of yours, April.'

Josh saw April blush and he was pretty sure he was blushing too.

'Where are the daddies?' April asked and Josh almost did a double-take at her phrasing.

'In the kitchen, making lunch with any luck,' Arbella said.

'Mummy doesn't cook,' April explained.

'Huh! The cheek of the girl! You know as well as I do that I'm better with paints than pots and pans. "The kitchen is a foreign country. They do things differently there."'

'L P Hartley,' Josh said.

'Yes, only adapted to suit me – hah!'

Josh liked the short sharp way she laughed, throwing her head back and barking at the heavens as her hazel eyes crinkled with mirth.

'Come and meet the daddies,' April told Josh as she propelled him towards the kitchen, obviously unable to wait a moment longer.

The kitchen was a small galley affair at the end of the house and two men were standing by a worktop chopping vegetables together. Josh tried to identify which was which, and it wasn't hard to guess for one was wearing a neat cream shirt and crisp blue jeans, and the other was wearing a long striped shirt in a crumpled linen and paint-splattered slacks.

'Daddies!' April cried as she entered, again taking Josh aback a little by the extraordinariness of it all.

The two men turned around as one, only they couldn't have

looked more different. The one wearing the neat cream shirt had fine dark hair, cut neatly around his face. He was clean shaven with delicate features and kind eyes. The other looked like a lion, Josh thought, with his tousled fair hair, stubbly face and amber eyes.

'April!' the lion said, coming forward and embracing her.

'Daddy George,' April said. 'I want you to meet Josh.'

'And so I shall!' George said, extending a large hand towards Josh. Josh shook it.

'Pleased to meet you, sir.'

'Sir, indeed! First time I've been called "sir"!' He laughed.

'And this is Daddy Jeff,' April said as the neat, crisp man came forward and shook Josh's hand with his more delicate one.

'Good to meet you,' Jeff said.

'And you,' Josh said, looking into a pair of gentle eyes which he immediately trusted.

'And April! How pretty you look.' The two hugged. 'Well, we're just about ready for lunch,' Jeff announced. 'I'll finish preparing. George – want to open a bottle?'

'Absolutely!' George said, his already wide grin widening even more. 'We have a nice bottle of white chilling.'

'Home-made gooseberry from three years ago,' Jeff said.

'Good vintage,' George declared.

'Best yet,' Jeff added.

Josh smiled, watching the happy dialogue of these two men. April's two fathers. She'd done well, he couldn't help thinking. Some people didn't even get one father while others had to put up with shockers. But these two men seemed pretty decent.

He watched as George poured the wine into glasses and handed him one.

'Take one through to your mum,' George said, handing April a second glass a moment later together with iced water for her as she was driving.

Josh took a sip and then spluttered. Then coughed.

'Oh, dear!' Jeff said. 'Too strong?'

Josh continued to cough. 'Just a little!'

George laughed heartily. 'Let's try you with the elderflower.' He took Josh's glass, emptied it down the sink and then reached for a second bottle in the fridge. 'You should find this a bit lighter.'

Josh felt a little nervous as he went to take a sip of the elderflower a moment later, but it was good and definitely less intense than the gooseberry.

'Thank you,' he said.

'We'll have to build you up to the gooseberry,' George teased. 'Shouldn't take too long.'

Just as they were leaving the kitchen, Josh took April to one side.

'Where does your name Channing come from? If you don't mind me asking.'

'Daddy Jeff. It's Jeffrey Channing. Daddy George's surname is Molesworth and Mum refused to have that for our names.'

'So she chose Jeff's name because she preferred it?' Josh asked in surprise.

'That's right.'

'But George is your real father?'

'They're *both* our fathers, Josh, I told you.'

'Yes, but it seems more likely that Daddy George is your birth father, don't you think? What with the art and everything, and his colouring is similar to yours, isn't it?'

'Have you been trying to work it out?' April asked. 'You really shouldn't, you know.'

'Why not?'

'Because it doesn't matter.'

'But aren't you the least bit curious?'

'No. Not really. And Daddy Jeff is artistic too in his own way.'

'Is he?'

'He knows how to *appreciate* art. That's just as important as creating it, I think.'

'Yes, I know, but wouldn't you like to know the truth?'

'You mean drag our fathers through the humiliation of DNA testing? That's barbaric!'

'But don't you think the real father has a right to know?'

'They don't want to know,' April assured him. 'And you're forgetting something vitally important here. If we all *did* know then one of the daddies might feel sad about it.'

Josh had to admit that he hadn't thought about that. 'But what if something had happened like they'd all fallen out?' he went on. 'What if your mum wanted nothing more to do with them? What then? Which father would you have seen? One of them? Or both?'

'What is it with all these questions?' April asked, sounding none too happy with Josh's fixation. 'None of us knows what the future holds.' A look of anxiety crossed her face and then she took a deep breath. 'But we're a family – just like yours. Only different.'

Josh took a sip of his wine and nodded. 'I'm sorry. I'm just curious about it all.'

'I can see that!' She took a sip of her water. 'Let me give Mummy her wine.'

He followed her back into the main room, passing a row of bright blue canvasses on the floor. April saw where he was looking and smiled.

'They're from Daddy George's Greek period. He went away for a few weeks to the Greek islands. I think we've got a brother over there.'

Josh almost spluttered on his wine again. 'You *think*?'

'Yes. Daddy George isn't convinced that the boy is his.'

Josh felt as if he'd been knocked face-down. This family was getting stranger and stranger the more he learned about it.

'Ah, I thought I'd lost you two!' Arbella said as April

approached her with the wine. 'What do you think of my two men, then?'

'Oh, well, they're great!' Josh said.

April laughed. 'He thinks we're very strange.'

'I didn't say that!' Josh cried in alarm, lest Arbella thought him uptight.

'You don't need to. It's written all over you,' April teased.

'It's a different sort of life from many,' Arbella announced. 'But it's a good life.'

'I can see that.'

Arbella smiled a smile which softened her whole face and made Josh feel a little less awkward.

'Now, where's that lunch?'

Lunch was served on a table which, minutes before, had been strewn with large sketches and pots of pens and pencils. April had helped her mother clear it while Jeff and George had laid the table and had placed all the bowls and plates of food out.

'Pick and mix,' Jeff announced. 'There's bread and salad, beans and pasta, some roast veg there and some hummus there.'

'A little bit of everything,' Arbella says. 'Kind of our motto in life.'

That, Josh thought, was something he was beginning to understand about this family.

Talk over lunch was easy and natural. Arbella and the two daddies asked Josh a series of questions about his work, promising to visit his bookshop in the near future and showing a genuine interest in the Nightingale family's business.

'The world needs more books,' Arbella declared. 'Physical books, I mean – not those awful digital ebook things that you can't touch or furnish a room with.'

'But digital books are so portable,' Jeff said. 'I read them on my commute.'

'Ah, nasty things!'

'Mummy has quite a collection of books,' April told Josh.

'I've noticed,' he said. There were several piles around the table, leaning precariously.

'You can't have too many books, can you, Josh?'

'Absolutely not,' he said, pleased that they'd found something they wholeheartedly agreed on.

As he ate, he looked around the table at them all. There were no visible signs of rivalry and none of them seemed to think there was anything unusual in the way they lived. Perhaps it wasn't *so* unlike his own family, he thought. They all made time for each other and certainly knew how to make a guest feel at home.

'More wine, Josh?' Jeff asked, seeing his empty glass.

'Ready for the gooseberry yet?' George said with a laugh.

Josh quickly placed his hand over his glass as the gooseberry bottle hovered dangerously close.

'I think I'll just have a water,' he said and everybody laughed. Yes, he thought, it was very much like Sunday lunch at Campion House.

The afternoon grew hot and, after being shown the gardens, they retreated inside and Josh was given a tour of the rest of the apartment. In truth, each room looked exactly the same because they were all stuffed full of books, art and plants. Josh looked at more art that day than he believed he had in the whole of his lifetime up to that moment. His mind was full of colour, shape, form and texture. And passion. He could feel himself vibrating with the passion that emanated from the pieces by Arbella and George.

'You've created a really beautiful home here,' he told Arbella as she closed the sketchbook she'd been showing him. 'And I love your work. All of it.'

She laughed. 'Well, *you* can certainly visit again! Artists do love to hear their work praised.'

'I think it's probably time we got back,' April said, breaking the spell Josh felt he'd been under and he found that he felt disappointed that it was time to go. He watched as April received two of the biggest bear hugs from each of her fathers. He turned to say goodbye to Arbella and she sidled up to him and whispered.

'She hasn't told you, has she?' Her voice was quiet and serious.

Josh frowned. 'I know she's a twin if that's what you mean, but she didn't tell me when I first met her, no!' He laughed.

'Mum? What are you talking about?'

Arbella shook her head. 'Nothing. Just telling him to take care of you.'

'Oh, Mummy! Don't embarrass him!'

The two women hugged.

'You got the paintings you wanted?' Arbella asked.

'Yes, thank you. I've popped them in the car. They'll look lovely in the shop.'

'Just don't sell them. Those ones *aren't* for sale!'

'Okay, I promise not to sell them even if a millionaire offers a fortune for them.'

'Some things are worth more than money,' Arbella told her and April smiled. She was obviously used to hearing that, Josh thought.

They walked down the stairs to a chorus of goodbyes and went back out into the garden. It was still warm and April wound the car windows down as they drove away.

'Two Aprils,' Josh said. 'And two dads. There isn't anything else you're hiding from me, is there?'

April glanced at him, her eyes clouding with anxiety as he noticed they did from time to time.

'No, of course not,' she said. 'What makes you say that?'

'Oh, nothing. I was just joking.' He paused. 'Well, your mum said something.'

'What?'

'That you haven't told me something. I thought it was about

you being a twin, but she knows I know that, doesn't she? I mean, we were all talking about it at lunch.'

'Of course,' April said.

'Then what did she mean?'

April didn't answer for a moment, but then said, 'Who knows what Mummy means half the time?'

Josh smiled and looked out of the window at the passing landscape. He wasn't going to press things, but he couldn't help thinking that there was something else that April wasn't ready to tell him yet.

CHAPTER ELEVEN

Sam was the first to quiz Josh. Bright and early on Thursday morning.

'Two fathers? *Wow!*' he said after Josh had filled him in.

'That's the word I keep using,' Josh told him, 'and you know how much I hate not being able to express myself properly. But she just keeps making me think or say *wow* all the time!'

Sam grinned. 'She is certainly a woman of many surprises.'

'Yes she is.' Josh sighed a very heavy sigh.

'What is it?' Sam asked, sounding concerned.

'I don't know.' He shrugged.

'Tell me.'

Josh looked out of the window across the road towards April's. They'd had a cup of tea together before opening their shops and she'd told him that her mother had rung the night before and had raved about Josh for a good half hour. The fathers had adored him too. He had the official family seal of approval.

'I'm not sure,' Josh said now. 'It's just something April's mother said about her not having told me something. I thought her mother meant about April being a twin, but that doesn't make sense because we were all talking openly about May over lunch.'

'Then what could it be?'

'That's it. I really don't know. But surely there can't be any more secrets.' He sighed again. 'It's probably nothing. I've more than likely misunderstood something. It was all so surreal yesterday and my head felt scrambled looking at so much art.'

'Was it good art?'

'Yes, actually. April's got two very talented parents. I mean, Jeff's talented too only in business. It's George and Arbella who are the artists.'

Sam cleared his throat. 'So, how does it all – erm – work with them? It sounds very Bloomsbury Group to me.'

Josh smiled. 'Yes, I thought that too. I think that's part of the charm for them – that connection to the artistic group that had no rules. But the thing is, it felt completely natural. They weren't just trying to emulate their idols – they were living the life they truly wanted to live.'

'But...' Sam frowned. 'Doesn't that get complicated? Don't they fight or get jealous of each other?'

'I kept asking April about it all and she kept saying I was making a great fuss over nothing and that it's all quite straightforward. They're a family.'

Sam nodded sagely and then chuckled.

'What?'

'I was just trying to imagine Dad sharing Mum with another – well – dad!'

Josh laughed. 'I can't see that working at Campion House. I think Dad would chase any would-be suitors off with his garden fork!'

'But what if...' Sam started and then stopped.

'What?'

'What if April wants a similar lifestyle?'

Josh did a double-take. 'I don't think that's likely, is it?'

'Why not?' Sam asked.

'Well, for one thing – you're getting a bit ahead of things. We...' He paused and looked down at his perfectly polished shoes. 'We haven't even kissed yet.'

'Wait a minute!' Sam said, his eyes wide behind his glasses. 'You haven't *kissed* her yet?'

'No.'

'What are you waiting for?'

'The right moment.'

'And when's that?'

Josh shoved his hands in his trouser pockets, feeling a little put out by his brother's pushy questioning.

'It might have escaped your attention, Sam, but I'm a gentleman.'

Sam smiled. 'It hasn't escaped my attention, believe me.'

'Well, then!'

'But let me just say – and please don't take any offence because I really don't mean any.' Sam paused, looking awkward.

'Well, get on with it,' Josh said at last.

'Okay. Here it is. Don't be *too* much of a gentleman, Josh.' He reached out and gave Josh's shoulder a pat which Josh read as a kind of *go get her* gesture that he didn't wholly approve of.

He watched as Sam left the shop, a thousand restless thoughts spiralling in his mind. Of course he wanted to kiss April. He'd be a fool not to; she was a beautiful woman. But they were still getting to know one another and that, in its own way, was delicious enough, wasn't it? He didn't want to push things too quickly. He wanted to enjoy the newness of it all, of each little moment they spent together. April seemed happy enough with that too, didn't she?

Josh sighed. Sam had sown the seed of doubt in his mind now and he wasn't sure what to think.

He spent the rest of the morning dithering around, which was very unlike him. He could feel the change in himself and it unnerved him. He'd truly never thought that he'd fall in love. It was different for his siblings – they had the open, warm and adaptable personalities to cope with love, and Josh couldn't help thinking that he didn't. He wasn't even coping with the thought of a first kiss, was he? And how hard could that be? He'd kissed a few girls before. Well, two. There'd been Melissa at college who'd shared a bottle of wine with him one summer's night, but it had just been that one tipsy kiss before they realised that they had absolutely nothing in common other than that bottle of wine. Then there'd been Holly who'd been a customer for a while. Theirs had been a mild flirtation over books punctuated by a few kisses, but it had never gone beyond that and she'd moved away after he'd given her a copy of *Tess of the D'Urbervilles*. Josh had to face it: he just wasn't the romantic hero type and he wouldn't be a bit surprised if he went and ruined this precious thing he had with April.

He was just mulling this over when the shop door opened, ringing the bell.

'Winston!' Josh cried, glad to see the old man back in his shop so soon. 'How are you and how's that brother of yours?' Josh asked. 'Monty, wasn't it?'

Winston guffawed. 'I've come out of the house to get away from him for a bit.'

Josh grinned. 'Oh, dear. Outstayed his welcome already?'

'You could say that.' Winston sighed. 'I feel bad. He's grieving his wife, you see. So *he* feels bad. But, ever since we were little, he's always had the knack of winding me up and making *me* feel bad. And now I'm feeling bad about feeling bad about him being here when he's feeling bad.' He let out a great big breath, releasing just a little of the tension he'd obviously been holding in. 'Does that make sense?'

'Kind of.'

'Anyway, that's where I'm at with it all.' He took his cap off, scratched his head and replaced his cap.

'Winston?'

'Yes?'

'Can I ask you something – about women?'

Winston looked startled by the question. 'What about them?'

Josh had never felt more awkward in his life. He should be asking his brother, Sam, about such things or maybe even his own father, but he just couldn't. It would be way too embarrassing. But Winston was different. He was a little removed and, well, he wouldn't be likely to tease him, would he?

'I need some advice.'

'And I'm the one you thought to come to?' Winston stroked his chin. 'Well, I didn't know I had that kind of a reputation.'

This made Josh smile and he felt himself relaxing a little.

'Is this about the pretty girl over there?' Winston asked, pointing across the road.

Josh nodded. 'I went to visit her family yesterday.'

'Well, you sure don't waste any time! Why do you need any advice from me if that's the speed you're working at?'

'Because – well – I haven't kissed her yet.'

Winston took this on board with a few slow blinks. 'I see,' he said at last. 'But you do *want* to kiss her?'

'*Yes!*' Josh cried. 'But *when*... I mean how do I know when the time is right?'

Winston's face seemed to wrinkle with deep thought. 'Well, I'm not sure,' he said. 'I think it's more about feeling. If you *feel* it's right. Don't over think it.'

Josh sighed. It was too late for that. He could do nothing *but* think about it now that Sam had said what he'd said.

'What did you do, Winston?'

'What did I do?'

'With Marguerite? What happened after the dance?' Josh gestured to a nearby stool and Winston sat on it with what looked like relief. 'Did you kiss her that night?'

A smile crossed the old man's face and Josh could see the delicious moment when he journeyed back into his own past.

'Well, we danced and we danced,' he said. 'Her friends soon stopped laughing. I told you they were giggling when I approached them?'

'You did,' Josh said. 'Must have been so intimidating.'

'But it was me who was soon giggling – on the inside! With the sheer joy of being in her company. Of having my arms around her and hers around me. Our bodies moving to the music – and there was all sorts playing that night. I've never been a musical man and my dance moves were nothing to write home about even as a youngster, but there were some pretty fast beats that night, let me tell you. And we didn't once tread on each other's toes. It's as if we'd been made for each other. That's what I remember thinking.'

Josh smiled. It was the same feeling he got when he was with April. He'd never looked to have a woman in his life, but she seemed to fit all the same.

'And then there were the slow dances,' Winston went on, his old eyes all sparkly now and full of youthful dreams. 'It's the slow dances you really come for, you see. Those upbeat ones are all very well – they're fun and all that – but it's the slow ones that help you get through the working week.'

'And that's when you kissed her?' Josh asked, eagerly waiting for the revelation.

Winston's eyebrows rose. 'Now, just you wait! I'm not quite there in my story yet.'

Josh laughed at his own impatience. 'Okay – in your own time.'

'Thank you!' Winston said, with mock sternness. 'Well, there was one particular slow dance. It was getting late and I didn't rightly know if there'd be another moment like this. Marguerite felt so soft and warm in my arms, our cheeks were pressed together and we were swaying to the music. I don't remember what it was now. Anyway, something sweet and romantic. It was all there – all the pieces for the perfect first kiss. And there was plenty of kissing going on around us that night, let me tell you. First kisses, chaste kisses, not-so-chaste kisses. It was all happening on that dance floor.' He paused.

'So what happened?'

'Monty.'

'What? What do you mean?'

'Monty happened,' Winston said. 'He came barging into the town hall, drunk as a frog or whatever that saying is, pushed his way through the dancers and clapped a great, sweaty hand on my shoulder.

'What was Monty doing there?'

'Spoiling my fun,' Winston replied without missing a beat. 'As far as I'd known, he'd never shown any interest in the dance hall until I did. He knew I'd be there that night and, after a belly full of beer, he'd decided to see what I was up to.' Winston shook his head at the memory. 'My brother was much more into an evening at the pub with his mates than I ever was. But he also liked the ladies and he knew they preferred the dance hall to the pubs.'

'So what happened?'

'He cut in.'

'What? Just like that – while you were dancing?' Josh was horrified by the idea.

'Just like that. He's very good at cutting in,' Winston confessed. 'Not only in dancing, but in conversation too.'

'But surely Marguerite wouldn't have liked that, would she?'

'Pah!' Winston's face was practically purple now. 'You'd be surprised what it is the ladies like. Monty, you see, has a way with the ladies. What you and I might see as rude, obnoxious behaviour, is often seen as being adorably cheeky by the ladies.'

'No way!' Josh felt indignant on his friend's behalf.

'Alas, yes.'

'So you didn't kiss her?'

'Now, let's not get too ahead of ourselves,' Winston said. 'The evening wasn't quite done.'

'Well, I can't wait to hear–' Josh was just about to say, 'what happened next' when the shop door opened. 'Ah.'

Winston turned around. 'Time for me to go?'

Josh gave an apologetic smile and he leaned towards Winston. 'As much as I'd love to hear more, this is one customer who won't tolerate being kept waiting.'

'Message received and understood.' Winston touched the peak of his cap as he climbed down off the stool.

'But come back soon and tell me what happened next, okay?'

Winston gave a little wink as he left the shop.

The feeling of contentment Winston had felt sharing his story and his memories of Marguerite with Josh was soon banished when he opened the door to his home and felt the all-enveloping presence of Monty once again. As usual, he was sitting in Winston's favourite chair, toast crumbs down his front and on the carpet around him.

'Where've you been?' Monty asked as Winston came into the room.

'I told you. I went to the bookshop.'

'You left me.'

'I asked you to come with me,' Winston reminded him, but he'd been relieved when his brother had declined his invitation. He'd needed a short break.

Monty waved an exasperated hand at him. 'I didn't feel up to it.'

'The fresh air and walk would have done you good.'

'Would it?'

'Yes!' Winston all but barked, and then felt bad. 'I'll make us a cup of tea.'

'Good idea. Want a hand?'

It was the first time Monty had offered to help with anything since he'd arrived.

'You're okay there,' Winston said. The truth was, he needed to think.

Having his brother there with him was proving to be more than a mild irritation. It was resurrecting all sorts of issues that had been locked away for years. Issues and emotions that Winston thought had been dealt with and forgotten, but clearly they weren't.

Because there'd been more to that night at the dance hall than Monty cutting in with Marguerite. Winston had just chosen to not think about it for a few decades.

CHAPTER TWELVE

Life seemed to be punctuated with an endless stream of lunches, Josh thought as he got up on Sunday morning and took a shower before breakfasting and tidying around his already tidy home. As he did so, he looked at his home with new eyes, wondering how April might see it.

Beige. That was the word that sprung to mind. His home was an unending blend of beiges, magnolias and ecrus. There was no getting away from it. Josh hadn't really noticed until now. The walls, curtains and other furnishings were merely a backdrop to his interior thoughts. He'd never really paid those sorts of things any attention. But visiting April's family home now made him see it all differently and he had to admit that what he saw no longer pleased him. Perhaps he should buy a few pot plants. Or paintings. Yes! He could commission some wonderful art from Arbella and George to brighten and enliven his place.

Or get some furniture painted by April. Even better – give her some of his dull and drab pieces to make over as she saw fit. Yes! That's what he'd do. He'd ask her advice.

He shook his head. Would April laugh at him if she saw his

boringly beige bachelor pad? Would she shake her head in despair and be put off him because he so obviously lacked creativity and imagination? He wasn't sure and yet he knew that he wanted to change the space around him. Meeting April and her family had had such a profound effect on him and he was unable to see the world as he had before. The world was full of pattern and colour, texture and shape and, in his own small way, Josh wanted to feel a part of that even if it was only by changing his furnishings.

It was with a renewed vigour and purpose that he left his house later that morning, driving the short distance to the Victorian home April shared with her sister, May. He couldn't help admitting that he'd be glad when this day was over. As much as he longed to introduce April to his family and his family to April, he felt like it was kind of an audition, especially after what had happened with the last lunch – what with April turning out to be May. He knew his family would be comparing and contrasting the two sisters. At the same time, he was longing to see her again and was looking forward to telling her of his new ideas for his home.

He rang the doorbell a little before noon.

'Oh, it's you,' May said as she opened the door to him.

'Hello, May,' Josh said, unfazed.

'April – it's him!' May called through the house, leaving him on the doorstep without inviting him in while she herself went back inside.

Josh flinched a little, wondering when he'd been relegated to a mere 'him' and finding it amusing and insulting at the same time. He followed her inside. May was standing beside the fireplace and had picked up a pottery mug of tea and was sipping it. She didn't offer to make him a drink and she didn't bother to strike up any idle conversation as they waited for April.

Josh was just about to say something inane like, *nice day, isn't it* when April appeared. She was wearing a lacy cream blouse over a sky-blue skirt and had a long necklace of sea-green glass beads around her neck. Her chestnut hair was loose and Josh felt his mouth go dry.

'You look lovely,' he said.

'She *always* looks lovely,' May cut in.

'Well, of course,' Josh said, wondering if this was some kind of test May was putting him through. 'That goes without saying.'

'Does it indeed?' May said.

'You look lovely too,' April said.

Josh smiled at her praise. He'd worn his best navy shirt and had polished his already highly-polished shoes and still wasn't sure if it was good enough.

'Ready to go?' he asked.

April grabbed her handbag from a nearby chair.

'Call me if you need me,' May said as the two sisters embraced.

Once outside, Josh opened the passenger door for April and made sure she was comfortable.

'What's wrong with May?' he asked when he joined her a moment later.

'Wrong?'

'She was very short with me.'

'Oh, she just objects to you. That's all.'

'*Objects* to me?'

'Of course. She doesn't like me seeing anyone. But don't take it personally. She'd object if you were a girlfriend too. She likes me all to herself.'

Josh frowned. 'Isn't that a bit – I don't know – stifling?'

'I'm not sure. I've never really known anything else.'

'Well, I'd find it stifling.'

'I guess I find it comforting in a way.'

'It seems like I've got a lot to learn about twins.' He smiled and then cleared his throat. 'Listen, April, I was wondering if you could take a look at something for me.'

'What is it?'

'My home.'

'Oh?'

He suddenly felt awkward. 'This isn't some sneaky way of getting you back to my place or anything,' he hastily added. 'I'm not that kind of man.'

'Josh – I *know* you aren't.'

'It's just that I need some help. Decorating.'

'Oh, I see.'

'Yes, and you will see. I'm actually...' he stopped, almost regretting this idea of his already.

'What?'

'I'm a bit nervous showing you if I'm honest. But I don't know how else to change things and I *do* want to change them.'

'Then why are you nervous about it?'

'Because it might put you off me if you see how dull and boring my place is.'

April laughed. 'It won't put me off you!'

'Wait until you see it first.'

Josh drove them back to his place, parking the car neatly and sitting for a moment.

'Are we going in?' April asked.

Josh turned to her. 'Promise you won't judge me too harshly?'

'Josh – it's *you* who is judging yourself too harshly as far as I can see.'

He looked at her kind eyes behind their pink glasses and immediately felt himself relax a little.

'Okay, then,' he said, getting out of the car and running round to open her door before letting her into his house.

Josh's home was a new-build. Not for him were the character cottages Suffolk was renowned for. All those bumpy old walls and uneven floors would not have suited Josh. Oh, no. He liked the straight lines and sureness that came from a brand new property with mains drainage and plumbing that could be relied upon, and windows that were double-glazed and doors that were a proper height. And he'd been genuinely happy with his new home until recently.

'Oh, I see what you mean,' April said a moment later, her eyes darting around his front room.

'It's bad, isn't it?'

'Bad is a very strong word,' April said. '*Bland* might fit better.'

'Yes,' Josh agreed. 'It's bland all right. Bland and boring and dull and dreary.' He let out a long, heartfelt sigh. 'Is there any hope for me?'

April turned to face him. 'It'll take a lot of work,' she told him seriously, 'but you're not *completely* beyond saving.'

'Good to know!'

'You've just got to learn to embrace...' She looked around and Josh couldn't help wondering what it would be like to embrace her at that precise moment. He swallowed hard and took a step forward.

'April?'

'Yes – you've got to learn to embrace colour more,' she finished.

'Colour?' Josh said. 'Oh, yes. I see.'

The moment had gone and April remained unkissed. Another time, he told himself, when she wasn't quite so preoccupied.

'Then you'll do it?' he dared to ask, trying not to stare at her rosebud mouth.

'You want me to do it?'

'I thought you could help me – perhaps take some of these bits of furniture and spruce them up a bit. Inject a bit of this thing called colour into my life.' He smiled, doing his best to make light of the disastrous choices he'd made in the past.

April nodded. 'Perhaps I could come round on Monday after work and we could make a list together.'

Josh nodded. 'A list sounds good. I like lists.'

'I thought you might.'

There was a pause when she looked around the room again. 'Are the other rooms like this too?'

'Pretty much,' he admitted. 'Although I chose quite a different colour for the upstairs landing. It's much darker and bolder.'

'Oh, what's it called?'

'Sand.'

April giggled. 'Another beige?'

'I guess so.' Josh shrugged. 'What can I say? I've led an introspective sort of a life and I can't say I've noticed all this other stuff before – all this beauty outside of the world of books. But, since meeting you and your family and seeing the way you live and the beautiful things you surround yourselves with, well, it's changed the way I'm seeing things too and I can't help thinking that life would be a lot better if I could learn to see things like you do.'

Josh smiled at April and watched as her face softened.

'That's the loveliest thing anyone's ever said to me,' April told him.

He watched her for a moment as her eyes appeared to be glistening with tears.

'April...' He took a step towards her. Would now be a good moment to kiss her, he wondered?

But she blinked, shaking her head and turning away from him. 'I'm getting all silly,' she said. 'One compliment and I'm floored.' She laughed and grabbed a tissue from her bag and dabbed her eyes with it. 'Shouldn't we be heading to your parents'?'

Josh looked at his watch. 'We probably should.'

They left the house together and got back in the car.

'Now it's *my* turn to be nervous,' April said.

'Don't be. Everyone will love you.'

'Did they love May?'

Josh hesitated before answering. 'They were confused by May.'

'Yes, she can be, well, a bit abrupt.'

'Why is that?' Josh asked as they pulled out into the road.

April shrugged. 'I'm not sure. She's always been that way. I guess she likes to get to the point. She doesn't mess around dressing things up in fancy words. She tells things like they are.'

'She certainly did that with my family!'

'Oh, dear! Was it really awful?'

'Erm, well, there were a few awkward silences.'

'I'm sorry.'

'Don't be. It'll be something my family will enjoy talking about for years!' Josh laughed and then caught himself. 'Sorry – that was insensitive.'

'No, don't worry. I totally understand. But don't be too hard on May. She's a softie, really. She just has a rather hard shell.'

'And you don't, do you?'

April smiled. 'It could probably do with being a little harder at times.'

'I don't think that would suit you.'

'You're probably right.'

They drove down the main road before turning down the country lane towards Wintermarsh. The early June sky was cloudless and the most delicate of blues, promising a beautiful day.

'Well, this is it,' Josh said a few minutes later as he pulled into the driveway of Campion House, the feeling of déjà vu weighing heavily with him, only how different this all felt, knowing for sure that this was April beside him. 'Ready?'

'As I'll ever be.'

They got out of the car and Josh took her hand in his.

'Just keep breathing,' he said as he walked across the driveway with her. Only, this time, it felt right. His stomach wasn't tied up in knots as it had been with May. It was as if he'd instinctively known she wasn't April. But April was here now and something told him that everything was going to be okay.

Josh tried not to laugh when he saw several members of his family at the living room window watching their progress. They were ready to pounce and, as soon as he knocked on the door, his whole family swooped in on them as if they could contain themselves no longer.

'Now, this is the real April?' Lara asked, her voice loud above the general commotion of everybody introducing themselves.

'I promise it is!' April said, seemingly unfazed by the whole experience even though she'd been palpitating with nerves just moments before. That was the thing with the Nightingale family, Josh found. They sounded scary because of their sheer numbers, but the reality was quite different – they were warm and welcoming and April seemed to be coping admirably.

'Well, it's wonderful to meet you at last,' Josh's father came forward and shook her hand. 'I'm Frank.'

'April.'

'It's so lovely to meet you!' Josh's mum was next with a big hug for the new arrival. 'Come and have a drink. Meeting us all is exhausting work!'

April just had time to glance back at Josh and smile before she was ushered towards the kitchen. Everybody followed except Sam.

'She seems lovely, Josh,' his brother said.

'She is.'

He leaned in slightly and whispered. 'Kissed her yet?'

Josh coughed. 'That is none of your business!'

'That must mean you have!' Sam cried in delight. 'Well done, bro. Well done!'

Josh gave a resigned smile and didn't contradict his brother. It was time, he thought, to have another chat to Winston.

~

Sunday lunch at Campion House was extra-special that day. The conversation flowed naturally and easily around the table, and there were none of the awkward moments that had peppered the Sunday when May had been April. Josh couldn't take his eyes off her. She looked totally at home in his family's dining room, he thought. Just as Callie and Jago and Ben did. And, when he finally did take his eyes off April to glance at his mother, he saw that she was smiling and she gave Josh a little nod of approval too.

'How's the shop doing?' Bryony asked April as a strawberry gateaux was served for pudding.

'Good,' April told her. 'Lots of commissions. Including a new and very interesting project.' She turned to look at Josh.

'What's this, then?' Polly asked.

Josh cleared his throat. 'I'm going to give my house a make-over. April is supervising.'

'You mean your very beige house?' Lara said.

'I do.'

'What a relief!' Bryony said. 'I've been telling you to inject some colour into your life for years!'

'Well, maybe I wasn't ready before,' Josh said, exchanging a look with April.

'Sometimes, you have to wait for the right moment for these things,' his mother told him.

'Exactly,' Josh said, his eyes never leaving April's.

'He's totally smitten with her!' Polly said in the kitchen as she, Jago, Bryony, Ben and Eleanor stacked the dishwasher and washed the glasses.

'I've never seen him look so happy,' Eleanor said.

'Well, it's about time,' Bryony said.

'And she is lovely,' Ben said. Bryony elbowed him in the ribs. 'Obviously not as lovely as you!'

Bryony nodded in approval.

'Do you think he's going to propose?' Polly asked.

'Oh, give him a chance!' Eleanor said in her son's defence.

'He has only just met her,' Jago said.

'I know,' Polly said, 'but you know when it's *the one*, don't you? And he does have that look about him.'

'I think it's wonderful,' Eleanor said. 'He's never brought a girl home before, has he?'

'And then he goes and brings two at once!' Bryony joked. Everyone laughed.

'I'd love to see them both together – April and May,' Polly said.

'Do you think we'll get the chance?' Jago asked.

'Maybe if there's a wedding in the near future,' Bryony said with a giggle.

'Now, you lot stop that with the teasing!' Eleanor said, pausing with a floral tea towel in her hand. 'But maybe we *should* start measuring up the garden for a marquee – just to be on the safe side.' Her eyebrows rose and a gentle smile spread across her face and everybody laughed.

Unlike the Sunday with May, April stayed well into the afternoon, accepting tea and biscuits and joining the family for the traditional dog walk. Josh took the opportunity to hold her hand again – a gesture that didn't go unnoticed by his family who smiled, winked and generally made him feel as self-conscious as possible. But he didn't mind. Not really. How could he when he felt so happy?

'How's May?' Frank asked as they walked along a wooded footpath lined with towering foxgloves.

'She's well, thank you.'

'We enjoyed meeting her,' Frank said.

April smiled. 'I'd like to apologise for that. We never meant to cause confusion or – well – make any trouble.'

'You didn't,' Eleanor assured her.

Grandpa Joe chuckled. 'We enjoyed every minute of it. In retrospect.'

Frank laughed. 'We have to admit to being a little baffled at the time. Josh reported one thing and we got quite another.'

'Frank, we don't need to go into all that,' Eleanor told him with a warning glance.

'It's okay – Josh filled me in and I'm so sorry about what happened. But please don't judge May too harshly. She's just a different sort of person.'

'She speaks her mind,' Josh put in.

'Oh, yes,' Lara said. 'She did that all right!'

'Anyway, *you're* here now,' Polly said, 'and that's the main thing.'

They continued their walk, Josh helping April over the stile that led into a large field where the pointer and spaniels took off at high speed. It felt good walking with April by his side, having her at the heart of the Nightingale family with his sisters and brothers, his parents and grandparents and nephew around them. For once, Josh wasn't on his own, watching those around him chatting and exchanging sweet glances with their loved ones, for he had somebody too.

When they returned to Campion House, tea was served in the living room. April asked to see the garden and Josh let his father do the honours, seeing him beaming as April asked him questions about what he was growing.

'And now Dad's in love with her too,' Lara said.

Josh blushed as everyone's eyes fixed on him.

When the pair returned from the garden, April glanced at her watch.

'I'm afraid I should be getting back.'

Everyone was on their feet in an instant.

'Are you sure you have to go?' Bryony asked.

'May will be expecting me.'

'Well, do come again *very* soon,' Eleanor said.

'That's so kind.' April smiled at them all, thanking them profusely and then Josh caught her looking at the one person who wasn't there to say goodbye to her.

Grandma Nell was sitting in her favourite chair, staring at the group, but seemingly unable to move. So April went to her, kneeling down beside the chair and taking the old woman's hands in hers.

'I have to go now,' April told her. 'But it was lovely to meet you.'

Nell looked into the face that was only inches from her own. 'How sweet you are,' she said. 'Come back soon.'

'I will.' April stood up and Josh realised that everybody had fallen silent as they'd watched the scene before them.

And then they left the house together.

'How did I do?' April asked once they were in the privacy of Josh's car.

'They loved you!'

'How can you tell?'

'You mean you didn't notice? They didn't stop smiling from the moment you arrived! And you totally made Dad's day by asking to see the garden.'

April laughed. 'I wonder what they're saying now.'

'They're probably deciding what to wear to our wedding,' Josh said and then blushed. 'I mean...' He swallowed hard.

'It's all right! Daddy Jeff's exactly the same. He likes to know exactly what's going on and to plan ahead.'

Josh relaxed a little. It was good that he could say what he wanted to April.

'And it was very sweet what you did with Grandma. It's easy to forget her sometimes.'

'She's a lovely lady. I'm sorry what's happening to her. It must be heartbreaking to see that.'

Josh nodded. 'She's forgetting so much these days, but I don't think she'll be forgetting you in a hurry.'

CHAPTER THIRTEEN

After the best Sunday of his life, it felt like something of a comedown to be back in the shop again on Monday morning, which was a strange revelation to Josh because his shop had been the centre of his entire world up until recently. How quickly things changed, he thought, as he looked out of the window towards A Little Bit Bloomsbury. He and April had exchanged a few waves that day and he was looking forward to popping over there for a cup of tea come mid-morning as they'd arranged. In truth, eleven o'clock couldn't come round quickly enough.

It was as he was glancing out of the window for the hundredth time that he saw Winston coming out of Well Bread, sticking his nose into the paper bag he was holding.

Without missing a beat, Josh was out of his shop.

'Winston!' he called.

Winston looked up from his paper bag as if caught doing something illicit.

'Josh?'

Josh beckoned him over and Winston crossed the road, Delilah by his side.

'Can I borrow you for a minute?' Josh asked, ushering him into the shop.

'What's the matter?'

'I need to know the rest of your story – no interruptions this time. I've got to know when you kissed her and how and what happened after that.'

A smile spread across Winston's face. 'Put the kettle on,' he said.

A moment later, Winston was perched on the stool behind the till, his paper bag in front of him and his mug of tea in his hand. Josh had decided to hold out for his cup of tea until he went over to April's. Besides, he was too anxious to hear the rest of Winston's story to think about drinking.

'So, where were we?' Winston asked, glancing fondly down at Delilah who had settled by his feet.

'Monty had cut in and was dancing with Marguerite and she seemed to be enjoying his company.'

'Ah, yes!' Winston said with a nod. 'Well, I could see that Monty had enjoyed a few drinks before he'd arrived at the dance, but it took me a little while to realise just how many. At first, he started slurring his speech. Then he started to fall over his own feet, stomping his great fat shoes on Marguerite's delicate ones.'

'Something *you* hadn't done all evening!'

'Well remembered,' Winston said, obviously impressed. 'So, after Monty cut in and proceeded to crush Marguerite's feet, he started to turn a very strange colour. I think it was red at first – as if he was overheating. Then he seemed to go green.' Winston chuckled. 'I knew what was coming and so did Monty because he rushed out of the town hall as quickly as he could and was bent double over the pavement by the time I caught up with him. I won't go into the gory details. Suffice to say that that is no way to impress a lady.'

Josh laughed. 'I imagine not.'

'Marguerite stood there shaking her head, but she was laughing too. Her friends couldn't stop. If it had been today, they'd have all had their cameras out and it would have been up on Twitface before you'd known it.'

Josh bit back a smile.

'So what happened after that?'

'I called a taxi to make sure Monty got home safely. Made sure he had money for it too.' Winston shook his head at the memory. Then I asked if Marguerite needed seeing home. She said I was very gallant and she placed her arm through mine. She lived just at the edge of town and it was a warm evening. The moon was high and bright and the sky was just like you'd see in one of them romantic movies. All inky and starry.' He paused as if recalling it.

'And that's when you kissed her?' Josh asked. 'Under the moon and the stars?'

'Now, hang on a minute – I hadn't yet walked her home. We were chatting as we walked. About everything and about nothing. I really can't remember now. It was one of those easy, senseless conversations that show you that you feel comfortable with a person.'

Josh nodded. He got that same feeling with April.

Winston took a sip of his tea. 'Well, we reached her home. I suppose we had to at some point. We couldn't make that starry walk last forever.' He paused. 'There was a little gate and she bent to open the latch and went through it, closing it between us. I was a bit disappointed, I can tell you, to have that gate in between us, but I waited to see what she'd do next.'

'And?' Josh's mouth was quite dry by this stage.

'She leaned forward – ever such a little bit. And I leaned forward too. I can't remember if it was her who moved first or me. I don't suppose it matters because we were both after the same thing: that first kiss.' Winston sighed. 'And what a perfect first kiss too.'

'What was it like?' Josh asked.

'It was like...' Winston's eyes took on a dreamy quality. 'It was like heaven.'

Josh smiled. 'Heaven.'

'There aren't many things in life that I'd describe as being like heaven, but that was one of them.'

'So you saw her again after that?'

Winston nodded.

'But you didn't marry her, did you?'

Winston shook his head. 'A lot happened after that first kiss,' he told him.

Josh was just about to ask him what when Winston hopped off the stool and picked up his paper bag of bakery bits.

'But let's save that for another time, eh?'

'Winston?' Josh called after him as he was about to leave the shop with Delilah.

'Yes?'

'Thank you.'

'For what?'

'For sharing your story with me.'

'Has it helped?' he asked, nodding across the road towards A Little Bit Bloomsbury.

'Yes, I think it has.'

Winston winked at him and then left.

For a moment, Josh stood there in the silence of his shop looking out towards April's. It was quarter to eleven and he knew he couldn't wait a minute more. He could see April moving around, her bright hair seeming to dance behind her. It was loose today. He liked it loose.

He took a deep breath. This was it, he told himself. It would be now.

He left his shop, turning the 'Closed' sign around and locking the door. He crossed the road and opened the door into April's shop.

'Josh!' she cried. 'You're early.'

There was a part of him that wanted to stride across the shop floor and take her in his arms and kiss her right there and then, but he lost his nerve as soon as he thought about it.

'Had a good morning?' he asked instead.

'Very good actually. I sold a little chair and the woman loved it so much that she's told me she wants at least three more like it.'

'Do you have three more?'

'Not yet!' April said. 'But I think I know where I can find some likely candidates and I can't wait to get started on them. What about you? Everything okay?'

Josh could feel himself growing distinctly hot under his collar. What would she think if he told her the truth? That he'd been thinking about kissing her all morning and had even asked a man in his seventies for advice on the subject? And that he'd spent the whole of Sunday evening flipping through and reading every novel he could think of in which there was a kissing scene. But they hadn't been very helpful at all. In fact, they'd made him feel even more insecure about the whole thing because he knew he was never going to match up to the heroes in novels.

'Okay,' he said at last, studying her beautiful eyes behind the pink-tinted glasses, his gaze then slipping down to her perfect mouth. He swallowed hard. It was too soon, wasn't it? Too soon for kissing. They'd only just met. Okay, so he'd met her family now and she had met his, but there was a protocol to be observed. Manners. Decorum. That sort of thing. He might not have read any guidance book about kissing, but he was pretty sure that now, here in the shop, was too early. It might have been all right for Winston and Marguerite under the starlight after dancing all evening, but this was mid-morning in Castle Clare.

'Josh? Are you all right?'

He nodded.

'You look hot.'

'No – no – I'm fine. Just a bit...'

'Can I get you some water?' She stepped closer to him – so close that he could smell the apple sweetness of the shampoo she favoured. And he could see her lips again.

'No water.'

'How about that cup of tea we were going to have?'

He nodded helplessly. If April went to make tea, it might give him time to recover himself.

'Good,' she said. 'Mind the shop for me.'

He watched as she went through to the back room and he sighed. What was going on with him? Why was he over-thinking this thing? Why couldn't he just get on with kissing her? Heaven only knew he wanted to.

Heaven.

He thought of Winston's word again. Didn't Josh want a little bit of heaven in his own life? Of *course* he did! So why was he hesitating and procrastinating like Hamlet?

'Here we are,' April said, coming out with the tea. 'Milk no sugar.'

'Thank you.' He took his tea and sipped it, grateful to have a distraction.

'I've been thinking about your place a lot,' she said.

'You have?' Josh was confused for a moment.

'The colours we could use, the changes we could make.'

'Oh, right. Yes.'

'So, what colours do you like?' April asked. 'I mean other than beige.'

'I *don't* like beige,' Josh told her emphatically.

April frowned. 'Well, you do pretty good impression of a man who *does* like beige.'

'I guess I do. But when I first moved in, I didn't pay the walls much attention at all. They were merely places to lean bookcases. I didn't really care what colour they were.'

April tutted. 'It's a terrible thing not to care about colour.'

'I know that now.'

They exchanged smiles.

'What about shapes? What shapes do you like?'

'Shapes?' Josh scratched his chin. What shapes did he like? He didn't think he'd ever been asked that question. At least, not since primary school, perhaps. He really couldn't think that he'd ever favoured a particular shape in his life. Except...

'Rectangles!' he blurted.

'Rectangles?'

'Books are rectangular, aren't they?'

'Oh, I see,' April said with a laugh. 'Any others?'

Josh puffed out his cheeks. It had been difficult enough coming up with one shape and now she wanted another.

'I'll tell you what. I've got some books in the back here. And magazines and things I often use with clients. We can look through them for inspiration. Will that make things easier?'

'It can't make them any harder!' he joked. 'Am I what you'd call an awkward customer?'

'No!' April said, all too quickly and then giggled. 'You just haven't found your style yet. But that's perfectly normal. Many people come in and ask for advice. They know they want to change their decor, but they're overwhelmed with choice and they just need a bit of help whittling things down a little.'

Josh nodded. 'Yes, help me whittle, please.'

'It will be my pleasure.' She disappeared again into the back room and returned laden with an armful of books, magazines and scrapbooks bursting with folded bits of paper stuck in at random angles. It was a glorious, arty mess. 'If you can't find anything in here, we're doomed.'

Josh took one of the magazines and started to flip through it. It was the sort that was filled with other people's homes both modern and ancient. There were sweet country cottages filled with floral curtains and cushions, and sleek modern apartments where light and space were paramount.

'Look at the colours people choose,' April told him. 'That one there – it's all neutrals, but highlighted with those acid greens, see.'

Josh grimaced at the effect. 'It looks like a space ship.'

April laughed. 'I take it you don't like it?'

'It's horrible.'

They flipped through some more magazines as they sipped their tea. Occasionally, Josh would lift his head to see if a queue was forming outside his bookshop, but it was a quiet day and he was glad of it.

'What about this?' April asked, pointing to a pink thatched cottage whose living room was a symphony of peaches and terracottas.

'Getting there, I suppose. It's a little too feminine, don't you think?'

'Perhaps.'

Josh picked up a book. 'Charleston!' he said, recognising the famous Bloomsbury home on the cover.

April beamed. 'This is one of my favourite books,' she confessed, stroking the cover. 'And one of my favourite homes.'

Josh nodded. 'Yes. It's a special place.'

'You've visited, haven't you?'

'Yes. But I think we paid more attention to the garden to be honest. You know what Dad's like.'

'Well, take a look at the rooms – they're like nothing else you'll ever see. It was only rented by Vanessa Bell. She and Duncan Grant invested so much time and passion into it. There's virtually no surface left unpainted. Chairs were painted, table tops were decorated, even the side of the bathtub was painted.'

Josh smiled. 'I don't remember that.'

'Really?' April looked a little perplexed that he could have missed such a thing.

'I don't think I'll be painting my bathtub yet,' he warned her.

'Well, that is a bit extreme for a beginner. But have a look through the book and see what you like.'

Josh did, turning the pages, his eyes widening at the bold use of colour and shape in every room, all hand-painted directly onto the walls.

'They've painted a dog on the wall of this room,' Josh said.

'We could paint Hardy and Brontë if you like.'

Josh laughed at the idea, trying to imagine the pointer and spaniel immortalised on the walls of his home.

'It's hard to truly appreciate it from a book,' she told him. 'It's a pity it isn't a bit closer – we could go and visit.'

Josh continued to look through the book, unsure that he could ever be even half as bold in his choices as the likes of Vanessa Bell and Duncan Grant.

'See anything inspiring?' April asked a few minutes later.

'It's all inspiring, but I'm not sure it's quite right for me.'

'What *do* you like?'

Josh closed the book. 'I like all those soft jades and warm ambers you wear.'

'You do?'

'I really do.'

April looked concerned for a moment.

'What is it?'

'But you want your choices to be about *you*.'

'They will be.'

'But what if we aren't always together and you've surrounded yourself with colours that – well – remind you of me?'

Josh felt concerned. 'Are you suggesting we're not always going to want to be together?'

'Well, you do have to think about these things.'

Josh frowned. There she was, looking all anxious again about something he didn't quite understand.

'What is it?' he asked her gently.

'Nothing,' she assured him. 'I'm just trying to be professional about this rather than making it too personal.'

'But I *want* it to be personal,' Josh told her earnestly.

'Let's keep looking,' she said, handing him another book as she opened a new magazine. He watched her slim fingers turning the pages, pointing out little details which she thought he might like. But Josh was only hearing half of what she was saying because he was thinking.

'Let's go,' he suddenly said.

She looked up from the magazine. 'Go where?'

'To Charleston!'

'But it's hours away.'

'I don't mind driving. We could make a day of it – a little holiday.'

April was smiling. 'Really?'

'Yes! It might help to inspire me.'

'I'm sure it will. It's my favourite place in the whole world!'

'Then we're definitely going!'

'Oh, Josh! I'm so excited!'

He smiled at her joy which seemed to be spilling out of every pore of her, and he was also smiling because he had an idea – a wonderful, foolproof, romantic idea.

Josh was going to kiss April in the garden at Charleston.

CHAPTER FOURTEEN

Slinking off on a little jaunt in the middle of the week felt wonderfully naughty to Josh. He rarely, if ever, took a holiday and, when he did, it was invariably in the UK – somewhere like St Ives or Lyme Regis where he could browse in a few bookshops and stroll along a beach. He rarely took time off during a normal working week, but this was something he'd felt impelled to do. April, he thought, was not only helping him to see the joy of colour, but the pleasure in spontaneity too.

Polly was minding the shop for Josh, and May was minding the shop for April, although she hadn't been happy to miss out on a trip to Charleston.

'I really feel I should go too,' she'd told Josh when he'd picked April up from home that morning. 'It could be useful for our business.'

April had looked at her apologetically. 'We'll go together another time,' she promised her sister.

Josh had been quite relieved when he'd got April away from her sister and into the car. He'd been a little fearful that April would suggest they take May with them and that would have put paid to the kissing business.

He took a long, deep breath as they drove off. He'd set the destination in the satnav and they were going to have a little break about half way for refreshments. All being well, they should arrive at Charleston around lunchtime.

'It's going to be a wonderful source of inspiration for you,' April declared with confidence.

Josh nodded. He knew he'd like it, but that wasn't the main reason for his suggestion of visiting. He wanted to take her somewhere beautiful – somewhere that was special to her. He only hoped that he didn't go and ruin the place for her if the kiss he was planning was a total disaster. Imagine that, he thought – April carrying the memory of being kissed badly in the most beautiful garden in England. Oh, the shame of it! No, he thought, this was going to go well. He'd channel the spirit of young Winston Kneller on that starry night all those decades ago.

After stopping for refreshments in a small market town, they continued on their journey, arriving at Charleston just before noon. A long track led to the car park and Josh was surprised at just how many cars were there in the middle of the week but then the sun was shining and the Sussex Downs were looking glorious. No wonder they'd been such a draw to the artists who had chosen to live and work here, he thought.

April looked so excited as they left the car. She'd brought a summer hat of sage-coloured straw with a wide ribbon around its brim, and she was wearing an apple-green dress starred with tiny sprigs of flowers. As ever, it took Josh's breath away just to look at her. By comparison, he felt deadly dull in his cream trousers and burgundy shirt. Maybe he should rethink his wardrobe as well as his home decor, he thought. But who was he trying to kid? Was he really going to start wearing orange and purple? He couldn't see it himself.

It wasn't possible to glide through the famous Bloomsbury house at your own pace; it was much too delicate for that, and it would be all too tempting for the fingers of well-meaning fans to reach out and touch the fragile textiles and do all sorts of mischief. So, after a light lunch in the cafe, Josh and April joined one of the tours, listening as the guide told them stories about the colourful occupants of the colourful rooms, pointing out special pieces in each room they entered.

The final stop on the tour was the artists' studio on the ground floor. It was a light spacious room with views out across the garden.

'Mummy and Daddy George would adore this!' April whispered to Josh.

'Have they been?' Josh whispered back.

'Oh, countless times! But they'd love it all over again if they were here now.'

Josh smiled, trying to see it all as if through an artist's eye.

As they left the house and entered the garden, April was almost buzzing.

'What did you think of the pillared bookcase painted by Duncan Grant?'

'It was extraordinary!' Josh said. 'I'd never have thought to have painted a bookcase.'

'I do it all the time!' April said with a laugh. 'And that dining room with those bold, dark walls.'

'Yes, I'm not sure black, grey and yellow are quite my own choices,' Josh stated, 'but I did admire the overall effect.'

'And those wonderful curvy figures on the fireplace in the studio. I mean, why shouldn't there be figures painted onto your fireplace?'

'And dogs painted under your windows and cockerels above them?'

'Exactly!' April said. 'And seeing those amazing yellow circles on Vanessa Bell's wardrobe again. One forgets the impact that they have. Oh, to be so close to all those wonderful objects and know that the hands that created them were those of the artists I love most in the world! After Mummy and Daddy George, of course.'

'Well, of course!' Josh said.

'I had the strangest feeling in some of the rooms,' she told him. 'Because so much of it was painted – the walls and the furniture and the paintings too, that I couldn't help feeling that I'd stepped inside one great big painting.'

Josh looked at her. 'You do think the most extraordinary things!'

'Do I?'

'You really do!'

'And what about the painted bath panels?' April went on.

'Again, I've never seen anything like it.'

'Didn't you love the slightly haphazard feel of it all too with one room light and another room dark? And some of the painting felt unfinished, didn't it? And there were lampshades that didn't quite sit right on their lamps.'

'Yes, I noticed that,' Josh said. 'Not sure that would work for me.'

'I thought you'd feel that way,' April confessed and slipped her hand into Josh's. It was so simple a move and yet it made him feel as if he'd been given the greatest gift in the world.

'Shall we look around the garden?' she asked.

He nodded.

The June garden was bursting with colour. Like the house, there was barely an inch that wasn't full of something wonderful and the tiny paths spilled over with floral delights. Summer had exploded in the garden at Charleston in a delightful painter's palette of jewel colours, rich and deep, blowsy and unrestrained with irises, alliums, poppies and roses.

The sun was hot on his skin and April's face was full of joy as she looked at the flowers before her, pointing to a large bumble-bee as it buried itself in the heart of a creamy pink rose. He could feel his heart thudding inside him as she turned around and he swallowed hard as she took a step closer towards him, her face filling with sunlight.

And that's when it happened. Him and her. Both together, moving towards each other to the soundtrack of swifts screeching over the Downs which shimmered in the heat.

The kiss.

It felt like it was going to go on forever. Soft and warm, sweet and passionate all at once. Josh was lost for what seemed like an eternity and it took him a moment to recover from it. He felt dizzy, almost drunk, as if he might tumble right over into one of the flower borders. He looked at April.

'What are you thinking?' he dared to ask her. She was smiling and her gaze was soft and hazy.

'I'm thinking,' she began, 'that this is heaven!'

They kissed again and most likely would have gone on kissing if one of Charleston's gardeners hadn't been coming down the path with a wheelbarrow full of tools.

'Excuse me!' she bellowed and the two of them sprang apart and leapt out of the way. Of course, there wasn't really anywhere for them to go and they both ended up neck-high in the borders, laughing. Josh had never felt so happy. He'd also never felt so alive. It was as if he'd drunk a special potion or swallowed a magic pill which had given him this inexplicable sense of euphoria. But he knew that this was better than any potion or pill because this was real.

~

Project Josh, as April was calling it, got underway in earnest the next day with a trip to the hardware store for paint and supplies during their lunch break. It was a very exciting moment for Josh. He truly felt like he was changing, like a colourful butterfly emerging from its drab chrysalis, and he did his best to hold the spirit of Charleston within him as he made his choices.

'Try and think like Vanessa Bell and Duncan Grant. What would they do with the space you've got?'

'Paint nudes and dogs over it all?' Josh answered.

'Well, we don't need to copy them *exactly*,' she said. 'But think boldly and brightly.'

After their shops had closed for the day, they went back to Josh's together, sharing a simple tea before they made a start. Josh loved watching April work. She had a natural flair for making a space unique just by moving a few pieces of furniture around and suggesting colours that simply sang.

Together, they worked hard – sanding down and priming the pieces that were going to be given a makeover, and choosing the colours for the walls that would set the new-look pieces off to perfection. With April's guidance, Josh had chosen a warm terracotta for the living room, a soft amber for his bedroom and a sky-blue for the landing.

'Does that go with the warm colours we've chosen elsewhere?' Josh asked, wondering if they were making a mistake with the cool blue colour.

'Light and dark, remember? Warm and cool. Rooms don't have to be the same colour or tone.'

'Right,' Josh said, thankful of the reminder.

The walls were completed quickly. They worked well with each other, listening to Josh's collection of classical music while they painted.

Most of painting was finished within a fortnight, the two of them working around the clock to decorate the larger pieces such as the bedroom wardrobe and chest of drawers. Other pieces, like the dining table chairs and the bookcases would take longer, but the change was well and truly underway and Josh couldn't believe the difference.

'I never dreamed it could look like this,' he told her at the end of one evening's marathon painting session. He'd made them a cup of tea and they were looking back at the work they'd done so far.

'You like it, then?' April asked.

'Like it? I *love* it!' Josh said. 'I love *you!*'

The words tumbled out of him before he had a chance to think about them, leaving him feeling stunned. April looked stunned too and there was an awkward moment when he wondered if she was going to flee or tell him that she loved him too. When she did neither, he felt both relief and panic.

'April?' he said, putting his tea down. It didn't feel right to be confessing his love to a woman for the first time while holding a Snoopy mug.

'Josh – I...'

'You don't need to say anything,' he told her, watching as her expression slipped from joyful to anxious. 'I didn't plan on saying that. And you know by now that I'm a man who likes to be in charge of his thoughts and feelings.'

'Yes.'

'But I obviously needed to say that.'

There was a moment's silence between them which didn't feel awkward exactly. But it did feel as though Josh had made a leap into the future and he wasn't quite certain that April had come with him. He watched, not quite sure what to say, as she finished her tea. Reaching out, he took her Charlie Brown mug and placed it next to his on the coffee table which was now a beautiful warm red with yellow, cream and pink flowers painted upon it.

'I guess I should be going,' she said.

Josh took a deep breath. 'Listen–'

She moved towards him, stopping his words with a kiss and, even though she hadn't told him she loved him too, and even though she seemed to be running away from him now, he felt the power of her love in that single kiss.

CHAPTER FIFTEEN

Josh pulled up outside Campion House and sat in the car a moment longer than he needed to. He could see his mother hovering at the living room window and, a couple of seconds later, she was at the door. He sighed and got out of the car.

'Josh, darling!' she said as he approached, wrapping him up in a warm hug as Hardy and Brontë welcomed him by pushing their noses into the back of his knees. 'The kettle's on and I've made a Victoria Sandwich.'

Josh smiled. Tea and cake – whatever the question was, they were the answer.

'It's quiet,' he said as he came into the house and took his shoes off in the hallway.

'Your father's out with a friend at some garden I've never heard of. He said something about permaculture, but I'm afraid I wasn't really listening.'

Josh grinned, knowing how his father often seemed to be speaking in a different language when talking about gardening.

'And Grandpa has taken Grandma to an appointment. They shouldn't be too long, though, if you want to see them.'

Josh nodded. It was nice that he had his mother to himself for a change. It was a rare occurrence in such a large household and, although he was the grand old age of thirty-one, he still craved a little of his mother's undivided attention every so often.

They moved through to the kitchen and he saw the newly-made cake on a stand in the centre of one of the worktops.

'Looks good!'

'Let me get you a slice. The kettle's just boiled if you want to do the honours.'

A few minutes later, the two of them were sitting at the kitchen table, drinking their tea and eating their cake and it felt so good to be there, Josh thought. There was such an easy atmosphere in their family home and each of the Nightingale children knew that they were welcome back any time of the day or night whether it was for tea, cake and a chat or anything else that was needed. Campion House would always be there for them and, for that, Josh was eternally grateful.

'Everything all right?' his mother asked him at last. 'You sounded worried on the phone.'

Josh had rung her earlier that day, but they hadn't been able to talk whilst he'd been in the shop. The truth was, he hadn't wanted to talk to his mother then either. Something like this needed to be face to face.

'I told her I loved her,' he said at last.

Eleanor sat quietly for a moment, giving him the chance to say more.

'I told her I loved her and she said nothing. She kissed me and left.' He ran a hand through his hair. 'She left me and I can't help thinking she moved away from me just a little. Emotionally. I don't know. I can't be sure. But she often has this look, this expression of...' he paused. 'It's like she's lost.'

He saw his mother frown. 'Lost?'

'It's like a kind of anxiety. I catch it every now and then – these fleeting, haunting looks. They pass quickly enough, but they leave me feeling helpless. Like there's something she's not telling me.'

'What else might she not be telling you? Surely you've had all the big surprises? Her twin and her two fathers.'

Josh nodded. 'That's what Sam said too.'

Another moment of silence elapsed between them in which Eleanor poured them some more tea and offered Josh another slice of cake which he eagerly accepted.

'You really do love her, don't you?' she asked him softly.

'Does it seem strange?'

'No!' his mother cried. 'Why should you ask that?'

He smiled and shrugged. 'Because it seems strange to me. It's all happened so fast. I feel like I'm spinning and yet I feel so in focus too. Does that make sense? There's a strange clarity about things now.'

'My dear boy, that makes *absolute* sense!'

'It does?' Josh was pleasantly surprised that his mother understood.

She smiled at him. 'When you fall in love, the whole world seems happy along with you. Colours are brighter, food tastes better, everything has a place and a purpose.'

He watched her as she spoke, her gaze softening.

'Falling in love is a wonderful feeling,' she said. 'And nothing – absolutely nothing – can top it.'

They exchanged smiles which told them that they knew exactly what they were talking about.

'I hope it's my father you're reminiscing about here!' Josh teased at last.

Eleanor laughed. 'Well, of *course* it is!'

They sipped their tea and Josh finished the last of his second slice of cake.

'So what next?' Eleanor dared to ask.

'I was going to ask you that,' Josh confessed. 'Do I come out and say I know that something's bothering her? Do I remind her that even her mother told me that there was something she was keeping from me?'

Eleanor pushed her plate away from her and sat staring into space as if willing the answer to materialise there.

'I'm not sure there's much you can do, darling,' she said at last. 'If she wants to tell you then surely she will.'

'But why would she keep it back if it's causing her so much pain?'

'I don't know. Are you sure there really *is* something?'

'What else could it be?' Josh asked.

'Maybe she's just fearful of commitment,' Eleanor suggested.

'You really think that could be it?' Josh wasn't convinced. 'Why would her mother bring *that* up?'

Eleanor sighed. 'Is it really causing a problem between you?'

'*Yes!*' Josh said. 'I can see her holding back and I don't know why when we're so obviously happy together.' He looked down at his hands in his lap, thinking of how empty they felt now when he wasn't holding April's. 'I want to reach out to her, but I'm not sure how.'

'Maybe...' his mother began, 'maybe give it some more time. As you say, this has all happened so quickly. Perhaps she just needs time to catch up a little.'

Josh nodded and that's when the front door opened.

'We're back!' Grandpa Joe called through the hall, immediately setting the dogs off.

Eleanor looked at her son, an unspoken apology in her face at being interrupted.

'Thanks, Mum,' he told her and she nodded just before Grandpa and Grandma entered the kitchen.

'Is that cake?' Grandma Nell asked, looking at the Victoria Sandwich. 'I like cake, don't I?' She looked to Grandpa Joe to confirm her suspicion.

'Everybody likes Eleanor's cake,' he told her.

'I'll do the honours,' Eleanor said, reaching across the table to squeeze Josh's hand before turning her attention towards the cake.

Josh returned home, entering his living room and switching on a lamp. He smiled as he saw the new warm colours of the room illuminated. How glorious it all looked now that the beige had been banished. April had made such a huge difference to his life in so many ways and it was now almost impossible to remember what his life had been like in the years when he hadn't known her. But those years had been long and there had been many of them. He'd thought he'd been happy, but he hadn't really known the meaning of the word, had he? And yet, there was a part of him that was intensely sad because he knew that April was hiding something and that it was hurting her to do so.

But perhaps his mother was right and that April just needed time.

The next day, Josh was surprised still not to have received a message from April. It had been two days since she'd left his home that night after he'd told her he loved her and it was the longest that the two of them had gone without speaking since they'd started seeing each other.

Josh was even more surprised when he saw that A Little Bit Bloomsbury was closed for two days in a row. That hadn't happened since it had opened for business, he thought.

When it opened at lunchtime on Wednesday, he walked straight across the road and entered the shop. April had her back to him, her bright hair tied up in a messy bun. But what a wonderful thing to see her again.

He reached out, touching her shoulders lightly with his hands.

'*Josh!*' April spun around revealing that she was, in fact, May.

'Oh, lord!' Josh exclaimed.

May's eyes were wide and her face glowed red with embarrassment. Josh was only grateful that he'd quashed his initial impulse to grab her and spin her around to passionately kiss her.

Recovering his composure a little, he asked, 'Where's April?'

May reached up to tidy her hair. 'She's at home.'

'Is she okay?'

May pursed her lips as if deciding whether to talk to him at all. 'Not really,' she said at last.

'Migraine?'

May took a moment to answer.

'May – please tell me. I've not spoken to her for days now and it's driving me crazy.'

'Yes, it's a migraine.'

'How long for?'

'Yesterday and today.'

'Can I see her?'

May shook her head. 'Best not.'

'She doesn't want to see me?'

May sighed. 'She needs rest, Josh.'

'Okay,' he said resignedly, wishing her tone could be a little less brusque. 'Can you let her know I asked after her?'

'Yes.'

Josh stood in the middle of the shop floor feeling as if he didn't belong there for the first time. Without April there, the atmosphere was quite different.

'Okay,' he said at last. 'Everything all right with you?'

'I'm fine.'

'I – erm...' he looked around the shop for something to admire. 'I like that stool over there.'

May turned to look at the stool. 'It's between coats of paint, but it has potential. It was a nasty purple when it came in.'

Josh grinned. He'd never known there was such a thing as a nasty purple before.

'I really admire what you're doing here.'

'Do you?' She sounded surprised.

'You're making something beautiful out of something ugly or ordinary.'

'Somebody has to.'

'Yes, but not everybody does, do they? I know I didn't until I met your sister. I suppose she's told you about my house?'

May's lips quivered into a very slight smile. 'She said it was a hundred different shades of boring.'

Josh laughed. 'That's true enough. But she saw it's potential.' He paused. 'She saw *my* potential.'

May's eyes narrowed a fraction and there was that feeling of insecurity growing tight in Josh's chest again.

'Don't get too attached,' May said in a voice barely above a whisper.

'What do you mean?'

'April isn't...' May bit her lip and turned away.

'What isn't she?'

'It doesn't matter.'

'What do you mean, it doesn't matter?' Josh was getting mad now as well as frustrated. 'You were trying to tell me something and, from your expression, it sounded like something important too. So tell me what it is, May.'

He waited.

'April isn't one for commitments,' May said at last. 'That's all.'

Josh sighed. So that was it, was it? That's what he'd been fearful of.

'Well, people change, don't they?' he told her.

'I don't think they do.'

'I'm changing, aren't I?'

'But you *want* to change. Some people *can't* change who they are.'

Josh shook his head, feeling like he was getting nowhere with May's riddles. 'Look, this isn't making any sense. Can you tell her I called, okay? And tell her I'd love to hear from her as soon as she's well enough to talk to me.'

He left the shop and a part of him wanted to hop into his car and go straight to April's home to see her because, although he didn't completely disbelieve what May had told him, he couldn't help not wholly believing it either.

Winston Kneller didn't normally sleep well. Was it old age? Was it his weak bladder? Or was it because he was aware of time passing faster than ever now and feeling that it was a crying shame to spend so much of it unconscious? He wasn't sure. But, what he was sure of was that his sleep had been even worse since Monty had come to stay.

As much as it pained him to admit, Winston just didn't get on with his brother. He never had. When he thought back to their childhood together, theirs had never been an amicable relationship and it had got progressively worse as they'd reached adulthood and the whole Marguerite business had happened. Having his brother under the same roof just as Winston was remembering the story of how he met Marguerite was forcing all sorts of emotions to surface once again. Emotions that had been long buried and – well maybe not forgotten – but definitely locked away as the years had passed and life had moved on. But they were clearly unresolved, Winston thought as he got out of bed at a ridiculously early hour, pulled on his old dressing gown and trudged downstairs.

Delilah looked up from her basket as he went into the living room, her tail giving a quick thump in welcome. She was used to seeing him up and about at funny hours and soon settled herself again.

Winston made himself a cup of cocoa because he knew caffeine would just make his situation worse. But he needed something warm and sweet to sip as he tried to quieten his mind.

It would never have worked.

He could still hear his brother's voice from decades ago.

I did you a favour.

He put an extra sugar into his cocoa and stirred vigorously in an attempt to try and banish the voices from his past.

He walked back through to the living room and drew the curtains a chink. The first rays of light were piercing the sky and he could hear the tentative notes of birdsong. It was a funny, in-between sort of time to be up and about, he thought. Even his young neighbours who got up early for their weekday commute into Cambridge would still be sound asleep. And Monty was too. Winston thanked his lucky stars for that small mercy. He was increasingly needing these quiet moments of alone time in his own home. In his own chair. He patted the arm of it now and slowly sipped his cocoa but, even though he felt a little calmer, his mind refused to leave the past and he saw a clear image of Marguerite standing before him by the garden gate in the moonlight.

'I hope I'm going to see you again,' Winston had told her after that heavenly kiss.

'I hope you will too.' Marguerite had smiled back at him. 'I'll be at the dance next week.'

'You will?'

She'd nodded and her face had looked all soft and dreamy and Winston had been tempted to steal another kiss, but he hadn't.

He'd carried the memory of that first kiss with him throughout that week. And what a long week it had been. He remembered counting the days as he'd laboured on the farm. The weather had been particularly irksome and the work particularly back-breaking. But, finally, Saturday night had come round again.

Winston finished his cocoa and put it down on the little table beside his chair, smiling as he remembered that second Saturday night.

He was just drifting into the most beautiful sleep when he heard a crash from upstairs.

Delilah barked and struggled out of her basket, her old limbs as stiff as Winston's as he pushed himself out of his chair.

'Monty?' he called up the stairs, climbing them as fast as he could before knocking on the door of the bedroom Monty was in, which was, of course, Winston's bedroom.

'Winston?'

'Are you all right in there?' Winston opened the door a crack. 'Good heavens!'

Monty was on the floor.

'I seem to have fallen out of bed.'

'Well, I can see that,' Winston said, bending to help his brother off the floor. Luckily, a good deal of bedding had fallen out with him, so his landing had been padded, but he'd managed to take the bedside lamp with him as well as a full mug of water. In short, it was all a bit of a mess.

'What happened?' Winston asked as he helped Monty to sit back up on the bed.

Monty took a moment before he answered and Winston couldn't help thinking that his big brother looked somewhat shocked and shrunken sitting on the edge of the bed in his pyjamas.

'I'm not sure what happened,' Monty said with a sigh, his right hand reaching to flatten his hair. Honestly, Winston thought, the man could be on his deathbed and still be worrying about how he looked. 'One minute, I was having this fabulous dream about Brigitte Bardot and, the next, I was on the floor.'

Winston guffawed. 'Maybe she kicked you out of bed!'

Monty laughed. 'I wouldn't have thought so!'

'Does anything hurt?'

'My pride?'

'Right,' Winston said, making to leave the room.

'What's that... can I smell cocoa?' Monty asked.

'I made myself a cup a little while ago. I couldn't sleep.'

'Sounds like just what I need,' Monty said, climbing back into bed. 'Thanks, Winston.'

Winston shook his head before making his way back downstairs to make a second cup of cocoa.

CHAPTER SIXTEEN

It was Thursday morning when Josh saw April. He'd noticed that A Little Bit Bloomsbury was late to open and he'd been keeping an eye out for the moment either April or May turned up at the shop. And, oh, how glad he was when he saw that it was April there that morning.

Alas, he couldn't shut up his own shop and run across the street to see her and the minutes passed painfully as he served one customer after another, willing his shop to empty. But then something wonderful happened.

'April!' Josh cried as she walked into his shop.

She crossed the floor towards him and, although there was a young couple in the shop browsing, they fell into each other's arms and kissed. It was something that Josh would never have dreamed himself capable of just a few short weeks ago. Public scenes of emotion – especially of the kissing sort – left him shaking his head in dismay, yet here he was kissing in the middle of his own bookshop on a Thursday morning.

'I've missed you,' he whispered in her ear.

'I've missed you too!'

'Are you okay? May told me you had a migraine.'

'I'm fine. I just had a wobble, that's all.' She buried her head against his chest and hugged him close to her.

'A migraine wobble?' he asked her, his arms tight around her.

She nodded and they stood like that together for a few moments, silently absorbed in the closeness of one another.

'You're okay now, though?' he asked.

'I feel *great* now,' she told him, 'and I want us to do something fun together. Like our Charleston trip. I *loved* that!'

'I did too,' Josh said with a smile. 'What do you want to do?'

'I want to see things – lots of *beautiful* things!'

'Like what?' He looked down into her face which was beaming.

'Like galleries and gardens and castles and museums! And woods and rivers and the sea! I'm desperate to see the sea!'

Josh laughed at her enthusiasm. 'I'm not sure we'll fit all those into one day.'

'I know. But we can have *lots* of days out, can't we?'

'I don't see why not.'

They hugged again and there was something in that embrace that made Josh suddenly feel invincible. Having April there in his arms, he felt as if he could accomplish anything and be anyone he wanted to be. He could truly be a colour-loving guy who kissed his girlfriend in the middle of his shop in front of customers and not feel self-conscious about it. He could be–

'Excuse me?' A man's voice interrupted him.

Josh relinquished his hold on April and felt his face flood with heat as he turned to see a customer, his hand outstretched with a book in it.

'I'd like to buy this. *If* you're not too preoccupied, that is!' the customer said with a grin.

Josh nodded and took the book to the counter, acknowledging

the fact that he still had a little work to do when it came to not feeling self-conscious.

Josh and April didn't wait too long to start their summer adventures. After handing over his shop to Polly on Saturday afternoon, he and April took off to the coast, arriving in Aldeburgh mid-afternoon. They bought fish and chips, hot and vinegary, and ate them as they admired the candy-coloured houses on the sea front and pottered along the little back streets where tiny cottages jostled together.

'You know M R James set his story *A Warning to the Curious* here? Although he called Aldeburgh "Seaburgh".'

'Stories are never very far from your thoughts, are they?' April observed.

He shrugged. 'I guess I am a bit obsessed.'

'*Just* a bit!' she teased.

Josh smiled. Being teased by April was a totally different feeling from being teased by his family. It was the kind of teasing he liked.

After finishing their food, they walked along the pebbly shore, listening to the gentle hiss of the waves and the raucous cries of the gulls before admiring the Maggi Hambling scallop sculpture which stood tall and proud against the sky. It was made of stainless steel but it had taken on a rosy glow in the evening light and they stopped to admire it, reaching out to touch its ridged contours and to read the words that had been cut into it.

Then, hand in hand, as they had been all day, they found a quiet spot and sat down on a shingle bank, looking out into the waves as the sun slowly descended towards the horizon.

'Thank you,' April whispered to him.

'For what?'

'Bringing me here.'

'But it was *you* who brought *me* here,' Josh told her. 'Honestly, I hardly ever think to come to places like this on my own.'

'But you should!'

'Well, I know that now,' he said, 'but it seems a bit sad when you don't have someone to share it with, doesn't it?'

'You shouldn't think like that.'

He nodded. 'You're probably right. But it's sometimes hard to muster up the enthusiasm when it's just you.'

'So what *did* you do with your time before you met me, then?' she asked him, her mouth curving into a smile.

Josh gazed out to sea. What did he use to do with his time?

'I used to sell books and then I went home and read books. Then I'd start the whole thing again the next day.'

'Is that all?'

'Pretty much!'

April laughed.

'I know! I'm a hopeless case!' Josh admitted. 'Until I met you.'

They knotted their fingers together playfully and then they kissed.

After their day at the seaside, Josh and April chose a city for their next adventure, driving into Cambridge and walking around the colleges and the streets full of students and bicycles. They toured the Fitzwilliam Museum, marvelling at ancient Egyptian artefacts, and the glass cabinets stuffed full of beautiful ceramics. Once they'd surfaced into the brilliant sunshine, they walked to the River Cam and did what every self-respecting tourist to Cambridge needs to do and climbed on board a punt. Josh couldn't believe that he'd lived so close to Cambridge for so many years and had never punted down the river. It was yet another joy which

April had brought into his life, he thought, as he gazed across the water towards the magnificent chapel at King's College.

'Before you say anything,' April said as they floated by, 'I know that your M R James was Provost of King's.'

Josh looked at her, dumbfounded.

'You see, I did my homework!'

'I'm impressed!' Josh laughed. 'But have you read any of his stories yet?'

'Not yet,' April admitted.

'Maybe we can find a copy of one of his collections while we're here,' Josh suggested.

April nodded and Josh thought that he saw that fleeting look of anxiety again, but she was soon smiling as they glided under a bridge and he thought no more about it.

He had to admit that it really did feel good to get away from everyday life once in a while. His little country bookshop might be his favourite place in the world, but it was wonderful to breathe in the fresh air and see new things. After all, there was only so much you could learn from books, wasn't there? They certainly didn't tell you how amazing it felt to be in the first flush of love in summer in England. Well, they might try. H E Bates might have gone some way towards capturing the essence of love in the summer, but they were just words on the page until you'd experienced the thing for yourself. That's how Josh was feeling now. Books had been at the very centre of his soul. He'd led such a book-centric life and he genuinely hadn't realised what he was missing out on. But, looking at April now, the afternoon light highlighting the freckles across her nose, her chestnut hair lifting gently in the breeze, he knew that *this* was real life and that those literary worlds he'd been living in for so many years were a very poor second now that he'd experienced the real thing.

After their punt, they made their way back into the centre of

Cambridge and Josh led the way to one of his favourite secondhand bookshops.

'I want to find you an old edition,' he told her.

'Are we still talking about M R James?' April asked.

'Of course!'

They found their way down a narrow side street and entered a shop with rows of shelves stuffed with goodies. Josh soon found what he was looking for and handed the prized tome to April.

'Oh, Josh! You really shouldn't,' she said as she opened the jacket and saw the price. 'This is *much* too expensive.'

'Nonsense! You should see what the first editions go for. Callie bought Sam one, but that's a story I'll tell you another time.'

'But I'd be just as happy with a cheap paperback.'

Josh did a double-take. 'You're having *this* one!' He took it to the counter and paid, handing it to April once they were outside the shop.

'I don't know what to say,' she told him.

'You don't need to say anything. Just enjoy the stories and maybe remember this day whenever you read them.' Josh smiled, but his smile quickly turned into a frown when he saw that look in her face again – that fleeting flit of sorrow or anxiety, or maybe even both. 'April?'

She looked up at him. 'Thank you,' she said.

'Are you okay?'

She nodded and then gave a quick, little smile that wasn't totally convincing. 'I guess I'm just tired. It's been a long day.'

Josh nodded. Maybe she *was* just tired and he'd been reading too much into things.

'Let's go home,' he said.

April was quiet on the drive back to Castle Clare. Josh occasionally glanced her way and asked if she was okay and if she needed anything, but she assured him she was fine. He noticed that the M R James book was on her lap and that she seemed to be clutching it as if it was some kind of talisman.

'I hope it isn't haunted,' Josh said.

April looked up in alarm. 'Hope what isn't haunted?'

'That book.'

She looked down at the book in her lap. 'How could a book be haunted?'

Josh smiled and told her the story about the first edition M R James which had come into their family – twice!

'I don't believe it!' April said once he'd finished.

'Don't believe I'm telling the truth or that a book could be haunted?'

'That the book could be...' She picked her book up and flipped through the pages.

'Don't worry – it's only with very special first editions,' he assured her.

'I'm glad to hear it.'

He switched the radio on, nodding to April to check that was all right with her, and they listened to a beautiful Vivaldi concerto until they reached home. Pulling up outside her place, he switched the engine off and turned to face her.

'Are you sure you're okay? You've been very quiet.'

She reached across and took his hands in hers.

'I'm good.'

'Just tired?'

'Just tired.' She swallowed and he watched her carefully. 'My eyes – they sometimes affect me that way.'

Josh nodded. He hadn't thought of that. 'I'm sorry to hear that.'

'It can get me down a bit,' she told him. 'I'm sorry if I seem – odd sometimes.'

He lifted his hands which were still wrapped by hers and brought them to his lips where he kissed her fingers tenderly.

'You're not odd. I just worry about you when you're quiet like that.'

'But I don't want you to worry about me.'

Josh shrugged. 'I can't help it!' They were still holding hands and he slowly felt her withdrawing them.

'You don't need to.' She picked her book up and made to leave the car.

'Hey!' he called after her. 'Where to next, captain?'

She turned back round, a big smile in place once more. 'Another day out?'

'Of course! Where would you like to go next?'

She looked thoughtful for a moment. 'How about London?'

'Yeah?'

She nodded, looking excited. 'What's your favourite London museum?'

Josh took a second to think. 'I'd have to say the Natural History Museum. What can I say? I fell in love with Dippy at an impressionable age! What about you? Which is your favourite?'

April smiled. 'It has to be the V and A.'

'Let's do both!'

'Can we?'

'Why not?'

April's cheeks were rosy apples of joy now. 'When?'

'I think I could possibly get Polly to sit the shop on Tuesday.'

'Okay. I'll ask May to do the same.' April leaned across the car towards Josh and placed her hands on his face and kissed him soundly. 'Thank you!'

'Thank *you!*'

They laughed and he watched as she got out of the car, clutching her non-haunted edition of M R James tightly to her heart.

~

Before their trip to London, Josh had invited April to Sunday lunch at Campion House again, but she told him that friends were coming to visit her parents and that she and May were spending the weekend in Norfolk. A weekend had never seemed so long to Josh. He walked around his house feeling utterly lost apart from the moments he spent texting April and anxiously awaiting her replies.

Sunday was an agony of teasing by his family round the dining room table.

'Leave your brother alone!' Eleanor told both Bryony and Lara as they mercilessly made fun of their lovelorn sibling.

'But he's texting under the table!' Lara complained. 'You don't let *me* do that!'

At last, Monday came round and he was able to cross the road from his shop to April's and take her in his arms and kiss her.

'I thought you were exaggerating in your last text,' she whispered to him.

'What do you mean?'

'When you said you wanted to kiss me to within an inch of my life!'

'I wrote that?' Josh was genuinely surprised.

'You don't remember?'

They kissed again.

'You wrote a lot of things,' she said.

'I missed you.'

'I missed you too.'

'I can barely wait for tomorrow,' he confessed.

'But we'll have to,' she said, nodding towards the shop window where they saw a man struggling along the pavement with what looked like a dilapidated bathroom cabinet.

'I think you've got a customer,' Josh said, kissing her quickly before leaving her to it.

As he left the shop, he remembered that he was running low

on teabags and so nipped round to the Co-op in Market Square, quickly spotting Delilah tied up outside.

'Hey, girl,' he said, bending to pat the dog's head. 'Your master in there, is he?'

Sure enough, Josh found Winston inside, filling a basket with a few things.

'Josh!' he said.

'How are you?'

'Can't complain,' Winston said. 'Unless you'd like to hear the latest, of course.'

'Cup of tea at the bookshop?'

'I'll see you in five,' Winston said. 'Oh – Josh?'

'Yes?'

'The Hobnobs are on offer.'

'Noted!'

Ten minutes later, the two of them were drinking tea and eating Hobnobs in the bookshop, Delilah resting beside them.

'He fell out of bed?' Josh said.

'Yep! Found him on the floor. Lucky he didn't break anything.'

'Indeed!'

'Like my floorboards!'

Josh laughed.

'Seriously, though,' Winston said, 'he could have knocked a hip out or anything.'

'Do you know what happened?'

'He said he was having a dream about the French siren, Brigitte Bardot.' Winston guffawed. 'Still thinks he could pull.'

Josh took a sip of tea as Winston dunked his Hobnob in his own mug.

'I've pulled,' Josh said in a stage whisper.

Winston's face broke into a smile. 'Did you – did you...'

'I kissed her!'

'Josh!'

'And we haven't stopped kissing since.'

'Well, this *is* good news!'

'I couldn't wait to tell you.'

'Well, I'm proud of you, boy! I know how anxious you were, but I knew it was only a matter of time, and now you've got those nerves under control, there'll be no stopping you. So to speak.'

Josh smiled. 'I'm still being a gentleman.'

'Naturally!'

They drank their tea.

'Listen – you never told me what happened next with you and Marguerite – after the heavenly kiss.'

Winston finished his Hobnob and wiped his mouth with the back of his hand. 'Well, Marguerite told me she'd be going to the dance the next weekend and I made sure I was all spruced up in my finest. Her friends weren't so giggly this time round and made sure we had plenty of privacy to talk and dance. Oh, Josh! What an evening that was. Is it possible to fall in love so quickly? I didn't really believe it until that second night. Of course, I'd been smitten that first night and I'd been carrying the memory of that kiss with me all week – through the tedium of all those back-breaking jobs around the farm, through the driving rain and across the muddy fields. I held that kiss close to me, wondering where it might lead, but never imagining that I'd fall for her so quickly.'

He took a sip of his tea.

'I suppose it was always too good to be true,' he went on.

'What happened?' Josh asked, concern in his voice.

'Well, the dancing went on for a few weeks. We got to know each other in that haphazard sort of way that young people do – a question here, a revelation there. All between dances too. We'd come up for air and I'd discover she had a younger sister called Annie, and then, at the buffet table, I'd tell her about the farmyard dog, Freddie, who'd taken a shine to me.' He grinned. 'It was all so easy between us.'

'Did you see her outside of the weekly dances?'

'Not at first,' Winston said. 'To be honest, Josh, I couldn't afford to take her out and was too embarrassed to even try. But I was saving up, see. Every penny I earned that didn't go on keeping me alive went into a little pot I kept at the back of my wardrobe. Because Marguerite was the sort of girl you didn't just take anywhere. You'd want to spoil her a bit.'

Josh nodded in understanding, knowing that he only ever wanted to do the same for April.

'Well, I finally saved up enough of my money. It took a few weeks, but I managed it, and I'd booked us a table at this little place that overlooked the river. Lovely spot. Long gone now, of course. Had to book it weeks in advance and I'd booked it before I had the money to pay for it!' He shook his head at the memory. 'Marguerite was so excited when I told her about it and I was counting down the days and the hours until we went.' He paused and Josh noticed the pained expression in his face.

'Winston?'

'Just give me a minute,' he said, bending to pat Delilah's head. 'It was Friday night. Our big night out before the dance the next evening. I'd had a haircut, ironed my best shirt and borrowed a jacket from a friend. I'd even polished my boots – a rare occurrence!' He gave a little chuckle, but then his face darkened. 'And then I went to get my money from the back of the wardrobe. Only it wasn't there. It had gone.'

Josh frowned. 'Who'd taken the money?'

'Can you guess who I was sharing a house with at the time?' He gave a dark laugh.

'Monty?'

'You got it in one.'

'He took your savings?'

'Not only that – he took my girl!'

'What?'

Winston nodded. 'I was in a terrible panic when I couldn't find the money, I can tell you. How was I going to explain to Marguerite? She'd been looking forward to the evening for so long. I couldn't let her down, could I? Only we couldn't go without any money. So I called round at hers. I remember it as if it were yesterday. Her mother answered the door and looked confused as to why I was there. I told her I was picking up Marguerite and she said she'd just left – with Monty.'

'Where were they?'

'At the restaurant I'd booked. Eating the food I'd saved up for.'

Josh's mouth fell open. 'But why did Marguerite go with him and not wait for you?'

Winston gave a long, low sigh. 'He lied to her.'

'What did he say?'

'He said that I'd been seeing somebody else for months and that I'd been stringing Marguerite along for laughs.'

'And she believed him?'

'I wasn't there to defend myself and he can be pretty convincing when he wants to be. Convincing and charming.'

'And she didn't see through it?'

'I don't suppose she wanted to,' Winston said with a shrug of resignation.

'But did you ever speak to her and tell her what had happened?'

'I couldn't. I thought about it, but I don't mind saying that she broke my heart a little bit thinking the worst of me so easily.'

Josh nodded, feeling the rawness of Winston's sadness even though these events had happened decades before.

'So what happened with Monty?'

'I moved out. Left him to pay the rent on his own,' Winston said. 'I kipped on a friend's sofa for a bit until I found somewhere else.'

'And did he pay you the money back?'

Winston shook his head. 'He said he was doing me a favour if she thought so little of me as to believe him.'

'Blimey, Winston! I can't imagine what you must have gone through.'

'And he left her shortly after that.'

'And you didn't think to get back together with her again?'

'Would *you*?'

'Probably not!'

'Anyway, I met Sally. Okay, it was a few years before I dared to let myself fall in love again, but she was a keeper so perhaps Monty *did* do me a favour all those years ago, eh?'

'And have you two talked it all out since then?'

Winston sighed. 'That's the odd thing. We never really have. I have a feeling that Monty just doesn't see what he did to me.'

'But you still see each other and talk and everything. How does that work?' Josh asked, unable to imagine anything like this happening in his own family.

'Well, we didn't for a few years,' Winston confessed. 'But then life happens, doesn't it? Weddings and funerals and you find yourself moving in the same social circles. I don't know.' He sighed.

'I don't know what to say,' Josh said honestly.

'There's not a lot to say, is there? Except "families", eh?'

'I don't know what I'd do if any of my family did something like that,' Josh admitted.

'I don't suppose you'll ever have to find out,' Winston told him. 'From what I know about your family, I think you're probably safe. I can't imagine Sam ever stealing your money or your girlfriend, let alone both!'

Josh let out a laugh at the mere thought. 'No, you're probably right.'

'We can't choose our family, though, can we?' Winston said.

'Maybe that's why so many of us turn to books, eh?' He looked around the shop.

'Fiction is the great antidote to reality,' Josh said.

'Maybe I should read even more of it.'

'Well, you know where I am if you need any recommendations.'

Winston nodded. 'Thank you. And thanks for listening to me.'

'It's been my pleasure, Winston. Although I'm sorry to hear the end of your story wasn't a happy one.'

Winston sighed again. 'But I can't regret the life I've had, can I? With my Sally and my children? And who's to say that it would have worked out with Marguerite? We might have only lasted a year or two. Even a month! Who knows? All I know is that life has a way of working things out.'

'You think it all happened for the best, then?' Josh asked.

Winston gave a little wink. 'I'm pretty sure it did.'

Josh smiled and watched as his friend left the shop, Delilah following behind him.

CHAPTER SEVENTEEN

Josh and April caught the train into London, holding hands and gazing out of the window together as they talked excitedly about the day ahead and all the things they hoped to see. It was wonderfully sunny and the people of London were wearing T-shirts and dresses. The Underground was unbearably hot, but Josh and April didn't complain. To them, it was a great adventure to be there – to hear the noise and see the sights that were so very different from the little market town of Castle Clare.

Getting off the tube at South Kensington, they made their way to the Natural History Museum. Josh's beloved Dippy was no longer in residence, but they stared in wonder at the blue whale skeleton which filled the space that Dippy had left in the fabulous Hintze Hall. They then marvelled at the rest of the collection, reminiscing about school visits with booklets to be filled in and how huge everything had seemed back then. Indeed, some of the creatures still had the capability to take one's breath away by their sheer size.

'It puts man in his rightful place doesn't it,' April said. 'We are not the centre of the world at all, are we?'

In the gift shop, April bought a piece of rose quartz which she thought Arbella might like and then they made their way outside, to walk the short distance along Cromwell Road to the Victoria and Albert Museum. April was now wearing a little blue cap whose peak shielded her eyes and Josh was beginning to wish he'd got a hat too because the sunshine was so bright, dazzling the London tourists who posed with the beautiful bulk of the Natural History Museum in the background of their selfies.

By this time, they were both more than ready for lunch. There were a few places to eat at the museum, but April wanted to sit in the courtyard and watch the playful little fountains.

After finishing his quiche salad, Josh sat back in his chair. He'd taken his jacket off and had rolled up the sleeves of his shirt. It felt good to feel the sun on his skin, he thought. He wasn't much of an outdoors person, but this – here and now – felt good and natural.

'You look happy,' April told him as she finished the last of her jacket potato.

'I am,' he said. 'I was just trying to think of the last time I took a day off.'

'It was with me, silly!'

'No – I mean *before* I met you!'

'Oh, that would be back in the Dark Ages then, wouldn't it?'

Josh laughed. 'We've only known each other a short time, but you know me very well indeed.'

'It's important to take time off,' April told him. 'Even when you love your work, you need to rest and refuel and go out into the world and be inspired.'

'I'm beginning to see that.' He reached across the table and took her hand in his. 'Do you want a piece of cake or another cup of tea?'

She shook her head. 'Let's go and see the collection.'

'Okay.'

They crossed the courtyard and headed back inside.

'It's like a palace of the arts, don't you think?' April said.

'That's a very good description for it.'

'I get so excited whenever I come here,' she confessed, 'and I always see something different and wonderful whether it's made from glass or silver or an object carved from wood or a piece of fabric. There are centuries of the finest craftsmanship here from all over the world and I want to stuff myself full of it all!'

Josh laughed. Her enthusiasm was infectious.

'So where do you want to start?' she asked.

'How about the Cast Courts?' Josh suggested.

'With Michelangelo's David? You know the original was carved from a single block of marble whereas the cast here was made up from hundreds of plaster moulds?'

'I can safely say that I didn't know that,' Josh said.

'It's still beautiful, though, and it saves travelling all the way to Florence to see the original.'

'Would you like to see the original, though? Isn't Florence *the* place to go for art lovers?'

April gave a thin smile. 'I'm not the world's best traveller. London's enough for me.'

Josh could understand that. He'd never been one to relish airports and queues and delays. And so they toured the world within the safe confines of the Victoria and Albert, taking in the glories of Europe, Asia and the Middle East. Josh soon felt heady with it all, wondering if his eyes could possibly take in any more beauty, but April seemed far from tiring and so he did his best to keep up with her. There was one moment when he felt anxious about her. She'd taken off her pink glasses. Josh didn't often see her without them on and he looked at her as she stood there without them, and he was quite sure that there were tears in her eyes.

'April! Are you okay?'

She nodded, but didn't say anything.

'What is it? Tell me!'

She gave a little sniff, still looking into the glass case in front of her. 'It's just so beautiful, isn't it?'

Josh looked into the case, wondering what it was she was looking at. He read the label. It was a sixteenth-century Spanish reliquary made from silver, with thirty-six crystal-covered recesses in which were reputed to be tiny fragments of bone or cloth believed to have belonged to saints.

'Yes, it's wonderful,' he said, not sure he was seeing quite as much in it as April obviously was, but he could definitely appreciate the craftsmanship and the beauty of the materials used.

'It isn't often that you get to see something like this, is it?' she whispered.

'I guess not.'

'All that beauty, all that history.'

Josh nodded, but he wasn't looking at the reliquary – he was looking at April and, even though she was professing to love this piece, it seemed to be making her intensely sad.

He reached out and laid a hand on her shoulder. 'April?

She didn't seem to hear him.

'Hey?' he said, his voice a little louder this time.

She turned to face him and there was fear in her eyes this time, he'd swear to it.

'Josh!' Her voice was a little cry and it was more than he could bear. He reached out, pulling her close and feeling the weight of her against him.

'What is it?' he asked, but she said nothing and so they stood there together in front of the glass display case as tourists passed them by with only the briefest glance of curiosity.

At last, April pulled away slightly, her face flushed with colour.

'Are you okay?'

'I'm sorry. I just felt a little faint. It must be the heat.'

'Do you want to sit down or get something to eat?'

She shook her head. 'Let's see some more things, shall we?'

'If you're sure you're okay,' Josh said, watching as she put her glasses back on and walked towards a different display.

The atmosphere changed after that although April didn't refer back to it and her voice and demeanour seemed bright enough, but Josh knew that what he'd witnessed hadn't been normal. Was she overtired again? Perhaps they'd overdone things. It was pretty warm, after all, and they were trying to cram a lot into one day.

'April – do you think we should call it a day?' he said a few minutes later, still anxious about her.

'No!' she cried. 'We haven't even seen the fashion collection yet and that's one of my favourite parts of the museum. Come on.'

Josh followed her, but he couldn't shake the deep-rooted anxiety that had settled inside him and that meant he was watching over April now rather than being relaxed in her company. He was, of course, still enjoying their day out together, but something fundamental had changed.

It was the same on the way home. April closed her eyes and rested her head against Josh, quickly falling into a shallow sleep. He held her hand as he gazed out of the train window and he couldn't help wishing that he understood just a little more about the woman who was sleeping on his shoulder.

But Josh didn't have long to wait before he knew more. After their trip to London, a few days went by when May was in the shop once more. Like last time, she was vague about her sister, telling Josh that she'd chosen to work from home for a few days. Josh wasn't totally convinced. If it had been as simple as that, why wouldn't April have told him? They'd called each other a few times since their day together and they'd swapped texts, but Josh hadn't had one for over a day now.

'Why don't you just go round there?' Sam said when Josh asked him for advice.

'What if I'm not welcome?'

'What makes you think you won't be welcome?'

He sighed. 'It's just a feeling I'm getting. April...' He paused. 'She sometimes seems to shut me out. I can't understand her. She does this half-pulling me closer and yet pushing me away at the same time.'

Sam looked confused so Josh told him about the strange incident at the museum.

'And she didn't say anything afterwards?'

'No, it's like it never happened,' Josh told him. 'Only she was completely wiped out on the train home and fell asleep on my shoulder.'

'Well, London wipes me out too. I'd have probably done the same thing. Only on Callie's shoulder – not yours!'

Josh gave a little smile.

'Just go round there,' Sam added. 'I think you need to find out what's going on. It's only fair. This thing between you – whatever it is – it's eating you alive and that's not good.'

Josh didn't say anything, but he knew his brother was right.

'Go and see her – right now.'

'But the shop–'

'The shop can wait. Your customers can wait. *Everything* can wait. But I don't think you should anymore. Honestly, Josh – you look like you're going to implode or something.'

Josh nodded, seeing the sense in getting things sorted. It was time.

~

Before he left for April's, Josh made sure that May was still in A Little Bit Bloomsbury. The last thing he wanted was her getting in the way of things. He walked into Market Square and bought a bunch of mixed flowers from the florists. He recognised that the orange ones were lilies, but he wasn't sure what the others were. Something scented and suitably beautiful. They were even wrapped in paper and not plastic so couldn't possibly offend on that score.

Walking back to where he'd parked his car behind his shop, Josh couldn't help noticing that A Little Bit Bloomsbury had shut. He shielded his eyes and peered through the window, but May had definitely gone and it looked as if it might be for the rest of the day for there was no friendly little note saying 'Back in five minutes'.

He cursed. She'd probably gone home which would mean he wouldn't have April to himself. Whenever May was around, she always seemed to come between them. Well, not this time, Josh vowed. He wasn't going to be fobbed off with May telling him that her sister needed rest and didn't want to see him.

He left the centre of Castle Clare, the flowers for April on the passenger seat beside him. He wasn't sure what to expect when he got there. If she did have one of her awful migraines, he truly might not be able to see her. But at least he could try and find out what was going on and he could leave the flowers for her with his love.

He pulled up outside the Victorian villa a few minutes later, sitting for a moment gathering his thoughts. Then he picked up the flowers and went to knock on the door. Sure enough, it was May who answered.

'What are you doing here?' she asked.

'I've come to see April. Is she here?'

'Shouldn't you be at work?'

Josh felt himself bristling at the tone of her voice.

'Can I come in?' he asked as May stood like a guard in the doorway, allowing Josh no access inside.

'She's in her bedroom.'

'Can I see her?'

May looked angry that he should request such a thing.

'I need to talk to her, May,' Josh said, standing his ground.

May sighed dramatically. 'Well, don't tire her. She's not well.' She stood to one side and pointed to the hallway through the door. 'She's in the room on the right.'

Josh followed the corridor and stopped outside the bedroom door. It was ajar and he knocked lightly.

'April?'

'Josh?'

He entered and saw her lying on the bedclothes, her hair a wild tangle and her cheeks pink and tear-stained. He noticed she wasn't wearing her pink glasses and that the curtains were drawn.

'April!' He almost flew across the room, sitting by her side on the bed and taking her hands in his when she sat up, the flowers dropping to the floor. 'What's the matter? Is it a migraine?'

She shook her head. 'No, it's not a migraine.'

'Then what is it? Why are you crying? I haven't heard from you in ages. I've been worried sick!'

She pulled a tissue out from her pocket and dabbed her eyes and cheeks. Then she took hold of his hands as he had taken hold of hers.

'What is it? Please tell me.'

'I don't know how,' she whispered.

'Tell me any way you want to, but please just tell me. It's more than just headaches, isn't it?'

She nodded and they sat for a moment in the quietness of her bedroom before she finally spoke.

'I didn't quite tell you the whole truth before. About my eyes.' She sniffed, but she was looking directly at him now, her hazel eyes still bright with tears. 'I have something called retinitis pigmentosa. Have you heard of it?'

'No, I haven't,' Josh said.

'Not many people have. It's quite rare, you see.'

'And what does it do?'

'Well, you know a bit about it already – my sensitivity to light and my headaches and migraines.'

Josh nodded.

'But that's not all,' she told him. 'My vision has never been good and...' she paused.

'Go on,' Josh encouraged.

'And it isn't going to get any better. In fact, it's only going to get worse as I get older, and it's already pretty restricted.'

'Is that why you've been in such a rush to see things this summer?' Josh asked as clarity dawned on him and he remembered the way she'd rushed around the museums trying to see as much as she could.

'Yes. It's been getting worse. A lot worse. I've spoken to my ophthalmologist and he's told me I should stop driving.'

Josh reached out and stroked her hair. 'I'm so sorry, April.'

'I feel so helpless – like the world is shrinking and I'll soon be confined to a tiny corner of it.'

'Oh, April! I had no idea. I'm so sorry.'

'Don't be. I've known for some time now.'

'But still – it can't be easy.'

'It isn't. Well – as you can see! I keep having little episodes. I go so long, trying to block it out, but then these waves of sadness come over me.'

Josh put his arms around her and held her close.

'There's something else, though,' she said. 'And I've been meaning to say this for a while now. It was wrong of me not to. But

I was so afraid of this all ending. I was having so much fun with you and...'

'What?' Josh suddenly felt scared.

'I don't think this is going to work.'

'What isn't?'

'You, me. Us. It's all too complicated.'

Josh pulled away and gazed at her in disbelief. 'Are you breaking up with me?'

He could see tears in her eyes again and she swallowed hard, nodding.

'It's for the best, Josh, really it is. I don't want you to feel obligated to me. I don't want you to ever feel unhappy that we can't do all the things a normal couple might want to do together.'

'But I won't, April. I promise you. I won't ever feel like that. I'm just happy to be with you.'

She shook her head. 'I don't want to be a burden to you.'

'Don't you think it's up to me to make that decision?'

'No.' The word came out quickly and bluntly and he stared at her in disbelief for a moment.

'April – listen to me! Since I met you, nothing's been the same for me. I feel happy – *truly* happy – for the first time in years. I always thought I was a happy person, but I realise now that that was just contentedness.' He shrugged. 'I was content with my life, my bookselling, being on my own in my boring beige house.'

'Josh–'

He leaned forward and kissed her. 'You have made all the difference in the world to me, April, and I'm not going to give that up so don't ever ask me to.'

'No, Josh!'

'Listen. I knew from the first moment I saw you that you were special. I really feel we have something precious here. Don't you feel that too?'

She nodded and a single tear fell down her cheek. 'But you don't understand.'

'What?' he asked gently. 'Tell me what I don't understand.'

She looked down at their hands all tied together in the space between them and, when she spoke again, her voice was barely above a whisper.

'I'm going blind.'

CHAPTER EIGHTEEN

April Channing had always known that she was going to lose her sight one day. Her family had prepared her for it and she'd taken it pretty much in her stride. Perhaps that's why she'd become so addicted to art books and galleries from a young age. It was as if she was trying to cram her eyes with as much beauty and colour as possible to see her through the dark days which she knew lay ahead.

As a teenager, she'd gone through a stage of blindfolding herself in order to practise being blind, but this had caused so many accidents in her family home including two broken easels and a pot of red paint knocked over on to white floorboards, so that April had had to give up. Anyway, a part of her thought it was slightly crazy to voluntarily lose her vision before she had to. Surely she should be making the very most of every single second of it. So she'd thrown the blindfold away and had, for the most part, put her fear of the loss of her sight into a box labelled *very dim and distant future.*

It mostly worked, not thinking about the future. Over the years, April had thrown herself into her studies and her passions, learning about colour and perspective, landscape artists and portrait artists, printers and furniture designers. She read every book on art and design from every library she could join and she saved up to buy her own books too, lovingly kept on a set of shelves they'd picked up secondhand from a car boot sale and which she had painted herself.

She'd never felt different. Maybe that's what came of being a twin. She always had somebody there with her if she was having a tricky day or an emotional wobble. April instinctively knew that their relationship was more intense than having a regular sister because May not only knew what April was thinking or how she was feeling, she'd know what was in her very soul. She could very often predict things like the choices April would make in any given circumstance and the next words to come out of her mouth. That happened so often that May would often answer a question before April had even asked it.

Growing up with May had been a privilege and a pain. To have somebody so close to you was wonderful in times of trouble, but sometimes April couldn't help hankering after a space to call her own. Was that awful? Was it a sort of twin taboo to admit something like that? She'd never confess it to May of course, but she knew that her sister felt it sometimes. Maybe it was April's condition that made her feel like that – knowing that, one day, she would truly be isolated in her own dark realm.

Not once did she ever bemoan her fate or wish that it was her sister who had been dealt the unlucky card. She'd accepted it peacefully.

But now that she could feel its stealthy approach, she began to complain. She felt true fear gripping her when she thought about it. Her vision was slowly closing down, a darkness eating at her eyes. She didn't want to go blind when there was so much to see in the world. How could she live not being able to see her twin ever again? Or Josh's handsome face? Or the treasures of her shop?

How would she be able to create things? Would she be able to hold a paintbrush again or experience the joy of an art exhibition? Or see her mother and Daddy George's latest creations? The thought of so much loss made her cry hot and silent tears. Those were the big losses. There were so many little ones too – like the thought of never seeing the colours of her bead necklaces again or the sight of a rainbow arching across the sky, and the shades of the sea and of spring flowers. To lose any one of those things would seem like a cruel fate, but to have them snatched away all at once seemed horribly wicked.

There was no consolation to be had for the loss of sight, was there? Nothing anyone could say could possibly ease the pain and, even though she knew she had the loving support of her twin, her mother and two fathers and, indeed, Josh, if she let him, she still felt like she was going through this alone. There was no escaping the inside of her head and that, she'd quickly learned, could be a very dark place sometimes.

She'd been experiencing more and more of her wobbles recently and had been so worried about the one she'd had in front of Josh at the Victoria and Albert Museum. She'd come so close to telling him then – in that dark moment of fear. She'd felt she could reach out to him, but she'd managed to recover herself and pass it off as faintness owing to the heat of the day. She'd been able to tell that Josh wasn't fooled. He'd known for some time that something was amiss and she'd been wrong to hide it from him.

Josh!

April had never counted on someone like Josh Nightingale walking into her shop and straight into her heart. At first, she'd thought it might be nice to have a mild flirtation. Nothing more than that. Somebody to chat to during the business days. What she hadn't expected was the great joy she felt every time she saw him.

May hadn't approved of course.

'He'll break your heart like all the others when he finds out,' she'd warned. But April didn't believe that. Josh was gentle and kind and, when she'd told him that she was going to be blind one day he'd held her hands oh-so-tightly and told her that he wasn't going anywhere.

And so she'd pushed him away as hard as she could.

'I don't want you here,' she'd said through the tears.

'I don't believe that, April.'

'You have to leave. Now!'

And that's when May had come in.

'Do what she says,' May had told Josh. He'd sat there for a moment, refusing to move, but then he'd got up.

'This isn't over, April,' he'd said.

'I think it is,' May had replied.

May was there now – standing over her in glowering guardian mode.

'You should have told him earlier,' she said.

'What – when he first came into the shop? "Hello, I'm April and I'll be blind one day!"'

'Yes.'

April sighed. 'I couldn't.'

'You shouldn't have let this thing go on for as long as you have.'

April glared at her sister. 'This *thing*?'

'Yes!'

'May – I'm in love with him!'

'Rubbish!'

'Why do you find that so hard to believe?'

May shook her head. 'You shouldn't let yourself get close to people who'll only hurt you.'

April found that she was gripping the bed sheets as if she meant to strangle them. 'Oh, that's right. You only ever want me to be close to you, don't you? You *hate* it when I make a new friend.'

'That's not true.'

'Yes it is.'

'I only want you to be safe.'

'But safe is so dull, May! I don't want to be safe.'

'You're talking wildly. You need to rest.'

'There'll be time enough to rest when I can't see anything.'

'Don't upset yourself.'

April could feel her heart racing now. She was losing control again.

'It's all right!' May raced across the room and was beside her and April felt the warm familiarity of her twin's embrace. 'You're all right. You're just having a wobble.'

April sniffed. A wobble. That had always been the way May had described April's little outbursts. It was like she was trying to belittle the enormity of the situation by turning it into something almost humorous. A wobble. Pass the smelling salts. It's nothing to be afraid of.

Only April was afraid. She was absolutely terrified and so she clung to her sister now.

'I didn't mean to get so close to Josh,' she said at last, once the waves of anguish had calmed a little. 'I thought I had everything under control.'

May stroked her hair in the calming way she always did. 'Well, at least he knows now.'

April moved back on the bed and hugged her knees up to her chest. 'But the look on his face, May!'

'Now, don't start crying again!'

'He looked so hurt.'

'He'll be fine. He's a grown man. You've just given him a bit of a shock, but he'll bounce back.'

April swallowed hard. The idea of Josh bouncing was preposterous.

'You really think it's for the best?' April asked.

'I really do. You've said so yourself a thousand times!'

'I know,' April said, hugging her knees tightly seeing as Josh was no longer there to hug. She'd have to get used to that, she thought. How quickly she'd become used to having him next to her – the warmth of his skin and the gentle strength of his touch. She smiled as she remembered their first kiss in the golden summer light of the garden at Charleston. She'd known he'd been trying to pluck up the courage to kiss her and had revelled in his sweet agony.

'What are you smiling about?' May asked, jogging her out of her reverie.

'Charleston.'

May grinned. 'See – you're over him already!'

Josh had left April and May's and got in his car, driving the short distance home. When he'd made his decision to see April, he'd had absolutely no idea of how things would unfold. But how could he have? He'd known she had problems with her vision and had a sensitivity to light, but he'd had no idea that she would lose her sight altogether one day.

No idea because she didn't tell you.

Josh sighed. He would try not to beat himself up about not realising what was going on with April. He hadn't known because she hadn't wanted him to. Although there'd been so many little signs that something was wrong – not just the tinted glasses and the drips of paint on the furniture, but that strange distance she kept sometimes, as if there were a sheet of impenetrable glass between them, and then there were the panic attacks and the overwhelming tiredness.

If Josh hadn't had a meeting with a rep that afternoon, he would have shut up his shop for the day. As soon as five o'clock came, he was out of the door because there was somebody he had to talk to about all this. Three somebodies in fact.

The address was programmed into his satnav, but he pretty much remembered the way through the Suffolk country lanes, heading north until he reached the border with Norfolk.

He recognised the track and slowed down, driving in the evening shade cast by the trees that lined it.

And there it was: Fairley Hall. The home of April's three parents. He hadn't rung ahead which was very unlike him. He'd been in such a hurry to get there. But now he wished he'd slowed down a little and thought things through. What if nobody was at home? Or what if they were and didn't want to see him? What if April had already called to tell them that she'd split up with him? A thousand different questions tormented him as he parked his car and he wondered if he should call in at all.

'You're here now,' he told himself, getting out of the car and running his hands through his hair. He felt a mess, but it was too late to worry about that. Anyway, he wasn't the important thing right now.

The front door that led out into the garden was ajar, propped open by a huge painting of a vague figure in greens and blues. Josh stared at it for a moment, noticing a huge hole in the middle of it as if a foot might have found its way through the canvas. He blinked and went through to the hallway and up the stairs to the apartment.

'Hello?' he called once he was at the top of the stairs.

He definitely felt jittery and shaky. A kind of nervous energy was coursing around his system. April was going to be blind. His April. He swallowed hard as he thought about the warm and beautiful young woman he had fallen in love with. When she'd told him she was losing her vision, he hadn't been able to say anything. He'd felt absolutely stunned. Words – which had been his lifelong friends and companions – had deserted him in that moment. All he'd been able to do was sit there and hold her hands as she'd told him about her condition, her beautiful hazel eyes swimming with tears. And then she'd told him to leave, and May had come and told him to go too.

How cruel life could be sometimes, he thought, rage surging through him. To take the sight of a talented artist like her – someone who saw the true beauty of the world. It was too horrible.

'Josh?'

Josh looked up. Somehow, he'd slid down the wall and had ended up sitting on the floor, but he had no recollection how that had happened. And there was April's mother standing over him, her face etched with worry.

'Arbella!'

'Let's get you up,' she said, bending and placing her arms under his.

'I'm okay,' he said, quickly righting himself and brushing his trousers.

'What on *earth* were you doing on the floor? And what are you doing *here* for that matter?'

Josh took a deep breath and looked at Arbella and she nodded.

'She's told you, hasn't she?'

'Yes.'

'Come on!' she said, in a no-nonsense sort of way as she put her arm around his shoulder and led him into the main room. 'George? Josh is here,' Arbella shouted above the sound of a radio blasting out some ear-piercingly high opera singing. 'Turn that bloody thing off!'

Silence greeted them a second later as Daddy George appeared.

'Josh! What a surprise. Good lord – were we expecting you? What's the time? What day is it? Have I missed something?'

'No, he's just turned up. He was on the floor,' Arbella told him.

'What?'

'April's told him.'

Daddy George cursed loudly and colourfully. In that respect,

Josh couldn't help thinking, his language was very much like his paintings.

'Time for wine?' George asked when he was done cursing.

Josh shook his head in case the gooseberry wine was about to make another appearance.

'I'm driving,' he said, glad of the excuse.

'Make the poor man a cup of tea, will you? And get me one too while you're at it.'

George nodded and disappeared.

'Come and sit down before you fall down again,' Arbella said, moving a heap of old newspapers and unopened post off a corner of the sofa.

'I don't know what happened,' Josh said honestly as he sat down.

'My daughter happened – that's what!'

Josh looked at Arbella, stunned by the simple truth of her statement. She sat on a wooden stool opposite and it was only then that he noticed Arbella had a streak of yellow paint across her right cheek and two paintbrushes sticking out of a messy bun. If Josh wasn't so miserable, he'd have smiled.

'Daddy Jeff not about?' Josh asked. 'I mean *Jeff*.'

'Not back from work yet. Ghastly commute from London.'

'Right,' Josh said, trying to imagine the horror of that for a moment. His own train ride in to London with April had been a delight with them holding hands and being oh-so-close for that blissful, uninterrupted hour. But he couldn't imagine what it must be like to have to do that day after day, and without the benefit of a romantic snuggle en route.

He closed his eyes as he remembered their day together and how April had wanted to see all the things she held dearest at the museum. It was because she'd known it might be the last time, wasn't it? God, how had he not known what she'd been thinking and suffering? Why hadn't he questioned her more?

'Why didn't she tell me?' Josh blurted now.

George came back into the room, mugs of strong tea on a tray with milk and sugar.

'I told her that she should,' Arbella said, 'as soon as I knew she was serious about you.'

'You tried to say something too, didn't you? When I came for lunch?'

'I guessed you didn't know then,' she confessed.

'She said she doesn't want to see me anymore,' he told them now.

George swore again.

'Why would she say that?' Josh asked, his voice fuelled by anguish. 'Isn't going blind bad enough without breaking up with the man you're supposed to be in love with too? I don't understand it!'

Arbella took a sip of her tea and then leaned forward and added another sugar. 'She thinks she's saving you.'

'From what?'

'From pain.'

'But I'm in pain *now*!'

'But that will pass – that's what's she thinking,' Arbella said with absolute certainty ringing in her voice. 'She's always said that she doesn't want to be a burden to anybody. Not even May although you can imagine how that went down.'

'How is May coping with all this?' Josh asked, thinking of the bristly sister with kindness and concern.

'She's known about it for as long as April has,' Arbella told him, 'and she's more ready than any of us.'

'I don't know what we'd do without her,' George said. 'She's a complete stalwart.'

Josh could well imagine it from what he'd seen of May, but there was a part of him that didn't believe there wasn't another way through this.

'But there must be something we can do – find an expert – someone who could operate?' he said.

'There's nothing,' Arbella said.

Josh shook his head. 'I can't accept that! There must be *something*!'

'Don't you think we would have found it if there was?' George cried. His eyes had taken on a wild look now and Josh felt bad for upsetting him.

'It's irreversible, Josh,' Arbella told him.

Josh swallowed hard at her use of the word. She said it so calmly that he couldn't help wanting to buck against it.

'But–'

'It's just the way it is. It's horrible and it's unfair and there's absolutely nothing we can do about it.'

They all sat in silence for a moment, the dark reality of it settling on Josh.

'What do we do?' he asked at last.

Arbella got up from her stool and perched on the arm of the sofa next to Josh, placing a hand on his shoulder.

'We live our lives to the very best of our ability. We don't dwell on the negative. We don't set a stopwatch and wait for the inevitable to happen. We see the beauty in every day, we spend time with the people we love, and we do the things we most want to do. That's what we do.'

Josh nodded. 'But she's pushed me away. How can I spend time with the woman I love when she doesn't want me in her life anymore?'

'Give her time, Josh,' George said. 'From what May has told us, April's had a bad week. I think she'll just need to come to terms with things herself first.'

'You think so?'

'Josh, my darling boy!' Arbella said. 'I have *never* seen April crazier about anyone in her life as she is about you. Like George said – give her some space and time and I'm sure she'll reach out to you again.'

Josh sighed. 'It's not going to be easy waiting to hear from her.'

'I know,' Arbella said. 'But she needs this time with May, so give it to her.'

'If you think that's for the best.'

'I really do.'

Josh left shortly after another cup of tea and a slice of something that Arbella thought was almond cake, but which had sat in a tin for so long that she couldn't quite be sure.

Driving back into Suffolk, he couldn't quite believe how calm Arbella had been about the whole thing. But they had lived with the knowledge of April's condition for a lot longer than he had, he reasoned. Still, it upset him that they seemed so resigned to the fact that April was going to be blind one day. Surely there was still some fight in them?

He cursed, slowing the car as he crossed a ford. Perhaps they *had* fought all they could over the years. Perhaps resignation was the sanest route. After all, as horrible as it was to admit, these things happened. Josh had quickly looked up April's condition on the internet and had read that one in four thousand people got it. Why oh why did April have to be so very unlucky? He'd known when he'd met her that she was one in a million, but he sincerely wished that she wasn't one in four thousand.

He withdrew inside himself for the next few days, thinking things over and coming to terms with April's news, hoping with all his heart that she would call him and say that she'd made a terrible mistake in breaking up with him. How many times his fingers had hovered over his phone, dying to call her or send her a text. He couldn't bear not hearing from her and knowing that she was in so much pain.

Each morning, he'd look across the road towards A Little Bit Bloomsbury, hoping that this would be the day that April would return to work, but it never was. It was always May in the shop. He gave her some space but, by day four, he was nearly going out of his mind and went over.

'Don't ask me anything,' May said as soon as Josh was through the door.

'What do you mean?' Josh looked at May, noticing how pale her face was.

'She's not speaking to me either now.'

'What?'

'She's shut me out. She won't even come out of her room. I have to leave the house to make sure I give her a chance to wash and eat.'

'God, May! You should have told me!'

'Told you what? You can't do anything! None of us can!'

Josh saw May's eyes flood with tears and he realised how hard this was all hitting her.

He crossed the space between them and put his arms around her. At first, she flinched. Like him, she wasn't an overly-demonstrative person, but he soon felt her exhale and then a sob rose from her and she let herself be held as she cried. It was all Josh could do not to cry himself.

'I don't know what to do!' May wailed. 'She's never *not* let me in before. But she won't even talk to me!'

He let her cry for a little longer until he felt the sobbing subside.

'Listen,' he said, doing his best to remain calm, 'she'll come back to us when she's ready, okay? And we'll be here. She knows we're here for her – that's the main thing.'

May sniffed and pulled a tissue out from her pocket and blew her nose loudly.

'What can I do, May? I feel utterly helpless at the moment.'

She shook her head, her cheeks still wet with tears. 'I don't even know what *I* can do. She's just disappeared somewhere deep inside herself. It's happened before, but she usually comes out of it quickly. Retreating then reaching out, I've always called it. But she's not reaching out this time.' May dabbed at her eyes again.

'Do you think I should go round?'

'No!' May cried.

Josh put his hands up in the air as if in defeat.

'I went to visit your parents,' he told her.

'What did you do that for?' May sounded genuinely confused.

'Because I wanted to try and understand what's going on. And – well – because you've never talked to me, have you?' Suddenly, Josh didn't want to hide anything anymore. He wanted it all out in the open.

May looked down at the floor and Josh felt instantly bad for having yelled at her.

'Sorry.'

'It's all right,' May said. 'I probably deserve it. It's just that, when it comes to April, I'm always so defensive.'

'I've noticed!'

May looked up and a tiny tickle of a smile flickered across her face. 'You might be the same if you had a twin.'

'I dare say I would,' Josh said, trying to imagine it for a moment. 'What's it like?'

May took a deep breath. 'It's like... it's like having a little piece of you wandering around the world outside yourself – quite independent and yet totally connected to you.'

Josh smiled at her description.

'I can't imagine life not being a twin,' May confided. 'I think it must be awfully lonely.' She smiled. 'April and I are so much a part of each other. One unit. It's always been that way. It's how we're seen by the outside world. We were always "you two" and never individuals. Anyway, we never minded. We liked it. And we have our own personalities, even though we're alike in so many ways. Everything we like, we like together. Growing up, we used to do *everything* together. We played the same games, read the same books and then we studied the same subjects at school and university. But it was more than that. I suppose, in some way, we were each other. I always knew what she was thinking and she always knew what I was thinking. That can be incredibly intrusive sometimes, let me tell you, but it can also be a great comfort too, because you don't need words to express yourself.'

Josh noticed the wistful look in May's eyes and thought how very much like April she looked in that moment – not just physically because there was never any disputing that, but emotionally too. There was usually a slightly sharper edge to May, but it had been whittled away as she talked so lovingly about her twin. Josh tried to imagine what it would be like to have somebody that close to you. He liked to think that he was close to his siblings and he'd always had a particularly close relationship with Sam, but they certainly hadn't done everything together in the same way that April and May had, and he couldn't claim to know what Sam was thinking at any given time.

May sighed. 'That's why it's so hard for me now. I know what she's thinking, but she won't let me near her.'

'And what's she thinking?' Josh dared to ask.

May looked at him, a look of true sorrow in her eyes. 'I can't betray that trust,' she told him, 'but it's dark.'

Josh nodded. 'I want to see her.'

'I know.

'I miss her.'

'Me too.'

They stood for a little while longer and then May did

something totally unexpected: she hugged Josh. He was so surprised by the gesture that, at first, he forgot to hug her back, but rectified the situation once he registered what was happening.

'I'm here if you need me,' he told her and felt her nodding.

'I'm here too,' she whispered against him.

CHAPTER NINETEEN

Winston had been sitting on his bed for a good half hour. It had been a strange time for him having Monty in his home. Strange and deeply unsettling. His talks with young Josh Nightingale had excavated quite a few unpleasant feelings from Winston's past and he'd been left feeling tired and confused by it all. There was a part of him – rather a large part – that was tempted to tell Monty to go home, but there was another part that remembered how very old and vulnerable his brother had looked when he'd fallen out of bed and landed on the floor. This was the brother who'd just lost his wife.

'And he's the only one I've got,' Winston told himself.

Yes, he thought, he could so easily wallow in the past, hating Monty for what he'd done and begrudging him now for monopolising his favourite armchair and for all his little selfish ways. But what good would that do, he thought? It would only compound the misery and Winston didn't want to carry the weight of it around any longer. Half an hour of wallowing was quite long enough, he decided, getting up off the bed and going downstairs.

Sure enough, Monty was sitting in Winston's favourite

armchair, toast crumbs down his shirt and his hair a mess. Without saying a word, Winston crossed the room and switched the TV off. There'd been some awful discussion show with people ranting loudly and not really listening to each other, and the silence that greeted the room was such a relief.

'Get washed and changed. We're going out,' Winston announced.

'Out?'

'Sunday lunch. My treat.'

Monty looked absolutely stunned by this. 'What have I done to deserve this?'

'Nothing,' Winston quipped and then instantly regretted it. He was already failing in his attempt to be magnanimous. 'I just think it's time we had a decent meal and a bit of a jaunt.'

'A jaunt, you say?'

'Well, don't get too excited. It'll just be the local pub, but I was thinking we should take a walk around the castle gardens afterwards and maybe sit by the river.'

Monty leaned forward in the chair, the crumbs on his shirt falling into his lap as he craned to look out of the window.

'It does seem a nice day.'

'That's settled then,' Winston said. 'Delilah can stay here. I'll walk her later when it's cooler.'

Monty smiled. 'I'll get changed then.'

Winston nodded, suddenly feeling anxious now that his plan was in progress. Anxious, but happy too.

Josh had been dreading Sunday lunch at Campion House. He hadn't yet told his family about April's condition. He'd needed to really try and understand his own reaction to it first before opening himself up to all the questions he knew would be fired at him from his family.

Of course, his mother knew something was wrong as soon as he walked into the kitchen.

'Josh!' She swooped across the room. From cooker to son in three seconds flat. 'What is it?'

He shook his head. 'Later.'

Her forehead wrinkled in concern. 'You promise?' She gave him a hug, instinctively knowing that he needed one.

Josh lost himself in the noise of the kitchen, taking it upon himself to wash and chop the lettuce that had been left out, listening to his sisters as they laughed and chatted about something. He wasn't quite sure what. He might have been there amongst them bodily, but his mind was elsewhere: in a little room in a Victorian villa with the curtains closed against the world. April's room.

Lunch was served and the conversations went on around and over Josh as he did his best to focus on his food. It was hard to enjoy anything much at the moment when he knew that the woman he loved with all his heart was suffering. And, all the time, he was aware of his mother's eyes upon him. Polly's too. She never missed anything. Sometimes, it could be a comfort to know that your family was looking out for you, but it was just making Josh feel more anxious now because he knew he had to break the sad news to them, and he could imagine their responses.

He had thought about not coming to lunch – of ringing up and giving some excuse – but he knew he couldn't lie and he had to tell them sooner or later, didn't he?

Finally, the torture of lunch came to an end and tea was served in the living room. The windows were open today and a warm breeze stirred the floral curtains and ruffled the top of Grandpa Joe's newspaper. Grandma Nell was snoozing beside him. He'd heard she'd had a couple of tricky days earlier in the week, getting confused and thrashing out at Grandpa, which was hard to imagine now as she slept so peacefully next to him.

Josh looked around the room at his family. Jago had brought his guitar and was quietly coaching Archie to play something new, much to the delight of Eleanor. Bryony and Lara were laughing about something. Probably about Lara's latest love at university. Sam, Callie and Ben were in deep conversation. Josh could hear snatches. Something to do with books. And Polly – Polly was looking directly at him.

'It's a shame April couldn't make it today,' she told him, her eyes never leaving his face.

'Yes, how is she?' his father asked.

Josh took a deep breath. There was no more delaying.

'There's something you need to know,' he began.

'Oh, you haven't broken up with her!' Lara cried.

'No, of course not,' Josh said, although April had kind of broken up with him, hadn't she? Anyway, he still didn't believe that.

'I think you've all noticed that April wears those pink glasses,' he said instead.

'Yes, they're very pretty,' Bryony said.

'Well, they're not exactly a fashion statement,' Josh told her. 'You know she has an eye condition?'

'Yes, she gets horrible headaches, doesn't she?' Eleanor said.

'I'm afraid it's more serious than just headaches,' Josh said. 'She has a condition called retinitis pigmentosa.'

'What's that?' Archie asked, looking up from his guitar.

Josh took a deep breath. 'It means her vision is very limited and she's extremely sensitive to light. And it means she'll lose her sight completely one day.'

A stunned silence greeted this.

'She's going to go blind?' Lara asked, her forehead creasing in concern.

Josh nodded.

'Oh, no!' Eleanor cried.

Polly's eyes misted with tears.

'Does she know when it will happen?' Sam asked.

'I don't think so. It's a degenerative thing, but her vision's suddenly got a lot worse this last couple of weeks.'

'That poor young woman!' Grandpa Joe said.

'How on earth does she work?' Bryony asked. 'And with her art too!'

'I'm afraid she isn't at the moment, but she's managed up until recently through sheer determination,' Josh told her.

'Well, she's certainly to be admired,' Frank said.

'Yes she is. She told me that nothing's ever stopped her from doing what she loves.'

'That's wonderful,' Jago said, 'and as it should be.'

Everybody murmured their agreement and then the room fell silent again. This, Josh thought, was a pretty weighty subject for a Sunday afternoon at Campion House.

Lara was the first to speak. 'How did you react when she told you?'

'How do you think?'

'Did you cry, Uncle Josh?' Archie asked.

'Very nearly.'

'It's so sad,' Polly said. 'To live with the knowledge that, one day, you'll lose your sight.'

'And she's always known that,' Josh said.

'It's probably had the effect of making her focus very strongly on what's important,' Frank surmised.

'But can you ever really prepare yourself?' Sam asked.

'No, of course not,' Polly agreed.

'It's just too awful,' Eleanor said. His mother's eyes filled with tears as Josh had known they would.

'And she's so young,' Grandpa Joe said.

'How does she feel about it?' Ben asked.

Josh let out a long sigh. 'She's only just told me about it, but I could tell she was frightened.'

'Of course!' Lara said. 'I would be petrified.'

'And – well – she's kind of shut herself away.'

'What do you mean?' Bryony asked.

'I mean, she's not seen me for a while.'

'Oh, Josh!' Eleanor cried.

'It's *killing* me!' he said and Polly was immediately up from her seat and he felt her arms around him. It was so unexpected and so very much needed that Josh burst into tears.

'It's okay!' Polly said. 'We're here. We're *all* here.'

Josh was lost. He'd never done anything like that before in his life, but he was too emotional to feel embarrassed by it and so he cried, letting out all the pent-up feelings he'd been holding in so tightly over the past few days.

Finally, once he felt like he could cry no more, he looked up. Everybody was there, speaking tender words and laying gentle hands upon him. He nodded and thanked them and accepted a hot mug of tea from his mother. When had she gone to make that, he wondered? How long had he been crying for?

It didn't matter, did it?

'I'm sorry,' he said nevertheless.

'You don't need to apologise,' Polly told him, and he saw that she'd been crying too. Actually, looking around the room, he noticed that everybody was looking distinctly red-eyed.

'It's a lot to take in, isn't it?' Sam said and Josh saw him squeezing Callie's hand.

'Is there anything we can do?' Eleanor asked. 'Does she need anything?'

'We could send her some flowers!' Archie said and Polly smiled fondly at him. 'Or chocolates! Everybody likes chocolates when they're feeling sad.'

'That's a very good idea, Archie,' Frank told his grandson.

'Will you try and see her?' Callie asked.

'May thinks I shouldn't. Not for a while at least. April's even shut her out at the moment.'

'Poor April!' Bryony said.

'But she'll want to see you again soon, I'm sure,' Sam told him.

'I hope so.'

'Of course she will!' Grandpa Joe said. 'I saw the way that young woman was looking at you when she was here. She's not going to give you up!'

'I wish I could be sure of that,' Josh confessed, taking a tissue which his mother handed him and wiping his eyes and giving his nose a good blow. He still felt on the verge of tears, but he was feeling a little stronger now. Having his family around him at such a time was definitely a comfort. He wasn't quite sure how he'd have coped on his own.

'Listen, Josh,' Sam said, 'From what I know of April, she seems like a strong person. Just think of how she came to Castle Clare to open her business. She didn't know anybody here at all.'

'Yes, it was a brave thing to do,' Eleanor said.

'And she's going to cope with this, especially with you being there for her,' Sam went on.

Josh nodded. 'I hope you're right. And I do think April's strong, but she seems to be in a dark place at the moment.'

'You're really worried about her, aren't you?' Polly said.

'I really am.'

'There's no use worrying,' Grandma Nell suddenly shouted from her chair, making both Josh and Polly jump. 'You can't change anything by worrying!'

'That's true,' Frank said.

'But I can't help it,' Josh said, turning round to face his grandmother who seemed very awake and lucid.

'She doesn't need you to worry,' Grandma Nell went on, 'only to be there for her when she's ready to come back to you. You've got to be strong. Strong enough for the two of you.'

Josh swallowed hard. Did Grandma Nell even know who she was talking about? He watched as her face gently clouded over with confusion again and she slowly closed her eyes. Grandpa Joe patted her hand and smiled at Josh.

'Listen,' Josh said, getting up, 'I'd better go.'

'You look exhausted,' his mother told him. 'Get an early night, won't you? You've got to take care of yourself.'

'I will.'

There were some extra long hugs for Josh as he left Campion House. He felt emotionally drained and yet wonderfully buoyed up by the love of his family.

Sunday lunch hadn't just been an ordeal for Josh. It had been one for Winston too. He only occasionally went out to eat. His meagre savings and pension meant he had to watch the pennies, but he'd been determined not to worry about that today. Today was not for worrying; it was for enjoyment.

And so Winston and Monty had made a slow progress into Castle Clare, choosing The George for the special occasion.

'Well,' Monty said, taking a sip of his beer after they'd placed their order, 'this is a rare treat.'

'Don't get used to it!' Winston said with a laugh.

'I can't remember the last time I ate out,' Monty confessed. 'Probably the funeral wake!'

Winston gave his brother a pat on the back as they took a corner seat.

'I still can't believe she's gone,' Monty went on. 'Did you feel like that? When you lost Sally?'

'I still do!' Winston confessed. 'I sometimes roll over in bed and my arm will reach out towards her and hit this cold empty space instead.'

Monty nodded.

'It's hard to break the habits of a long marriage,' Monty said. 'I'm still making two cups of tea each time I put the kettle on.'

'It'll get easier,' Winston told him. 'It'll take time, mind.'

They sipped their drinks and Winston looked around the pub at the young couples who hadn't yet experienced the pain of losing a long-term partner. He looked at the families and envied them the many happy years to come, knowing that it all rushed by in a flash. There was a part of him that wanted to tell them – to be the warning voice from their future, encouraging them to switch their phones off and simply talk to each other. Or not talk. Just be with each other. Look at the wonder of the person who is sitting beside you and in front of you. Don't look at that mindless screen on your phone. That isn't real; that isn't human. It won't love you back.

He sighed. Old age was turning him into an amateur philosopher. It was a good job the food arrived when it did.

'Well, this does look good, I must say!' Monty said, his eyes widening with delight at the size of the roast before him. 'Yorkshire puddings too!'

Monty nodded. It was, indeed, a rare treat. He really must try and do it more often, he thought. Having a meal cooked for you and not having to face a sink full of dishes at the end of it would be worth scrimping and saving a little each month.

They ate in companionable silence with an occasional grunt of satisfaction emanating from the pair of them. It wasn't until the end of the meal that Winston decided he had to say something. He didn't want to, but his head was so full of it that he knew he had to try and shake it off.

'Listen, Monty,' he began. 'I want to say something. Something that's been bothering me for some time now.'

Monty dabbed his mouth with his paper napkin. 'If it's me not pulling my weight around the house, I apologise. I've been in a bit of a fug, haven't I?'

'No, no. It's not that. Although, I don't mind if you do a spot of washing up every now and then.'

Monty leaned forward slightly. 'What is it, then?'

Winston shifted uneasily in his seat. 'It's... it's about the past.'

'The past?'

Winston looked down into his lap. There was no backing out now. If he wanted to get things clear between them, he had to go on.

'Marguerite,' he mumbled into his lap.

'Who's she?' Monty asked.

Winston's head snapped up and he looked at the confused expression on his brother's face. Was it possible that he'd forgotten?

'*Marguerite!*' he said again as if repeating her beautiful name might jog Monty's memory. After all, there weren't too many Marguerites about, were there?

'Not that little filly from the dance hall? Is *that* who you mean?'

'Yes, that's who I mean!'

'What about her?'

Winston frowned. 'You took her from me!'

'Took her? My dear brother – she willingly came with me. There was no taking involved.'

'You stole my money, Monty! You stole my money and you stole my girl!'

Monty looked genuinely perplexed by this. 'Is that really how you see it?'

'I see it like that because that's how it was!'

He shrugged. 'Well, I suppose I was a bit of a rat in those days! But I don't recall stealing your money.'

'It was hidden in the wardrobe – all my savings from my job. You must have searched for it to find it.'

Monty frowned. 'Ah, yes. I might well have done. Sorry about that. I was a bit short that week.'

'A bit short?' Winston cried. 'Those were *my* savings! Do you know how hard I'd worked for those? How many hours of hard graft on that bloody farm?'

Monty patted his pockets. 'I can probably reimburse you if it's still bothering you.'

'It's not about the money!' Winston said, his voice causing heads to turn now – something he was horribly conscious about. He sighed, doing his best to rein things in a bit. 'Well, it was at the time. But how could you have taken it knowing that was all I had? And you knew I'd been saving to take Marguerite out. You *knew* I liked her!'

There was a dreadful pause when the two brothers looked at each other: Winston with his hard-as-glass stare and Monty with his rheumy eyes which seemed full of incomprehension.

'Do you mean to tell me you've been carrying this around all these years?' Monty said at last.

'Well, I've not been dwelling on it every minute of the day, if that's what you mean,' Winston assured him. 'I have had a life to lead.'

'But it's come between us, hasn't it? I can tell by your face right now. You've hated me for it, haven't you?'

Winston shifted his beer mat a little. 'Hate's a pretty strong word.'

'But you have, haven't you? Tell me you haven't hated me? Go on!'

Winston sighed. This was all so very awkward.

'All right, I might have hated you for a while.'

'Well, I can't say I blame you!'

'I simply couldn't understand how you could do that to me –

your own brother! You knew I liked Marguerite. You knew she was special to me and that I wanted to treat her right. I told you I was saving up for that date, didn't I? And you swooped on in, stole my money and took my girl. And, on top of it all, you lied about me.' Winston's voice had risen again. 'You told her I was seeing someone else and that I didn't care for her!'

Monty shook his head. 'I don't remember that.'

'That's what you told me later. You really don't remember? You said you'd done me a favour!'

Monty's mouth dropped open and there was another awful silence between them.

Finally, Monty let out a deep sigh that seemed to come from the very centre of him.

'God, Winston! I don't know what to say? I know I've never been the best of brothers and I know I've done some pretty rotten things in my time, but I had no idea that they ever left their mark on anybody – not like this!'

'Well they do! They have!'

'Yes, I can see that.' Monty's face twisted itself up in an agonised expression. 'What do you want me to say? I'm sorry? Because I truly am. Really. I was just a young kid mucking around. I never meant to hurt you.'

'But you did, Monty.'

Monty's forehead puckered in pain and he reached a hand across the table. Winston stared at it as if it was the enemy.

'I'm sorry. I'm *really* sorry!'

Winston glanced up and then down again at his brother's hand on the table, knobbly and blue-veined just like his own. Probably crammed full of arthritis too, just as his was. And, as he looked at it, all the anger he felt drained right out of him. The truth was, he felt completely disarmed by his brother's repentance and, although he was grateful for it, he genuinely hadn't expected it. So he reached his own hand across the table and placed it on Monty's.

'Can you forgive me?' Monty whispered, his face looking pale and pinched. Winston stared at him for what seemed an eternity and then he nodded.

'Course I can, you silly sod! But you're getting the next round in.'

One of the most wonderful things about a Sunday in June was that, even when the last lingering guest had left Campion House, there was still a good hour to enjoy in the garden and Frank was making the most of it. Eleanor had seen him sneaking out of the back door as soon as Lara had left out of the front. Now, two cups of tea in hand, she ventured out to join him, leaving Grandpa and Grandma to rest in the living room.

The garden was deep in shadow now, but the air was still warm. Eleanor inhaled, the summer scents of the garden filling her with a peace she desperately needed after the stressful news they'd had earlier that day. She still couldn't believe that the beautiful young woman Josh had fallen in love with was going to go blind one day. Life could be so cruel, Eleanor thought, as she looked around the garden, taking joy in the way the last rays of the sun were playing in the tops of the trees. She could only imagine what it must be like to carry the knowledge that you were going to lose your sight one day.

Finding Frank leaning over one of his raised beds, she gave him his cup of tea and the two of them stood shoulder to shoulder sipping together.

'Just been staking the sunflowers,' he said. 'Six different kinds this year.'

'Is that enough?' Eleanor teased.

He threw her an amused glance. 'Probably not.'

They drank their tea, looking over the garden together as a

robin landed on the ground which Frank had disturbed with his fork earlier on.

'I still can't believe Josh's news,' Eleanor said at last.

Frank shook his head. 'That poor girl.'

'I don't know how she's coping.'

'He's fallen for her fast,' Frank said.

'That can happen you know.'

'I know!'

They exchanged a glance which said that that was what had happened between the two of them.

'I've never seen him react like that before,' Eleanor said. 'My little boy!'

'Not so little now.'

'He'll *always* be my little boy.'

They watched the robin for a moment as it hopped around, examining the earth for movement.

'I wish there was something we could do,' Frank said. 'Something like this makes you feel so helpless, doesn't it?'

'Yes.' Eleanor could feel her eyes blurring with tears and then Frank's arms were around her, his sunkissed cheek next to hers.

'We can be there for him, can't we?' he said softly, 'as he'll be there for her.'

'Yes,' she told him, kissing him tenderly. 'We can.'

CHAPTER TWENTY

Josh waited as long as he could, watching May as she came and went from the shop each day. For three whole days, he watched and waited, and then he went across the road just as a customer was leaving.

'She's still not called or texted me,' he blurted as soon as he was in the shop.

May looked up from a bookcase she was sanding down and pushed her chestnut hair out of her face.

'I need to know what's going on,' he told her.

She put the piece of sandpaper down, wiped her hands on the front of her denim overalls and sighed.

'She's still in a bad way, Josh.'

'I want to see her.'

'She's only just started talking to *me* again. I'm not sure if she's ready for you yet.'

Josh was pacing up and down the shop floor now. 'Well, it's a good sign she's talking to you, isn't it?'

'I don't want her getting stressed.'

'And what about me?' Josh said. '*I'm* stressed! I'm going out of my mind! And I hate thinking of her isolating herself like this.'

May crossed the shop and reached out to touch his shoulder, halting him in mid-step.

'Look, I can't make any promises, but I'll tell her you were asking after her, okay?'

'Her phone's switched off, isn't it? She's not even been looking at my messages, has she?'

'She's not been doing much of anything,' May told him.

Josh sighed. 'I need to see her, May.'

May looked up at him and nodded. 'I know you do.'

The next day, May called in at Josh's bookshop and told him to call at theirs that evening. He could barely think straight for the rest of the day and moved around the shop like a kind of ghost-Josh, only half there. He'd longed to be able to see April again but, now that the moment had arrived, he felt distinctly frayed around the edges.

Customers came and went. Phone calls were made and answered. Finally, the time came and he promptly left the shop, nipping round to the florists to pick up the pink roses he'd ordered earlier that day. They looked fresh and wonderful, their sherberty-pink petals deeply scented.

He laid them gently on the passenger seat of his car and drove the short distance to April and May's, rolling his shoulders back as he walked up the path to the front door.

It was May who answered, as he knew it would be, and she took one look at the flowers he was holding and sighed.

'Great! Just *one* more thing to remind her of what she'll not be able to see in the future.'

Josh cursed, feeling incredibly stupid.

'It's okay,' May said quickly. 'They're lovely.'

'They're scented,' Josh told her as if that might make all the difference in the world.

May leaned forward and sniffed them. 'They're nice.'

'You're sure they won't upset her?' Josh asked, anxious now.

'No. I'm sure she'll love them.'

'Can I see her?'

May nodded. 'But – Josh – listen! She's still very fragile. Don't tire her, will you?'

'I won't. I promise.'

May looked anxious, but nodded him through. Ever the guardian, Josh thought. But he was here now and he was going to see April.

He made his way along the hallway, stopping outside her bedroom door which had been left slightly ajar. He could hear music coming from inside. Mozart, he thought. Something light and beautiful featuring a harp and a flute. He knocked on the door.

'April?' he called softly.

'Come in, Josh.'

He entered and saw her sitting on her bed as if she hadn't moved an inch since his last visit.

'April!' he cried, dropping the flowers and flying across the room to wrap her up in his arms, all thought of remaining calm now gone. 'God, I've missed you!'

She laughed. 'I've missed you too!'

'I thought I was going to go crazy not hearing from you for all that time!'

'I'm sorry! I'm so sorry! I didn't mean to worry you.'

'When you said we shouldn't see each other again, it almost broke me.' He held her close, feeling the warmth of her cheek against his own and smelling the sweetness of her hair.

'It almost broke me too,' she whispered to him.

They held each other as if nothing else in the world existed outside of the little unit they made, but then April pulled away. She wasn't wearing her pink glasses and it was then that Josh noticed that her curtains were partially closed and a blind had been pulled down half-way.

'Are you feeling okay?' he asked her, gently stroking her hair.

'A little stronger than I was. I'm afraid I disappeared for a while, didn't I?'

Josh nodded. 'I didn't know what to do.'

'Neither did I! I think I went a little crazy. But May got me an appointment with my ophthalmologist and he was really understanding. He told me some things I needed to hear and put my mind at rest. At least a little. For now.'

'That's good,' Josh said, 'and something else I've been thinking. This thing – this blindness – it might not happen for years and years. I've been reading a bit about it.'

April reached out and squeezed his hands. 'That's just one of the things my doctor said.'

'And it's been making me feel so sad thinking of you shut away in your room like this. Especially when we had so much fun together on our days out. We did, didn't we?'

April nodded.

'And we can have more – *lots* more! There's nothing I want to do more than to be with you, April, and to make the most of the time we have. Because none of us are ever really sure what we do have. But I'm hoping it's years. Years and years of us together, having fun, and loving life – just as you've taught me to do.'

He watched as her smile slowly slipped away like a vanishing rainbow.

'Listen, Josh,' she said, her tone serious. 'I've loved our time together and my feelings for you... well, they're like nothing I've ever had before.' She paused and Josh lifted her hands to his mouth and kissed her fingers gently. 'But I've been thinking about this a lot and I really think it would be for the best if you saw May.'

Josh frowned. Had he heard her correctly?

'What do you mean?'

'I mean, you should see May instead of me.'

'April!'

'No – listen! It makes sense. She's a *much* better bet than I am. And she's very like me in so many ways.'

'Are you being serious?'

April looked at him, her face completely earnest. 'Yes, of course I am.'

Josh took a moment for it to sink in. 'I can't believe you really think I can just switch my feelings from you to May. Is that what you're asking me to do?'

She nodded. 'It shouldn't be so hard. After all, she's practically me, isn't she? And, if you do see May, you can go on seeing me too. We'll never be far from each other. So we can remain friends, can't we? We'd be a happy little trio.'

'You mean like your mother and fathers?' Josh said, horrified by the thought.

'No – not *exactly* like that! I wouldn't ask that of you.'

Josh sat perfectly still, April's hands still held in his.

'What do you think?' April asked him at last. 'It's a good idea, isn't it?'

Josh took a deep breath. 'It's a terrible idea. In fact, it's the *worst* idea I've ever heard!'

'Josh – no listen a minute–'

'No – you listen, April,' he said tenderly, 'I'm not dating your sister. She might look like you, but she *isn't* you. That's a vital component in all this, don't you think?'

'I know she can seem a little bit brusque around the edges.'

'That doesn't matter,' Josh said, 'because I'm not even thinking about May. I'm thinking of you and how I want to be with you even if you think I shouldn't be. I want to help you through all this – not abandon you when you need me the most.'

'But it's not fair on you, Josh.'

'But it's what I want. *You're* what I want.' He sighed. 'April – you know how I feel about you, don't you?'

April looked down at their hands which were still joined together and nodded. 'Yes, because I feel the same way too.'

'Then why are we even having this conversation?'

'I just want to make sure you know what this is,' she said. 'It's not going to be easy.'

'I know.'

'And I'm not sure how I'll respond to everything.'

'Well, if the last few days are anything to go by, I think we've got an inkling.'

April gave a weak smile and it was then that Josh suddenly remembered the flowers which he'd dropped as he'd rushed across the room earlier. Getting up from the bed, he picked them up now and handed them to April.

'Oh, Josh! They're lovely.' She held them up to her face and inhaled their scent. 'So gorgeous.'

'They're the same colour as the roses you loved in the garden at Charleston – remember?'

'I remember!' she said, her gaze soft and dreamy.

Josh sat back down on the bed and April reached out to him again.

'I don't deserve you,' she whispered.

He frowned. 'Why on earth would you think that?'

'Because I've done nothing but hide the truth from you since we first met and then I did my best to push you away.'

'But I keep coming back, don't I?'

'Yes! You do! Although I really can't think why.'

He kissed her in response. 'And I always will come back. If

you insist on pushing me away again, that is. Which I hope you won't!'

April put the flowers on her bedside table and then launched herself into Josh's arms.

'I won't. I promise,' she told him. 'Not ever, *ever* again!'

CHAPTER TWENTY-ONE

When Montague Kneller had arrived on Winston's doorstep, he had not been a welcome sight. But, now that he was leaving, Winston couldn't help but feel a little sad. He'd somehow got used to the company of his brother – awkward at first, it had to be admitted – but it had been something of a comfort to have a companion in his home again. A human companion, that was, he thought as he glanced at Delilah in her basket. Monty had just given her a treat from a little bag of biscuits he'd purchased in the pet shop in Castle Clare. And Winston had been given a very expensive bottle of malt whisky. It had, Winston thought, been a peace offering for the past.

'Right, right,' Monty said now as he stood in the hallway with his suitcase, patting the pockets of his jacket and his trousers. 'I've got everything, I think. Yes. *Glasses, keys, wallet, nerve. Especially nerve.* Wasn't that what you used to say?' He glanced up.

Winston blinked in surprise. 'You remember that?'

'Oh, yes,' Monty told him and then he sniffed. 'I remember not always behaving well too.' He paused, shuffling his shoes from side to side before looking back up at Winston. 'I know I've not always been the best of brothers and I know I've said and done things that – well – haven't always been fair or good or forgivable.'

Winston swallowed hard, unable to say anything.

'But perhaps we can go forward afresh,' Monty suggested. 'Perhaps we could see more of each other. Maybe even take a little holiday somewhere, eh? Get a dog-sitter for Delilah. What do you think? It would be my treat of course.'

Winston nodded. 'I'd like that.'

'Good! I'll look into it. And, maybe you can come to my place sometime,' Monty said. 'I've got a spare room, you know. Or you can have mine if you want. Whatever suits you best. And Delilah would be welcome too.'

Again, Winston was speechless and so he simply nodded.

And then Monty did something Winston would never have expected in a million years: he walked back through into the living room and knelt down by Delilah's basket and gave her head a rub. 'Goodbye, old girl. Come and see your Uncle Monty soon.'

Delilah looked up at him, looking as confused as Winston felt.

'Right, I'd better get going,' Monty said, standing back up with a groan. 'Knees.'

'Yes. I've got knees too,' Winston said.

'The Kneller brothers are getting old,' Monty announced.

'Who would've thought it?'

They chuckled together and then Monty leaned forward and gave Winston a hug, and all the years of resentment and misunderstandings seemed to melt away.

'Well, be seeing you, brother,' Monty said, picking up his suitcase.

'Safe trip home. Let me know once you're back.'

Monty nodded and Winston stood in the doorway, watching as the taxi pulled away, his brother's hand waving from the open window.

Closing his front door a moment later, Winston pulled out a

hankie from his waistcoat pocket and dabbed his eyes. Foolish to get emotional, he told himself, but there it was. He *was* emotional and it had been the very last thing he'd expected to feel as his brother left. Relief, yes – emotional, definitely not. It was something he'd have to tell Josh about, he thought.

Life could be so totally unpredictable sometimes. And wonderful.

It was a good turnout for the July book club. As ever, Callie had got there early to help Sam set the room up, and Polly and Jago were there too. Josh was the next to arrive with April, and Winston arrived with Delilah at the same time as Flo. Then Antonia and Honey and a couple of holidaymakers, Judith and Edward Robins, who were staying in a cottage nearby and had seen the club poster in the window of the shop and had asked Sam if it was okay to join them. They were in their seventies and hadn't read a word of Virginia Woolf, they'd confessed, but wanted to come along and meet some locals. Sam was only too pleased to welcome them.

Honey Digger got things started by placing a large floral bag in the middle of the room.

'Savouries!' she announced. 'For a change.' She reached into the bag and brought out a large tin full of biscuits. 'Sourdough crackers.'

Winston frowned. 'Sourdough?'

'It's all the rage, you know, and very good for you too,' Honey assured him. 'Beneficial for your gut health.'

'Nothing wrong with my gut health,' Winston said, patting his rather protruding belly and then belching. 'Oh, pardon me!'

Sam bit his lip in an attempt not to laugh.

'Well, *I've* brought something *sweet*,' Antonia announced. 'Because everybody loves sweet things.' She reached into a sturdy brown paper bag and brought out a plastic container filled with iced buns of every possible colour. Honey peered at them.

'Very... colourful!' Honey said.

'Certainly beats *brown*,' Antonia said, glancing at Honey's sourdough crackers. 'I detest brown food.'

'Brown food is very good for you,' Callie said. 'Wholemeal and wholewheat.'

'But sugar is good for the soul,' Sam said.

'Then you'll have a bun?' Antonia said, shoving the plastic container under his nose.

'I will. And a cracker too,' Sam said, ever the diplomat.

'I'll get some plates,' Honey said, disappearing into the tiny kitchen.

Five minutes later, everyone had either a cup of tea or coffee and a bun or cracker, or both like Winston. The chairs had been arranged in a friendly circle and everyone had taken a seat.

'I'm afraid I didn't bring any nibbles this time,' Flo Lohman announced.

'Well, that's a relief!' Antonia said under her breath.

'My hens seem to be broody or laying their eggs where I can't find them,' Flo continued.

'Well, there's certainly plenty to eat here,' Jago said as he munched on a cracker.

'Okay, everyone!' Sam said, clapping his hands together. 'Shall we make a start? We've got a couple of special guests tonight – Judith and Edward who are holidaying in Suffolk.'

Everybody said hello.

'We haven't read the book, I'm afraid,' Judith said with a blush.

'Don't worry,' Winston told her. 'I don't think many of us have read it either!' He winked and Judith's blush deepened.

'So,' Sam began, 'how did we all get on with the Virginia Woolf? I do hope at least a few of us have read it!'

There was an ominous pause and Sam scanned the faces of the group.

Winston shifted uneasily in his chair. 'Not one of the most riveting reads, I have to confess,' he said.

'But it's always good to challenge oneself,' Polly said.

'Well, I got hopelessly lost,' Flo admitted.

'Where did you get lost?' Sam asked.

Flo flipped through her copy of the book and then turned to the opening and scanned the first page. 'Paragraph three,' she said.

'Oh, dear,' Sam said.

'I ploughed on. For two whole weeks, I ploughed on every evening,' she told him, slapping the book with her hand. 'But, in the end, I stopped trying to make sense of it as a story and just concentrated on finding beautiful sentences.'

'Well, that's a unique way of approaching a novel,' Callie said.

'Some of the sentences *are* exquisite. I underlined a few like the one about the colour of a hollow wave ...' Flo flipped through her book and a hen feather floated out and settled on the floor between her dusty shoes. 'Oh, well, I can't find it now.'

'But surely a novel needs to be more than a few nice sentences,' Honey suggested.

'Does it?' Sam said. 'Isn't that exactly what a novel is?'

'Oh, this is becoming too confusing for me,' Flo said.

'It's like being back at university,' Josh joked.

'If it is, I'm glad I never went!' Flo confessed.

'What did you think about it, Honey?' Sam asked.

'Well, I don't normally read this sort of thing, I have to say,' Honey began.

'She's a Mills and Boon reader,' Antonia said.

Honey visibly bristled. 'There is nothing wrong with wanting to read a romance. Romance is the very essence of life after all, isn't it?'

Winston nodded sagely. 'She has a point!'

'But I do like to read outside my comfort zone every so often. Only – well – not *too* often!'

'So what did you make of *Mrs Dalloway*?' Sam pressed.

'It's romantic in its own way – the longing for the past and Clarissa's need for everything to be just right,' Honey said. 'She takes a pride in things, doesn't she? She doesn't want anything to disrupt her party.'

'Like what happened to the young man?' Winston chimed in.

'What happened to him?' Edward asked.

'Well, I don't think we should spoil the ending in case you want to read it,' Sam said.

Edward looked disappointed by this.

'Clarissa's response is rather callous, though, don't you think?' Josh said. 'She seems more concerned that the mood of her party has changed rather than a young man who–'

'No spoilers!' April cried, laying a hand on his arm.

'I liked how those two storylines came together,' Polly said. 'It's like real life, isn't it? People's lives overlap and intersect in messy and unpredictable ways.'

'And it all takes place in a single day,' Callie added. 'Don't you think that's amazing? It's a novel about all those little moments and thoughts, feelings and memories and how these all go to make up the passage of a single day.'

The group paused for a moment as if to consider this.

'But there are pages and pages of speculation about who was in a car, for goodness's sake!' Flo said. 'What does it matter?'

'I think Woolf was challenging what a novel should be,' Sam said. 'She was pushing the boundaries.'

'You mean she didn't know how to write a decent plot?' Winston guffawed.

'Shall we get a writer's opinion on that?' Polly suggested. 'What do you think, Callie? Can a novel have no real plot?'

'Well, the writer in me wants to shake Woolf hard and cry,

"You've not got enough story here". But I also like how brave she's been in following her muse and seeing where it takes her. She had a vision and she was brave enough to explore that and put it out into the world.'

'Yes, it's always good to challenge yourself in your art, I imagine,' Sam said.

'But she does head hop a lot,' Callie added.

'*Head hop*?' Flo said. 'What's that?'

'It's when the reader is taken inside the head of one character and can see what they're thinking, but then hops inside another character's head within the same scene. That's kind of frowned upon in the world of publishing.'

'So how did Virginia Woolf get away with it?' Jago asked.

'She's Virginia Woolf!' Callie replied and everyone laughed.

'What a wonderful term that is: head hopping!' Flo chuckled. 'Imagine if you could do that in real life – hop into each others' heads and hear one another's thoughts.'

'It probably wouldn't be a very good idea,' Sam said.

'Why? What have you got to hide?' Callie teased.

Sam felt himself blushing which made Callie laugh.

'But why does she write in such long sentences?' Honey asked. 'Look at this one on page seven starting with "And everywhere". It goes on and on and on! I can't see a full stop anywhere!'

'Yes, but she uses semi-colons most effectively,' Antonia said in a superior tone.

'A semi-colon's no good to me when I want to put my lamp off and go to sleep!' Honey said hopelessly.

'Let's talk a minute about Woolf's use of the long sentence,' Sam said. 'What effect does it have, do you think?'

'It makes my eyes sore!' Flo said.

'But what else do you think it does?' Sam asked.

'I think it creates a sense of excitement,' Callie said. 'One of urgency and breathlessness like the author can't get everything down on the page quickly enough – she has so many thoughts in her head and there are so many stimulating things to describe!'

'I like that,' Sam said. 'And I loved that the two protagonists witness the same incident in the street. They're so physically close and yet light-years away from each other.'

'It makes you wonder who you're standing next to in the street, doesn't it?' Jago added. 'And what their story is. I often think of things like that when travelling on public transport. I'll see someone across the aisle of the train or something and I'll think, "This is the only time our paths will cross. We'll never see each other again. I'll go off and live my life and you'll live yours."'

Winston scratched his head. 'This is all getting very deep, isn't it?'

Everyone laughed and Honey picked up her plate of crackers and passed them around. Not to be outdone, Antonia reached for her intensely-coloured buns and did the same.

'I have to say that I didn't like all the Peter Walsh stuff,' Jago said as they got back to discussing the book. 'I couldn't really see the point of it all.'

'I think,' Sam said, 'it shows how full a life is and how many other lives we touch so deeply, and how all of that – all of those little moments that we have – are only just a memory away.'

'True,' Winston said, nodding.

'April? What do you think?' Sam asked, noting that she hadn't contributed to the discussion yet.

'I think,' she said slowly, 'I think we're all judging this book too harshly. We're bringing all these preconceptions about what a book – a novel – should be, and we seem shocked to find something different within its pages. But, if you forget about all that's come before and all that's come since, you find something vibrant and unique. Something totally of itself.'

Sam saw Josh looking at April with something between wonder and love in his expression.

'Woolf said in her diary that, although it was original, she found it a struggle to write, but that's exactly what she found interesting,' April asserted. 'I'm sure there are some writers who are content to write the same novel over and over again, but Virginia Woolf wasn't one of them.'

'I agree,' Sam said. 'It's definitely original.'

'And a struggle!' Flo laughed. 'For Woolf *and* for her readers!'

'I listened to an audio version,' April went on. 'It was read by Juliet Stevenson and her voice was just perfect for it – clear and crisp and yet there was a warmth to it too.'

Antonia grimaced. 'I don't think listening to an audio book is *real* reading, is it?'

Sam frowned and he could see Josh bristling on April's behalf, but Sam was wrong if he thought April needed defending.

'And why is that?' April asked. 'Why is *listening* to a book less of a reading experience than seeing the words with your eyes?'

Antonia looked a little flustered at being challenged in this way. 'I mean,' she said, her face stony, 'that you can't possibly take in all the information properly.'

'I don't understand,' April said.

'Memory, child!' Antonia snapped. 'The eyes remember better than the ears when reading.'

'What makes you say that?' Sam asked, genuinely interested.

'It's just known,' Antonia said unconvincingly.

'So, by that token, you're saying reading aloud to children is a waste of time because they won't remember anything?' April asserted.

'No, I didn't mean it like *that*.'

'We love an audio book, don't we?' Judith said and her husband nodded.

'We listen to them together on long journeys.'

'We've got *Northanger Abbey* on the go at the moment, haven't we?'

'Audio books are a vital part of life for the blind and the visually impaired,' April went on. 'There are nearly forty million blind people in the world. Are you saying that they should be denied the pleasure of audio books?' She was speaking calmly, but there was a steely edge to her voice that made it clear she would not brook any nonsense on this subject.

'You've misunderstood me,' Antonia said, sounding flustered now.

'Have a bun!' Winston said, leaning forward to pass Antonia one of her own buns – the last one left: a strange shade of cerulean.

'I'm sorry,' Antonia said. 'I didn't mean to offend anybody.'

The room was silent for a moment. Nobody had ever heard Antonia apologise before.

Sam cleared his throat. 'I'm sure nobody was offended, Antonia. We were just having a healthy debate, weren't we?' He looked across the circle to April who nodded.

They talked a little more about the book and finished the crackers.

'So, our next book?' Sam announced.

'Please don't tell me it's a sequel to this one!' Flo said.

'Yes – *Clarissa does Christmas*!' Winston joked.

Sam laughed. 'No sequel, I promise. Actually, we were talking about this last week, weren't we?' he said, turning to Callie.

'We thought it might be nice to read a non-fiction title. We've had three novels in a row now,' Callie said.

'How exciting!' Honey said. 'What have you in mind?'

'I came across a delightful copy of *84 Charing Cross Road* by Helene Hanff a couple of weeks ago and read it again in one evening. I'd forgotten what a joy it is. I think you'd all like it,' Sam told them. 'It's written completely in letters between an American bookworm and an English bookseller.'

'Oh, I read that years ago!' Flo said. 'It's charming, isn't it?'

'It is a bit of a classic,' Polly said. 'Good choice, Sam!'

'Does anyone have any objections, then? Or maybe any other suggestions?'

Everyone agreed that Sam's choice sounded like a good one.

'That's great!' Sam enthused. 'So, we'll see you all in September. Let Josh know if you need to order a copy of the book.'

Everybody got up and Polly and Jago helped to stack the chairs which would be returned to the village hall in the morning.

When the last of the group had left the shop, Sam breathed out a long sigh.

'That got rather heated tonight, didn't it?' Callie said, walking up behind him and linking her arms around his waist as he closed the shop door.

'Yes! I'm wondering if it was a mistake choosing *Mrs Dalloway*. Maybe Castle Clare just wasn't ready for the Bloomsbury Group.'

'Oh, *don't* think that!' she said. 'It's good to challenge people and get them talking about things they might not necessarily like or agree about. That's exactly why they join book clubs, isn't it?'

'I'm not so sure. I think it's more about the company and the nibbles.' He grinned. 'You know, at one point, I felt sure Josh was about to fly across the room at Antonia. I've never seen him look so protective of someone before.'

'April took care of herself, though, didn't she?' Callie observed.

'She absolutely did!'

'They're wonderful together, aren't they?' Callie said wistfully.

'I've never seen Josh so happy,' Sam said with a smile.

Callie nodded. 'I really think those two can face anything together.'

CHAPTER TWENTY-TWO

It was on a sunny Wednesday morning in July when Winston and Delilah popped into Josh's bookshop.

'Winston! How are you?'

Winston smiled and scratched his head. 'Yes,' he said, looking a big vague.

'Everything okay?' Josh asked, putting a pile of books down on the counter and giving Winston his full attention.

'Monty just rang me.'

'How is he?'

'He's well. He's – he's booked us a holiday.'

'Really?'

'Yes. A little break at the end of the summer. You know, once the schools have gone back and all.'

'Where?'

'North Norfolk coast. A nice hotel just outside Wells. We've got our own rooms with balconies and en suites, can you believe it? And they allow dogs too!'

'Sounds perfect!'

Winston shook his head. 'Monty said we should spend more

time together, and he even mentioned a holiday, but I didn't really believe it would happen. At least, not so quickly.'

'It sounds like you two are getting on well these days.'

'Yes. It's like a new chapter, isn't it?'

The two men smiled at each other.

'Winston? Can I ask you something?' Josh said.

'Ask away.'

'How long were you married for?'

'Fifty years.'

'And how did you know?'

'Know what?'

'That she was the one for you?'

Winston took a deep breath as his mind seemed to somersault back through the decades. 'It's kind of like that feeling you get when you start a film,' he said.

Josh frowned. 'What do you mean?'

Winston scratched his chin. 'You know you can always tell if you're going to like a film? Sometimes, even before the opening credits are over, I know if it's my sort of thing or not and if I'm going to stay tuned or switch it off. Well, that's what it was like with Sally. I saw her one day and couldn't take my eyes off her and knew I'd never want to switch her off.'

Josh grinned. He wasn't sure about Winston's choice of analogy, but he felt the deep truth behind his words.

'Judging by the look on your face, you don't want to switch this one off, do you?' Winston asked now before glancing out of the window to the shop across the road.

Josh could feel his face flaming in embarrassment. 'I never thought anything like this would ever happen to me.'

Winston frowned. 'Why on earth not?'

Josh shrugged. 'I don't know. I guess I had myself down as the happy bachelor type. You know – married to my work. Married to my books.'

'So you're talking about marriage, are you?' Winston asked with a grin.

'Maybe,' Josh said, thinking about that for a moment as he walked to the window. April and May had been working at A Little Bit Bloomsbury together today and Josh had joined them earlier for morning coffee.

It had been an extraordinary few months since Josh had met April in May. And May in June. Or had he met May in May too? Yes, he had. Only he'd thought May had been April, hadn't he? Gosh, it was all so confusing.

'I still can't tell them apart,' Winston said as he stared out of the window, shielding his eyes against the summer light.

Josh looked across to see April and May placing a newly painted table in the window. Both of them glanced up at the same time to see Josh and Winston watching them and that's when one of them smiled.

'Ah, yes!' Winston said. 'I *can* tell them apart after all. There's no mistaking the look of love, is there?'

ALSO BY VICTORIA CONNELLY

The Book Lovers Series

The Book Lovers

Rules for a Successful Book Club

Natural Born Readers

Scenes from a Country Bookshop

Christmas with the Book Lovers

Other Books

The Beauty of Broken Things

One Last Summer

The Heart of the Garden

Love in an English Garden

The Rose Girls

The Secret of You

Christmas at The Cove

Christmas at the Castle

Christmas at the Cottage

The Christmas Collection (A compilation volume)

A Summer to Remember

Wish You Were Here

The Runaway Actress

Molly's Millions

Flights of Angels

Irresistible You

Three Graces

It's Magic (A compilation volume)

A Weekend with Mr Darcy

The Perfect Hero (Dreaming of Mr Darcy)

Mr Darcy Forever

Christmas With Mr Darcy

Happy Birthday Mr Darcy

At Home with Mr Darcy

One Perfect Week and Other Stories

The Retreat and Other Stories

Postcard from Venice and Other Stories

A Dog Called Hope

Escape to Mulberry Cottage (non-fiction)

A Year at Mulberry Cottage (non-fiction)

Summer at Mulberry Cottage (non-fiction)

Secret Pyramid (children's adventure)

The Audacious Auditions of Jimmy Catesby (children's adventure)

ACKNOWLEDGEMENTS

Special thanks to my Great Uncle Peter and to my dear friend Bridget for giving me valuable insights into what it's like being a twin.

ABOUT THE AUTHOR

Victoria Connelly is the bestselling author of *The Rose Girls* and *The Book Lovers* series. With over half a million sales, her books have been translated into many languages. The first, *Flights of Angels*, was made into a film in Germany. Victoria flew to Berlin to see it being made and even played a cameo role in it.

A Weekend with Mr Darcy, the first in her popular Austen Addicts series about fans of Jane Austen has sold over 100,000 copies. She is also the author of several romantic comedies including *The Runaway Actress* which was nominated for the Romantic Novelists' Association's Best Romantic Comedy of the Year.

Victoria was brought up in Norfolk, England before moving to Yorkshire where she got married in a medieval castle. After 11 years in London, she moved to rural Suffolk where she lives in a Georgian cottage with her artist husband, a springer spaniel and her ex-battery hens.

To hear about future releases and receive a **free ebook** sign up for her newsletter at www.victoriaconnelly.com

Printed in Great
Britain
by Amazon

32408807R00158